CLEARWATER

To Glen & ... my friends!
Real & ...!
7-28-05

[signature] Woodall

by Bobby R. Woodall

Woodall, Bobby R.
ISBN: 0-7443-0335-4
Clearwater/Bobby R. Woodall – 2nd ed.

SynergEbooks
1235 Flat Shoals Rd
King, NC 27021
http://www.SynergEbooks.com
Fax: 1-336-994-8403
Phone: 1-336-994-2405
Toll Free: 1-888-812-2533

Cover Art by Carl A. Posey   http:www.apparenthorizon.com
Cover Art design for paperback by Barbara Quanback
Contact the author via email at bwoodall@voyager.net

Printed in the USA

CLEARWATER

Acknowledgment

This book is dedicated to my wife, Laurel Ann, for without her faith in me this would not have been possible. I also want to thank my children, John Richard and Heather Lee for putting up with my idiosyncrasies. To all of my friends that let me use their names in my novel, I thank you.

I want to thank the following people; Ann Maloney from Bartlesville, Oklahoma. Judy Lumley and her daughter Crystal from Marlow, Oklahoma for their invaluable assistance, Kathy Rasener from Columbus, Indiana for getting me on the web, Susie Roush of Columbus, Indiana for letting me print hard copies when my computer failed and to Anita McHenry in Columbus, Indiana for getting me started with a word processor. Jessika Josette Mastroantonio of Grand Rapids, Michigan for her moral support. Also David Curtis of Tawas, Michigan for providing his excellent knowledge about weapons.

ONE

Sheriff Lee Wildman and Floyd Bills, a wrangler at the Corey ranch, were riding out to the spread five miles from town. The sheriff had received a report of a few cowboys harassing the people in the tent revival. The revival had located on the land adjacent to the Corey spread. There were plenty of water and a grove of cottonwoods afforded shade to the gathering. Lee was taking his time. He figured on the cowboys to be long gone and the holy rollers having enough time to calm down. The sheriff didn't see any sense in working up a sweat just because some local cowboys had let off a little steam.

"I've been young once," the sheriff recollected to himself. "A long time ago."

He smiled to himself at the remembrance. At least no one had been hurt or killed although the messenger had ridden into town with his horse all in a lather. Lee was thinking back to what had taken place this morning in town.

The dust was swirling as the cowboy pulled his mount to a halt in front of the sheriffs' office. He jumped off his horse, not bothering tying the reins and came running into the sheriffs' office, his face flushed with excitement.

"Hurry sheriff!" the cowboy shouted, almost out of breath. "There's been a whole lot of shoot'n out at the Corey ranch!"

"Hold on, son," Lee said, sitting back in his office chair and smiling and using the toe of his boot to pull out a chair from beside the desk. He was not going to get excited, after all he had a cushy job to worry about. "Calm down. Sit."

The cowboy was so agitated he could barely sit in the chair. When he sat, he crossed his legs nervously. Then he uncrossed them and his left leg started to bounce.

While this little tableau was going on, Lee arose and went to the coffee pot. He poured a cup of coffee and slid it across the desk in front of the cowboy. The sheriff couldn't help but smile as he saw the cowboy pick the mug of hot liquid from the desk and hastily drink it. Lee knew the coffee was piping hot, for he had just taken it off the potbellied stove a moment ago. He silently chuckled when the cowboy sputtered out the coffee on the front of his shirt. The wrangler immediately started to wipe his shirt with his hands. Then he took the back of his hand and wiped his mouth. Suddenly the cowboy jumped from the chair and rushed out the door.

Lee waited for a moment with a smile on his face. The smile caused the wrinkles in his forty-year-old face to widen as the smile grew broader. He reached up and stroked his mustache, white with age, as was his hair. His blue eyes were such that sparkled when he was happy and turned rock hard when he was mad. Lee's build was of medium height. He stood five feet, eight inches and had no desire to be taller.

"I'm tall enough to reach the ground," he jokingly told people. "Besides I'm afraid of heights."

They would grin, then take one look at his eyes and see the seriousness in them as they turned ice blue. Mostly, they suddenly find they had business elsewhere. No one yet had dared to comment on his size, at least not to his face.

Shortly the cowboy returned and sheepishly sat down. He slowly raised the offending cup to his lips where he softly blew on it and took a sip, then looked up at the sheriff and shrugged his shoulders. He took a deep breath.

"Guess I forgot to mention the trouble out at the Corey place?" said the cowboy, looking sheepishly and fidgeting in his chair.

"Yep," Lee answered, taking another sip of his coffee. "I guess you did at that. But now that you're calmer, why don't you tell me the story. Start at the beginning if you don't mind son."

"Of course sheriff," the cowboy gulped, sitting on the edge of the chair, seemingly afraid the chair would move of its own volition.

"Name's Floyd Bills. I've been working for the Bar de Har for going on five years. First, as a temporary full-time helper in the kitchen. I'm only a cook, but some of the guys have been teaching me to be a fair to a middling wrangler. Last night a bunch of us boys got to drinking. We started early because of our boss, Mr. Corey, was going to Oklahoma Station for some needed supplies. You know, we use up a lot of foodstuffs, building materials and clothing. Mr. Corey was gonna get us some things. "

Lee wondered if the cowboy was ever going to get to his story or not. It seemed as if this cowboy never got the chance to talk to anyone. Now that he had a captive audience he was bound and determined to milk it for all that it was worth. Lee smiled and sipped the remainder of his coffee.

"Anyone hurt?" Lee asked, getting up from his desk and moving over to the stove for more coffee. Glancing at the cowboy, he raised his eyebrow and asked, "Refill?"

"Don't rightly know? No thanks, sir," Floyd answered, taking another sip of the by now greatly cooled down coffee. He grimaced at the lukewarm temperature of the coffee. "One thing I don't like is barely warm coffee," he thought. "Least ways it's free," Floyd smiled, as he drank the last of the tepid liquid.

"Well, we'd best find out. You reckon?" Lee asked, resigned to do his duty as sheriff. He drained the last of his coffee and placing the empty cup on the side of his desk.

He stood and reached to the wall back of him. Lee removed his gun belt from its resting place on the wall rack and strapped it on. Then nodding to Floyd, jerked his head toward the door.

The two went outside to their mounts. Lee mounted his Appaloosa while Floyd crawled on a dun gelding. Together they rode at a leisurely pace out of the small town. They paused long enough to let a lady with her arms full of packages cross the street. She grinned at them and nodded her head when Lee tipped his hat to the woman. After she had passed, Lee and the cowboy continued to ride toward the Corey ranch. He noticed that the cowboy wanted to hurry, but Lee took his time.

"Got to enjoy the countryside now and then," he thought. "That's the problem with the world today, all the time hurrying. If they don't watch it, they'll end up running right smack dab over themselves." Chuckling at his down-home philosophy, Lee clicked his tongue and spurred his mount faster.

Clearwater, Indian Territory was an ordinary town populated by ordinary people that did ordinary things. There had been cases of public intoxication and wife abuse. Once there had been reported to the sheriff's office of seeing a gang of outlaws riding by on the outskirts of town near the old Dellasburg Road.

As the sheriff, he was duty bound to check all these happenings. Lee had thrown Cooty Brown into the hoosegow after he had found out that the damages incurred by the drunk at the saloon were going to be paid.

"It'd do to have the Cooty sleep off his night in jail," he thought. "Besides the bleary-eyed cowboy could get a free breakfast courtesy of the sheriff," Lee was also, besides being a very strict enforcer of the law, a compassionate man.

"Long as no one's hurt," he figured. "What harm could it be in being soft on an occasional drunk?"

Then there was Dawn And Scott Harvey. Scott had the bad habit of taking out his frustrations and anger on Dawn with his tongue, while Dawn took hers out on him with a cast iron skillet to his head. He had gone to the Harvey house, talked to the wife Dawn and her husband Scott. While sharing a cup of coffee, he was able to talk sense to the husband. When he rode from their house, he stopped and looked back over his shoulder. Lee smiled. The couple were holding hands and walking back into their house. Ridding out to check on the tracks left by the desperadoes and dismounting, he'd gone to look around for tracks. They had disappeared by now. He had sat back astride his horse and pondered the possibilities.

"I'm supposed to check out the trail of the bandits," he thought. "Now that they were out of my reach?" he pondered. "I think not."

At the present, he was on his way to investigate this latest means of lawbreaking. Lee knew it was a fair piece to the Corey place. The duo would arrive at dusk. Smiling to himself, he also knew Jeff Corey's wife, Judy, put out a good spread of victuals.

"Of course, I'll be invited to sit and eat with the bunch," he reckoned. "The absence of her husband would make Mrs. Corey thankful for the presence of the sheriff. Got to keep the citizens happy," he thought, as he noticed that the wrangler rode abreast of him.

The mere idea of the approaching feast made his mouth water, so he nudged his animal to pick up the speed. It wasn't long before he was riding ahead of the cowboy. The cowboy had to urge his horse to keep up with the sheriff.

Lee smiled as a chipmunk crossed the road, got to the other side and sitting on its haunches, started to chatter at the intruders to the chipmunk's territory. Its little squirrel cheeks were puffed out, filled with berries and Lee saw that it was missing its usual two black stripes bound by white bands on either side and down the middle of its back.

"Must mean an early winter?" he thought, nudging his horse . "My paw had taught me that when I was a child and I took it as gospel truth," Lee concluded, chuckling. "An old wife's tale,"

After he had calmed down Mrs. Corey and straightened out the mess with the holy rollers, Lee suddenly remembered what he had offered a fellow lawman earlier in the week.

Lee Wildman was the sheriff of the town of Clearwater. Earlier he had been on a simple process-serving jaunt, as a favor to the U.S. Marshal in Tahlequah.

"An errand boy for the feds," he smiled to himself. "Guess that I might's well get the job done today."

After making sure that Mr. Corey would be notified of the situation and saying his goodbyes, he tipped his hat and started out of the ranch. In a moment he applied the spurs to his horse and heightened up the pace to a small canter.

The sun was bearing down unmercifully on the lone horseman, as Lee rode slowly across the wide expanse of the plains. Its rays seemed to be boring into the back of his neck, the air was dry, heavy and there was no breeze. Even the saddle was becoming uncomfortable as the heat from the leather seem to radiate upwards. Heat waves shimmered in the distance and the rocks seemed to move of their own fancy.

Lee finally pulled back on the reins and stopped at the base of some hills. He reached to his neck and unloosened his bandana. Taking his neckerchief in his calloused hands, he began to wipe the sweat as it trickled down his face. The sheriff pushed his hat up farther up on his head and squinted into the distance. He held his hand up over his forehead to see if he could discern any movement on the prairie. Seeing nothing move, he clicked his tongue and rode his horse forward at a steady trot while determinedly looking to either side of the trail. The sheriff was man hunting now. He pulled his hat lower on his head and his smile was replaced by a grim line.

Suddenly he was fired upon. The sheriff immediately pulled his rifle from the boot and quickly rolled from his saddle. Lee moved the lever on his weapon and smiled in satisfaction when he heard a shell being seated in the rifle's chamber.

"Okay Mr. Shooter, I'm ready for you now."

Lee removed his hat and placed it to the side of the rock. Peering over the edge of the rocks, he sought out the position of the shooter. He figured his ambusher to be hidden behind a small hillock to his right, at least that is where the sound came from. Lee scurried to a more protected position in the rocks. The minion of the law thought that he detected a rifle barrel as the sunlight glinted off it.

The Clearwater sheriff was a patient man and he could afford to wait. That was the name of the game, hurry up and wait.

"There's too many graves in boot hills across the Southwest, 'cause of some people refusing to have patience," he thought to himself, as he looked once again toward the hill. "I can wait until perdition if I have to wait that long."

A few moments went by and he figured it to be long enough. Taking a quick peek over the rock, he saw no movement. Lee cautiously moved to the side of his horse. He started to stand, when suddenly he could feel the passing of air, as a bullet whistled by his ear. Quickly he ducked and hunkered down behind some rocks. A moment later he heard the report of a large bore rifle echo off in the distant horizon.

The sheriff carefully raised his rifle to lie atop the boulder. He squinted one eye, breathed, relaxed, took aim, squeezed the trigger and fired. A small puff of dust appeared in front of where he thought his quarry was hiding. Shifting his position, he hurriedly rolled to his left as a bullet ricocheted off the rock he was hiding behind. Once again, he breathed, relaxed, aimed and squeezed the trigger. This time he did not see any puff or for that matter anything.

Lee rolled to a more secure place behind a group of small boulders. These rocks were next to a cottonwood tree. He slowly stood up behind the tree trunk. Taking a deep breath, Lee glanced around the edge of the tree. The lawman heaved a sigh of relief when he wasn't fired upon anymore. Cautiously, Lee walked to where his hat lay and picked up the Stetson. He brushed the dirt off it, smoothed out a dent in the felt and placed the hat firmly on his head.

"Here I'm acting like an old woman," he thought, he started to grin self-consciously to himself as he stepped out in the open.

Lee held his rifle at the ready and advanced toward his horse. He shoved his rifle back into the boot and swung up in the saddle. Pulling on the reins, he wheeled his mount and rode to where he thought his attacker was last hidden. Getting closer, he automatically placed his hand on his gun's butt.

Lee rode up to the spot where he thought his prey had supposedly been to lie in wait. It was evident by the spent shell casings that this was the place. He dismounted and squatted to run his hands over the tracks left by his attacker's horse.

"The man must of been here a long time," he thought, as he saw the ridges on the horse tracks were already starting to crumble and the nearby animal droppings were beginning to harden under the hot sun.

"Do I want to pursue this matter?" Lee questioned himself, as he saw the trail went to the edge of the Red River. Making a quick decision about his jurisdiction, he turned back toward town. He tried to justify this latest happening as someone hunting. But there had been three shots.

"A dumb hunter," he thought. "Or at least a poor shot."

Shrugging his shoulders, he picked up the pace toward town. The small town sheriff had no thought of the events that were to transpire. These events would be tantamount to almost causing the town to go bankrupt and would cause him to reevaluate his position as it's chief law officer.

Lee sat astride his horse and gently let the reins droop over the mount's shoulders as he fished in his pocket for his tobacco makings. He stopped his horse and crossed his leg over the pommel of the saddle to roll a cigarette. Dragging a stinker across his thigh, he applied the burning match to the end of the cigarette. The sheriff took a deep drag and let the smoke trickle out of his nostrils and lips. Raising the reins once more, he put his heels gently into the side of the horse and continued the journey to *his* town, Clearwater, Indian Territory.

As he rode toward town, he took a survey of the surrounding area. To his left was the Red River and to his right but farther north the rolling hills surrounding Clearwater. Lee noticed that the Red River seemed to be swollen as a pregnant woman. He knew that it would not be long until the river overflowed its banks inundated the adjoining lands. Like the Nile River, the result was rich bottomland. The land was not only in great demand for its nourishment of the grasses, but provided a wonderful home for the wildlife.

TWO

He lay still on the cold hard bunk and laced his fingers behind his head so they rested on his dirty black curls. The prisoner stared at the four gray walls that separated him from freedom. A six-by-six foot adobe cell that had barren walls. Solitary confinement was his dungeon. He was segregated from the others.

"A condemned man needed no visitors or other contact with people," he was told by his jailers. The convicted felon had seen no one since his incarceration. But he remembered everyone; the prosecutor, his poor excuse for a public defender, the solemn jury and especially the small, grave, pompous and self-righteous judge.

The judge with a flowing black robe was perched behind a tall bench, like Zeus gazing down from his lofty perch on Mount Olympus at the feeble humans below. And like Zeus, the judge seemed to pierce him with a fiery look, as he brought the gavel down with such a force that a water glass tipped over to the side. The spilled water slowly meandered off the side of the high bench to drip on the hard wooden floor, as the glass continued to slowly spin on top of the bench. His Honor's imposing figure frowned at the guilty man and sentenced him with a single and final bang of the gavel. The magistrate's hair and eyebrows were white with age and his mouth seemed forever turned down. It was like being in the mere presence of the condemned was distasteful for him. The judge was a diminutive man and seemed delighted that he could wield his power. Because of his Lilliputian size, he thought it fitting to sit in judgment on anyone of bigger dimensions. Like Gulliver, only this time with the roles reversed. A panel of fellow lawgivers in the Indian Territory appointed the magistrate, on the simple account that no one else wanted the job.

The jurist was a disappointed man doing a disheartened duty. He was last in his class at a college back East.

"At least, there had to be someone last," he thought. By being last, he did not have the opportunity afforded him by any prestigious law firms. Thus, he was a back-woodsy type doing a back-woodsy type of job in a back-woodsy way. Of such was the law on the frontier in 1879.

The state's prosecutor was dressed in a fine broadcloth green suit with a vest from which a gold colored watch fob dangled in the front. The short, young and already starting to being bald strutted around in front of the jury box like a feisty bantam game rooster. This barrister had combed over what was left of his hair to cover his balding spot, making it look like a cobweb was placed on his balding pate. He was an up and coming lawyer, who would stop occasionally to take a quick snort of the pungent powder from his silver-looking snuffbox. A new celluloid collar, maroon tie, shiny black boots and an off-white cotton shirt finished out his ensemble. The one thing that stood out was his delicate looking hands.

These anemic looking hands and his stage voice, seemed to mesmerize the jury as he told the exploits of the criminal. He would list the crimes of the defendant in a singsong voice. Then he would shout them louder to reemphasize them. His voice went up and down the scale. One minute, it would be high like a woman's, the next minute he would drop its volume to a low rumble. Like a violinist, he played on the hearts of the jury. The prosecutor knew just when to pluck the strings and when to slide the bow in a long glide across the stretched catgut. He considered himself a maestro, raising his pasty hands in a crescendo, holding these appendages high and then suddenly dropping them in a climax of some long forgotten piece of music known only to him.

The hands were also used to the utmost at his effort of being somewhat an actor. They seemed to flutter in front of the jury, as a bird fluttered in front of a rattlesnake. Constantly moving, never resting, they hovered near the jury box. He would wave them up and down and side to side. Then with a flourish, he would pivot on his feet and as the viper was poised to strike, stand up on his tiptoe and then bring his finger to point at the defendant with finality.

Seeing he had everyone's attention, he held this poise for a moment. The courtroom was hushed. Quickly, he advanced on the defendant, stopping within paces of where the killer sat. Then the prosecutor, still gesturing with his hands, raised again up on his toes, gave the jury a piercing glance and in a demanding voice asked them for the most severe of punishments.

"Hang him!"

His lawyer seemed to him a poor whimpering fool, as he sat there with downcast eyes and never objected to the theatrics of the prosecutor. Once he started to raise his hand, only to let it fall down in futility. He was better defending a labor dispute or a land contract than to practice criminal law. This mild and meek servant of the law only looked sideways at him and gave a feeble smile.

A jury of twelve men, who were bored with the proceedings, seemed to take all of the prosecutor's antics in stride as they ho-hummed. They used long fans, pieces of paper and one took swinging his hat to the flying pests. The men were as interested in justice as they were expected to be. All they wanted to do is to get this predetermined trial finished. That way they could hurry home to get on with their drab lives. So, not even retiring to another room, they nodded to their foreman. He, feeling his importance, hurriedly stood and announced the jury had reached a verdict. They had voted unanimously.

"Guilty!"

The convicted man was taken to stand before the judge. The felon stood looking bored at the proceedings. Glancing up at the judge with defiance in his eyes, he said nothing in his defense. The prisoner was ready to accept anything, as he had been raised to give no quarter and taken none. He was resigned to his fate.

"Do you have nothing to say before I pronounce the sentence?" the gravely-voiced jurist asked, expecting no reply. He began to shuffle papers as if the judgment was a certainty. Now he was looking down at the defendant with an expression of extreme dissatisfaction.

"Then by the power vested in me by the federal government, I hereby sentence you to hang by the neck until you are *dead, dead, dead!*" the judge said, bringing the gavel down with a final force. He looked up and immediately dismissed this breaker of criminal laws as if it a duty to be done and he had done it.

The Indian Territory had no permanent place for lawbreakers. An outlaw's haven the rougher element that called it. Temporary jails and makeshift enclosures were the only means available for confinement of criminals. The land was ruled only by the strict laws set by the individual tribes of Indians. Often, death was the only means meted out to criminals and these were only to the Indians. An Indian could be put to death for the slightest infringement on tribal laws. Swift, but sure, with no complaints from the ones who were forced to pay, once it was measured out.

The cavalry provided the federal government's arm of enforcement. Then it was only if federal laws were broken. The officer in charge and the federal marshals determined these laws. There was a U. S. Marshal service in Tahlequah, but that was on the eastern side of the Indian Territory.

A traveling marshal often rode a circuit as a judge. He dispensed out quick retribution on the frontier. These traveling purveyors of justice had to be fast on the draw and what was more important, a sure shot. Usually, one's fate was determined by not only who shot first, but who was more accurate. Criminals who had run afoul of the law or who thought that they were quicker, soon found out that being fast did not do the trick. Sure they could get the first shot off, but they invariably ended by giving a vacant look toward the western sky, as their life blood slowly ebbed out of their bodies. Repeatedly it was the old adage, those who live by the gun, will surely die by the gun.

Two deputies led the judged man to a waiting horse. He was roughly forced to climb atop and was taken to the new jail many miles from what one would call civilization. This jail was the combined effort of a few ranchers in the Territory. They wanted a secure place to hold law breakers. It was a square enclosure made of adobe clay and had four one-hundred feet long walls surrounded by ten feet high walls. Guard towers were placed at the corners.

The guards were the volunteers from the ranches. They liked this form of work instead of riding the range all day and night in all kinds of weather.

"It's a easy job," some say. "There's good food and adequate sleeping quarters."

The guards had little worry over their charges, although a few had escaped. But these were quickly recaptured and brought back in bad shape. The prisoners had eyes gouged out, fingers and toes missing. And of course, more dead ones it seemed to be returning lately. But there being no returnees alive, their form of a cemetery was fast becoming filled to capacity.

"Had to shoot him," one guard said, winking at the other guards while undraping the tarpaulin that covered the body and letting it fall heavily to the ground.

They would unceremoniously drag the body off to a small cemetery. There it would be placed in a shallow grave without a marker. Then later while drinking his coffee would tell his fellow guards how the prisoner had stopped and waited to be shackled but grew nervous.

"Saw no reason in having to shackle him and spend all night trying to sleep with one eye open," one said. "So I just raised up and shot him. Of course, he's resisting arrest. You know, squirming as I tried to place the leg irons on him."

All knew that even if a prisoner gave up, that he would not make it back to the prison alive. Either way, the escapees always ended dead. There was an understanding among the guards that there were to be no survivors.

"I mean," their boss said, while wolfing down his dinner in a comfortable room decorated with various articles of the cowboys; spurs, weapons in gun racks and ropes festooning the walls, "if a man doesn't want to do his time, then they'll know that we're not going to beg them to stay. After all, we can't go mollycoddling everyone. 'Sides, it costs money to track them down and that's money that could, or should be spent on seeing to the welfare of the poor devils that we've now."

It was by such mentality that he found himself incarcerated. So now he was locked up and awaited his fate. Tomorrow they would take him from the cell, march him down the long windowless hallway and out the door to the dusty courtyard.

There, standing in the middle of the courtyard, stood the omen of his death; the scaffold awaited him. A guard would lead him up the thirteen steps to the top of the wooden structure. A gentle and a sad-eyed priest would mumble a few words out of the Good Book. He would be positioned over the trapdoor. The bald executioner would cover the convicted man's head with a black cloth hood. He would then slip the noose around the slender neck, making sure the knot was securely under the left ear and look to the warden.

The warden stood off in the shadows of the prison walls. He seemingly wanted to distance himself from the unpleasant but necessary duty. With a slight nod from the warden, the hangman would reach out and grasp the lever to the trapdoor. He quickly pull it. Once the trapdoor was released, the thin framed body that was home to *David Shannon White* would fall into oblivion.

"However, that's tomorrow," he thought. "Today I'm going to escape!"

"David," a burly guard asked, chuckling, while unlocking the cell door. "Ready for your last meal?"

"Sure," he replied, reaching behind his bunk for the spoon that he had recently stolen from the mess hall. He had sharpened it by spending countless hours rubbing it against the hard adobe walls. It was a small weapon, but nevertheless a weapon.

"A person's got to make do," David reasoned. "In the right hands it's extremely deadly. And in my hands, more so," he thought, as he palmed the whetted weapon and tensed for the door to open.

As the guard opened the door, David suddenly pushed hard on it. The metal door swung back hard forcibly striking the guard in the face. Utensils and food went crashing to the floor. Reaching for the falling guard, David turned his burden over and grasped the guard around the neck. Placing his forearm around the guard's neck and with his other hand, he abruptly shoved. David gave a sudden twist and smiled when he heard the breaking bones in the guard's neck. He was proud of his quick kill and grinned evilly.

Knowing he still had to get out of the cellblock, David reached down to the guard's belt and retrieved the keys. The condemned man quickly looked out the cell door. Seeing no one else, he broke into a run down the dimly lit corridor. David reached the end of the hallway. He stopped and peered out the window of the door. He could see two guards walking a prisoner between them; two burley men on either side of a scrawny looking prisoner, as they had their arms underneath his. They were not walking him as much as they were dragging him. Trails of dust were coming up behind the trio.

"Must of got him out of the *hot box*?" David thought ruefully. "So be it. Better him than me."

The hot box was an eight-foot wide three-foot deep hole dug in the ground. It's cover was a sheet of tin that had holes punched in the top for air. Once a day usually around eight in the morning, the guards would pull aside the tin and lower a small pail of refried beans. At this time they would pull up a pail containing the prisoner's waste. A prisoner could quickly lose his mind there. At night, he would almost freeze to death and during the day, the box quickly became unbearable. The hot rays of the sun hitting the tin made it a crude oven.

The killer saw another guard heading for his cell block. He hid behind the door and waited. In just a moment, he heard the key being turned in the lock. Tensing, his body felt ready for action, while quivering with excitement. The door swung inward. David waited for the guard to close the door.

"One grunt and you're dead!" he said, as he quickly grabbed the guard around the neck with one arm. Then he pressed the sharpened spoon into the guard's throat. David pulled the guard into a vacant cell and with a quick stroke slashed the guard's throat. Warm blood gushed freely on his hand. Looking down at the lifeless form he felt proud of his latest accomplishment. Dragging the corpse to a bunk, he laid the body on it.

He took the gun from the guard's holster and held it in his hand, smiling as the light from a torch hanging in the hall shimmered on the weapon. After strapping the holster and cartridge belt around his waist, he slid the gun up and down in the holster. Then he quickly unloaded the gun. Taking a solid stance, he whirled about. Drawing the gun quickly from the holster, he aimed the weapon at the wall. He pulled the trigger to test the tension, quickly dropped into a crouch and dry fired it a couple of times.

Pleasure washed over him. David shoved the gun home in the holster. It felt good to him after all this time being locked up. He felt so good that he bounced around the small cell for a moment. Then he reached for the cartridges and reloaded the gun.

David got a blanket from the bottom of the bunk and covered the guard, taking care to arrange the blanket. He pulled the blanket snug up to the guard's neck. Then he turned the guard's head toward the wall.

"Now he looks like someone asleep," he murmured. "He's actually dead to the world." Laughing inwardly, he turned and went to the entrance.

He looked out the doorway again and seeing no one, made a mad dash across the courtyard, then stopped. Standing in the shadows of the walls, he took a moment to look closely at the instrument of death. At night the scaffold looked dark and foreboding. David was going to cheat the hangman. Glancing back over his shoulder, he saw that there was no one to raise the alarm.

"So far, so good," he thought, as he finished his scramble across the open and dusty courtyard.

Once in the safety of the other side, he pulled an empty water barrel to the wall. After he scaled the wall, he ran down an arroyo between the wire fences that had been stretched around the inside perimeter of the prison walls. Now only a guard tower with a sharpshooter and another wall stood between him and his bid for *freedom*! He had gone too far to let this little problem deter him.

At the end of the gully, he glanced up and saw the guard tower. It loomed as a silhouette against the night sky, illuminated by the full moon like a specter of death. He grasped a tree limb and started slowly to climb. The tree was once the hanging tree, now it seemed to lean gracefully against the wall of the tower. By taking his time he went from one limb to the other. By now David reached the edge of the tower.

The wind started to blow harder against him. A hot humid breeze made his hair stick to his forehead. His locks were starting to fall down in his eyes, obscuring his vision for a moment. He was afraid to brush the curls as his toehold was not all that secure. Branches from the tree seemed to reach out and try to impede his progress. Nevertheless, he brushed them aside and held on tightly.

"That's all I need now, to escape the noose, only to fall and break my fool neck!" he muttered to the wind, noticing the irony of the situation. Minutes went by; he thought it was an eternity. David looked carefully over the edge of the tower.

"What luck!" In the glow of the lantern, he saw that the guard was nodding off to sleep

The killer quietly crawled over the edge and moved silently toward the unaware slumbering form. He stopped suddenly as the guard began to stir. The guard had only shifted positions by rolling over on his side. In just a moment the guard had placed his hands across his chest and was starting to snore peacefully into the night.

David reached out and slowly took the guard's fallen weapon. He raised the rifle above his head and brought it crashing down on the unsuspecting victim, sending bits of gore to splash against the gray tower walls. Once this was done, he easily scampered over the walls and was determined to place as much distance between him and the prison as possible.

"Pulling guard duty was a cushy job." he remembered overhearing one of the guards saying. He began to laugh at this statement.

"So far, I've killed three men, escaped from prison and now I'm on my way to Mexico! Not bad, if I say so myself," David smiled, in appreciation of his night's work, mentally rubbing his hands in glee.

David spent two nights in the arid land living off an occasional rattlesnake, kangaroo rats and any other small animal he could snare, getting his moisture from the white and purple blossoms of the Yucca plant. His lips were starting to get parched, cracking at the corner and his hands had formed blisters on them.

He made a temporary hat by taking a dried clump of grass and weaving it into a sort of hat. David thanked the many hours spent being locked up, learning to work with braiding material, taught by a captured leather worker. The convict had shown him how to braid rope so that it would take form and give him the utmost strength from it.

"If I can do that with rope," he thought. "Why not grass?" So he made a sturdy hat out of the tall Johnson grass. At first he wandered in the desert. He was lost! Finally he sat on a rock next to a small sapling and thought to himself.

"I can't believe that I escaped that hell-hole," he muttered to the wind. "Looks like I'm destined to roam aimlessly here in the desert until all people will find are some bleached bones."

Suddenly, he stood and remembered what his father had taught him. By always keeping the sun over his left shoulder in the mornings and his right shoulder in the evenings, he knew he would be headed south. He moved steadily forward. He arrived at the top of a small hill at sunup and saw a sod buster's shack lying before him. David looked at the bright ball as it started its customary journey across the sky. Shadows were starting to shorten around the small shack.

Silently, he ran to the side of the hovel, where he pressed his back to the walls and stealthily crept along the wall. David heard snoring coming from inside of the structure as he went toward the opening.

"Must be sleeping in," he thought, as he pulled to the side the blanket used for the front door and quickly dropped on his belly. Like a rattlesnake, he slithered inside. Like the snake, he was silent, swift and ever so deadly!

David looked to the far wall and spied two huddled forms asleep on the corn shuck bed. He arose slowly, looking about him. Then he reached out and grabbed the sod buster's shovel leaning against the wall. He swung the spade with no remorse at all and caved in the skulls of the two bone-weary occupants, spraying the dirty walls with bright red blood. David was quick in ransacking the hut, but found nothing of use for him. He then strode boldly out the door of the shack.

Once outside of the dwelling, David made a quick survey of his surroundings. His darting eyes quickly saw a bony sway-back mare that was hobbled to the side of a makeshift lean-to. He could see the ribs sticking out of the sides of the animal and immediately felt sorry for him, but just as quick, any sign of mercy rapidly left him.

"After all," he thought. "It's *me* to take care of, not some dumb animal."

David walked to the crib and gently slid his hand over the back of the horse. He spied a rope hackamore on a peg attached to the wall. Hurriedly, he moved to the wall and took down this piece of homemade harness from its resting place. He slowly moved it over the muzzle of the mare while speaking softly to her. David released the animal from the crib, found an old decayed leather saddle and placed it upon the weary animal. He swung up on the creature's back. The dumb brute grunted under the unaccustomed weight and at first balked at moving. Cruelly, David dug his heels into the horse's side. The nag started forward at a brisk pace. He rode away from the latest means of his thievery without a backward glance. Laughing to himself, he headed to *Mexico*!

The killer rode for an hour, then halted to rest his mount. Not because he felt any pity for the animal. He just did not want to have to walk any farther in this God forsaken land than was meant for him to walk. Then he walked his mount for a spell. It was far better for the animal to walk than for David to trudge. This went on all day and he only stopped when nightfall overtook him. The light of the full moon shining brightly gave off the only illumination. His visibility was excellent, as was his hearing.

He watched with humor as a sidewinder slithered sideways across the trail, disappearing into the brush. The small sound made by another resident of the wilds was picked up by its mate. The soulful sound of a coyote was echoed by another, and before long, the sounds blended together to make a nightly symphony. This cacophony of sound was unnerving to some, while to David it was sweet music to his ears. The desert was lively and at the same time secretive.

"Like me," the escapee thought, wiping the sweat from his eyes. "Lively, but cautious."

David regarded himself as a resident of the badlands. He had no home to speak of and everything he had was just for survival.

"Killing those people was the means to the end. I needed a horse; they had one and who can blame me for taking it. Certainly not me! They should not have made their horse so readily available. No one could blame me for seizing the opportunity afforded to me. Strike when the metal was hot and tonight, it was blistering!"

To his evil mind, he had no compunction in killing. It had to be done and who else but him could do it. He had killed before, raped a few and once had set fire to an orphanage just to see and hear everyone scramble and scream as the cruel fire ravaged the burning wooden structure. His eyes had seemed to light up as he watched a man carry a burned child to safety, but dimmed as he saw them look at him suspiciously. David quickly made an exit to another town and more killing.

"It's in my blood," he used to tell the barflies that hovered around him like moths around a flame at border saloons. "I can't help it," he once said, as he was busy drinking whiskey in an out of the way saloon. "Not that I want to," he silently thought to himself. "It's in my *blood*!"

"You've got bad blood!" his mother screamed to him. She had once told him that when he was only nine years old. It was the day before she ran off with a drummer leaving him and his father to work their tired out old farm in the hills of northern Arkansas.

No matter how much the White's tried, they could not make a go of it. Eventually, David's father took to drinking more and staying away from the farm. Finally walking out of David's life forever. After some time had elapsed, the townspeople came and took David away. He was shuffled from family to family until at the ripe age of twelve, he injured a neighbor boy in a fracas and was sent to a correctional institution near Huntsville, Alabama.

David endured two years there. He would often toss and turn and cry himself to sleep at night. When the cotton was in full bloom, he often developed allergies. Wheezing, Sneezing and coughing, the small boy would go about his dreary jobs at the home. It was during this stay he made a vow to himself.

"Never trust anyone but yourself and then have some doubts about that," he muttered to himself. "From now on, I just worry about David Shannon White."

It wasn't too long before a sickness of the mind slowly rooted itself into his fragile brain. He would have nightmares about some one tormenting him and chasing him down a long never ending tunnel. It seemed as if he would run two steps forward and then one back, a sort of prisoner's shuffle. No matter how hard he tried, he could not escape the reaching and clawing hands at his back. Waking up in a sweat, he would look wildly at his whereabouts. Seeing the bleak walls and the solitary opening which was passed off as a window, he would sigh and roll over on his cot trying to go back to sleep. This reoccurring nightmare plagued him for many months, stamping a horrible image of being pursed into his young mind.

The horse's ears perked up as it smelled water. David knew the Red River must be over the next hill. He also remembered that crossing the expanse of water was only the beginning of a long and treacherous trek through the western part of Texas. There would be more wasteland, more people and more danger. But he also realized that once across the Rio Grande River was what awaited him. *Freedom*!

David, in his mind's eye, could see the sweet señoritas and savor fine tequila. His mouth watered at the thought of tasting the tortillas and refried beans. Maybe even swing in a hammock and sucking suds.

"Ah, that'll be the life for me," he thought, while riding his stolen horse along a sandy trail. David rode up to a small knoll. He could barely see until the moon came out from behind a cloud. It was full. His vision improved greatly. David dismounted and looked down the hill. Below was the faint outline of a town. Beyond that, he could see the dark boundary of the Red River. This expanse of water separated Texas from Indian Territory, as it weaves its dark waters, hunting ways of least resistance through the arid land to end in the Mississippi River around Shreveport, Louisiana. It was supposed to be shallow at this time of the year.

David gazed down at the town and saw it was all quiet. There were few lights on, but outside of that it seemed lifeless. He knew that to survive in Mexico, he would need money. Here was his golden opportunity. This small town was bound to have a bank, and therefore, money. Money that he needed to live on in Mexico. He figured on making one last big haul. That way, he could squander his life as he chose. He did not believe in doing anything hard.

"That's for fools," he thought, as he cruelly rode his cayuse up and down the small hills. "All I need to do is break into the cracker box of a bank. I'll take what money and other valuables I can find deposited on the premises and ride like crazy to the border, letting the locals worry about the absence of their money," he considered. Inwardly, he chuckled at the thought of the proud citizenry waking up to find their life earnings were now safely stored in his saddlebags.

David rode to the edge of the town, stopping to read the sign that proclaimed the town of Clearwater, Indian Territory. The sign was in a state of disrepair. He dismounted so that he could read the piece of wood in the dim light.

"Just hope that the sign's no indication of this burg," he thought. He did not want to make a detour to a poor town. "If the sign's evidence of needed repair, what could the town offer me?"

Swinging up into the saddle, he guided his mount so that he could keep to the rear of the buildings. He reined in at the back of a livery stable and dismounted. Taking the reins of the horse, he tied them to a short fence post. Bending over a little, he then scampered to the back of the structure. David immediately halted his forward progress when he heard voices from inside the stable.

"Got two pairs," Tom Schellenburg chortled, in a victor's voice, pushing back his hat to reveal straight black hair, which he was all the time pushing out of his eyes. He took a deep breath and laid his cards down on the top of a nail keg. "Two aces and two sevens!"

"That's good, old son," Gary Sandusky said, spreading his cards to show a full house, queens over jacks. "But not good enough. Read 'em and weep, my friend. If I'm not mistaken, I do believe that beats you."

The two had been playing cards the biggest part of the day and on into the very early hours of the morning. They had to play in the stable as Chris Barker, the other stable owner and the town's blacksmith was away on a hunting trip. Chris was due back later in that day with the spoils of his hunt. Tom was eagerly waiting for Chris's return.

He was now in charge of the stable. A tall, lanky and a congenial person, Tom was also the town's mayor and sole owner of the local newspaper, *The Clearwater Crier*. The young man loved to be the first to tell of the news of far away places.

Tom's father, Jasper K. Schellenburg, with Chris shared ownership of the livery. Jasper was the more outgoing of the two. Chris was aware of his size and was the one who actually did all the backbreaking work. Whereas, Jasper would buy the supplies, Chris would patiently pound the anvil. The townspeople found that they could talk and joke with Chris. Jasper seemed not to have any empathy toward people. He was aloof most of the time, even condescending.

Jasper had asked Tom for help with the stable as he was going to St. Louis to buy supplies. Tom being a dutiful son, readily complied as he figured on only being away from the paper a few days.

"But only 'til Chris gets back," Tom said yesterday to his father.

Tom wanted to return to his paper. He loved the feel of ink and the musty smell of the newspapers fresh off the one-handed printing press. But he loved his father too much to deny help when needed, his mother dying in childbirth. The people did have to give Jasper credit, for he had raised Tom alone. This was Jasper's one redeeming quality, as far as the citizens were concerned, for Tom turned out to be a well-liked man. The gangly man was elected mayor by a landslide last year.

Originally, Jasper would buy his supplies from a traveling drummer, but he wanted to get out of this town for a while also. Being a widower made him want to see brighter lights and city people. Jasper also thought to be tied down to the town was beneath his dignity.

"One-horse town," he would scoff to the people, as he hooked his fingers in his purple suspenders, strutting around the city. The people would look at him, smile and think to themselves, "A country bumpkin."

Jasper was dressed up in his Sunday-go-to-meeting attire. A plaid top coat over a brown suit, cream color white shirt, five-buttons high top shoes and a green on white polka-dotted tie. A straw skimmer adorned his bald head. His head would be bobbing in the sea of humanity as he meandered through the city crowds.

Gary was the deputy sheriff. Medium build, with ash colored hair falling to his shoulders. He wore all black, like an undertaker. His hat had a leather hatband studded with small turquoise stones. A vest, trousers and Mexican vaquero boots were also all in black. The only other colors were an off-cream colored shirt with red garters at the sleeves and a bright red bandanna loosely tied around his neck.

A Colt .45 pistol was strapped to his right leg in a leather holster that was securely tied down with a leather thong. He had fought in the range wars in New Mexico after the war between the states. The ranchers of Lincoln County, New Mexico caused havoc among themselves, with fighting over whom should have what and how many of what. It was during this little range war that a small-time cattle rustler, William H. Bonny, also know as Billy the Kid, came to notoriety.

"Greedy guts," Gary had thought at the time, but took their money in return for hiring his gun out to them. "If I don't offer my gun to the highest bidder, someone else will do it," he rationalized. Gary was fast with it and often resorted to it when in need, which seemed all the time then. His shootings had always been in self-defense though.

Because of this fighting between the ranchers and his fast draw, Gary wore his hat at a cocky angle, as if to dare anyone to say anything to him. He would saunter down the main street, with his eyes constantly darting.

"A chip on his shoulder," some would say behind his back, but always with a grudging respect. No one dared to accost him, as they knew him to have a quick temper. Or least ways, do it and not expect him to do anything about it. Many had tried, yet few lived to caution others not to be so foolhardy.

The townspeople had hired Gary to be sheriff Lee Wildman's chief deputy. A laugh to Gary, because there were only two people on the work force, Lee and him. They covered 515 square miles with the town of Clearwater, Indian Territory being the focal point of the surrounding area to farmers, cattlemen and the townspeople.

The sheriff had a working relationship with the deputy U.S. Marshal out of the Tahlequah federal office. The marshal answered to the chief marshal in Denver, Colorado who in return answered to 40-year-old Judge Isaac Parker at Fort Smith, Arkansas. Judge Parker was also known as "the hanging judge." His court jurisdiction was not only the Western District of Arkansas, but encompassed the Indian Territory.

Lee had jurisdiction only in Clearwater, but the marshal had allowed Lee to mete out justice to the immediate area. So far, no one had defined *the immediate area*, therefore, Lee was a law unto himself. Since the law was obeyed and properly enforced, no one thought it necessary to complain.

There was talk of hiring more deputies but, as of yet, no one had really applied for the position. Though many asked, they all said that it was too dangerous. Besides, there was not enough pay. These reasons were the two main concerns the applicants had voiced.

Gary had wanted to settle down and this opportunity was a godsend for him. He was tired of being a loner and having to always look over his shoulder for someone who wanted to plant him in an unmarked grave out on the desolate prairie. He still could not control his temper very well, but to give him credit, he tried.

"Well," Gary said, getting to his feet and yawning, placing his hat on his head and turning to go. Then he pulled his timepiece from his pocket and flipping open the cover, peered at it intently. He had to squint to make out the time, as the lantern did not shed that much light. "It'll be daylight before too much longer. I guess I'll get a little shut-eye. See you later, Tom."

"Right," Tom said, stretching his sinewy arms over his head. "I'd better check on that filly of Miss Thomas. I keep telling her that horse's going to foal any day now. She wants me to keep an eye out for it and to be sure to let 'er know when the event is going to take place, as if she could help any. Just goes to show you that women can be very puzzling at times! I'll also check and see if Chris has made it back yet from his hunting trip. My mouth waters at the thought of clamping my teeth down on the venison he brings home. See you later, Gary."

"Jasper never seemed to let poor ole Tom have a moment's rest," Gary thought as he waved his good-bye and started toward his room at the jail. "I'm glad that I'm already born, that way Jasper wasn't my father."

He shook his head in disbelief and continued onward. The deputy would stop every so often to rattle the door handles of the businesses. He was tired and half-heartedly glanced at the door of the bank. Gary just sauntered by the bank, as he did not see the key gleaming in the moonlight.

"All's quiet tonight," he thought, as he turned toward the jail, visions of upcoming sleep already making his eyes drowsy.

Unbeknownst to him, an escaped killer was lurking in the shadows of the stable. David watched the receding back of the town's law. He waited until the deputy went inside the jail.

"Now I only have to be on the look out for that other feller," David thought, as he drew back more in the shadows. Patiently, David waited for the town to become silent. Presently, he heard Tom move about in the stable.

After Gary had left, Tom headed toward the back of the stable. He looked in on the Thomas horse, gave her some oats and crawled up the ladder to the hayloft. Tom sat on the clean straw, pulled off his boots and placed them at the side of the blanket he had spread upon the straw. Then he took off his jeans and unbuttoned his shirt. Afterwards he stripped down to his long underwear and tossed the jeans over a rafter by his bedroll. He noticed the loose boards on the floor by the opening of the hayloft. Tom put the thought of fixing the boards from his mind, he had other things to concentrate on instead. The small town mayor was not mindful of how these loose boards would play a big part in the future of the town.

Tom lay on the clean straw and placed his hands behind his head. He stared up at the livery ceiling and thought of how much he missed sleeping in his bed at the newspaper office. The smell of printer's ink and the often musty smell of the newspaper brought fond memories to the town official. He smiled.

"The smell of clean straw's also an added benefit of sleeping in the stable," he thought.   Then he remembered why he was here instead of there and grinned. Sure, it was to help his father, but simultaneously, he could keep an eagle eye on that horse of Miss Laurie Thomas. Thinking of her beauty, he smiled and drifted off to sleep. His snores bounced off the overhead rafters of the livery. They mingled with the soft breathing of the horses, mules and cattle patiently chewing the hay or their cuds in the stalls below.

THREE

David White stayed where he was for a moment. When he thought he had waited long enough, he slipped into the entrance of the barn. He held his hands out in front of him to make sure not to bump into any obstructions. Looking like a sort of ghost, he was walking stiff legged and with his hands thrust out in front of him.

Slowly he made his way to the front of the barn, stopping his forward movement when a horse snorted, after he mistakenly bumped into the side of the stall. He could hear the loud snoring of Tom above, but figured that to be a help, for when the snoring stopped, David knew that the sleeper was awake and that he must be more careful. Upon reaching the doorway, he squatted beside the entrance and looked out on the sleepy little hamlet.

The moonlight allowed him to see the buildings as if it were still dusk. David thanked his stars for the bright moon. He smirked as he cast his gaze about him, his beady eyes darting here and there were taking in everything.

Across the street was a telegraph office and a general store. Along with these businesses, a leather shop and restaurant were on the same side of the street. The newspaper office was on the corner. Next to the newspaper office was the leather shop. A sign hanging to one side of the leather shop door said:

HAIR CUTS
SHAVES
UNDERTAKING
TEETH PULLING
SURGEON

To the right were the saloon and the sheriff's office and across it emblazoned in bright large letters was THE CLEARWATER COMMUNITY COMMERCIAL BANK. The large edifice sat squatting like fruit in a bowl.

"Ripe enough to pick," he thought. "A fat plum and I'm just the man to pluck it."

The bank was separated from the sheriffs' office by an alley. The hotel next to it boasted of cane chairs and benches on the front porch. Potted plants were siting either side of the hotel door like door attendants. The sound of merriment, glasses tinkling and the loud pinking of a piano let David know the saloon was going full swing. The bank stood formidable across the alley from the sheriffs' office. The jail had a brick front and bars were at the window. It looked black and foreboding.

"At least it's closed," David muttered, as he looked at the darkened windows of the building. He could not discern whether the jail had occupants or not. The killer was just thankful that he was not one of the guests of the county.

He then glanced back at the object of his desires. According to the letters emblazoned in gold-colored paint across the window of the bank, Gale L. Loughmiller was the president; Ron Edwards, the vice-president and chief teller. Ron was also the only employee of the bank and according to Gale.

"That's all we need," he said. Gale did not want too many people to know of the bank's assets or his sometimes nefarious dealings. "The less that knew, the better," it seemed to him.

A short time later, cowboys were seen streaming from the saloon. David knew the saloon would be closing down for the night. He waited. The cowboys mounted their horses and galloped out of town. That left one horse at the hitch rail. The horse stood there and patiently awaited its owner. Finally, the owner showed up.

David saw a cowboy come staggering through the saloon's batwing doors. The cowboy stumbled down the steps, went to the hitching rail and untied the lone horse. He pulled his means of conveyance from the hitching post and then the fun began. David smiled as he watched the drunken cowboy try to get up on his mount. The man would get one foot up in the stirrup and the horse would shy away. The wrangler and horse went around in circles for quite awhile. Finally, he got up on his saddle. The bowlegged equestrian grabbed the reins with both hands. He wheeled his steed and started slowly down the street toward the outskirts of town.

"I wonder, how far he thinks he's going to get," David mused to himself, as he saw the drunken cowboy was leaning precariously in the saddle. He watched the receding back of this modern-day paladin of the plains and his transportation fade into the darkness of the still night.

David moved quietly from his hiding position. He ran to the side of the watering trough in front of the bank. He immediately dropped to his knees, breathing heavily, as he had not done much physical activity in a long time. After catching his breath, he was rising from this position when he heard a noise. Ducking his head and he hurriedly scooted back into the shadows cast by the lights from the saloon.

It was only the bartender coming outside to move a few chairs back into the saloon. He was preparing to close for the night. He gathered the chairs and took them into the saloon. In a moment, the bartender returned, placed his hands behind his back and stretched. The barkeep scratched his belly, then looked up and down the street. The bartender was short, portly and sweating profusely. He had on baggy trousers held up by red suspenders. His belly hung so far over his belt, it seemed to defy the law of gravity. Black garter belts held up the sleeves of his sweat stained white and blue striped shirt. Boots that were run down at the sides with the leather drooping over the heels were his footgear.

The bartender took a soiled handkerchief out of his rear pocket and proceeded to wipe his damp brow, which was glistening in the light of the moon. He wiped his forehead and blew his nose. Placing the soiled napkin back in his rear pocket, he hitched his trousers up a little. Then the barkeep pulled the saloon doors shut tightly, locked them, paused to stretch again and hurried down the street.

David watched him vanish around the corner of the street. He waited. The town was quiet as a tomb and appeared to be as empty as his stomach. The customary cur was asleep.

"Nothing like a yapping dog to spoil a man's plans," David thought. "Time to make my move," he muttered, as he slowly left his concealment at the partially filled watering trough.

David hurried to the side of the bank. The building had one large front bay window. Hurrying to the alley, which separated the building from the sheriff's office, he looked and saw another window about five feet from the ground. Its mate was further toward the back. All the windows were dark.

"The side window's the one I want," David thought, as he moved forward to the alley.

He looked around and his gaze fell upon a water barrel under a rainspout. David ran to the barrel and saw that it had water in the bottom. Emptying the barrel of its contents, he drug the hogshead underneath the window. David climbed atop the cask and he was happy to find that he could reach the windowsill. The killer took out his sharpened spoon and began to pry at the caulking in the panes of glass and achieved nothing. It was taking too long, by his reckoning, so he peeled off his shirt. Taking his shirt, he wrapped his hand in it. Then turning his head to shield his eyes from the flying glass, he broke out the window. He looked around to see if anyone had heard the noise. David discerned no movement so he turned back to the window and raised the sash. He wiggled into the opening.

David came down on top of a desk barely missing the upturned spike that held receipts. He jumped off the desk and found himself in front of a teller's cage. The light from the moon made checkerboard shadows in front of the teller cage. Other light filtering in a window cast shadows on the interior of the bank. They reminded David of part-time guards guarding the bank's contents. Like shadows they posed no threat to him and he happily walked among them. He moved behind the small wooden barrier in front of the cage and quickly pulled out each drawer to reveal . . . *nothing!*

"I'm a killer, not a safecracker," he thought, as he looked at the vault. It was too hard for him to break into. In the dimness, he could see a door beside the vault. "That must lead to the bank president's private office," he thought.

David grinned as he started toward the door, pausing long enough to grab a candle and a handful of stinkers from the side of a teller's cage. Making sure the drapes were pulled and satisfied that it was sufficiently dark for him, he drugged the lucifer across the wire mesh, held his hand up to protect the match and applied the flame to the candle. He held his hand in front of the flickering wick of the candle as he started toward the door. His progress slowed as the flame began to flicker. Reaching the door, he stopped and, holding the candle in his left hand, opened the door. The glow from the candle cast an eerie glow on the scene.

The room was twenty feet by fifteen feet, with a back door. He checked to make sure the back door was locked. Satisfied, he surveyed the room. An oval rug took up half the floor. On the wall above a large oak desk hung a picture of the president of the bank. He was shaking hands with some senator from back East. A heavily draped window was at the left of the desk. On the opposite wall were pictures of various railroads. Inside to the left of the door was a coat rack. The rack held: umbrellas, mackinaw, slickers and a woolen coat. On the top of the rack were a black felt bowler, a railroad conductor's hat and a woman's straw hat with a red ribbon.

David went to the desk and sat down in a swivel chair. He spun around to begin his search of the drawers of the desk. He pulled out the top drawer, which revealed paper clips, cloth bands and a pair of scissors. David shut this drawer and reached down to pull out the bottom drawers. One had a pile of dirty rags while the other had bank papers; some deeds, notary seal and blank bank drafts.

"Hrump!" David exclaimed. Disappointed with his find, he began to shut the drawer with the rags quietly. "So far," he thought, "nothing that I can use."

It was while shutting the drawers he heard a metallic click in the lock at the back door. He glanced at the door and saw the doorknob start to turn. Thinking fast David hurried across the room and quickly hid behind a sofa in front of the draped window. He pulled an overstuffed chair to one end of the sofa. The chair slid softly on the carpet. This chair helped to conceal him; he felt more secure.

"Sure the bank has the money?" a squeaky voice softly asked.

"I saw 'em bring it in this afternoon," a deep voice replied, also in a muffled tone of voice. "We just go into the front room where the vault's at. I place the dynamite.

Boom! We sashshay over and clean out the vault. Then we waltz out the door and hightail it to the border. Just live high off the hog and have pretty señoritas at our beck and call. We'll have enough money to get them to do anything we want."

"I can hardly wait until that bank clerk sobers up in the morning and finds his bank key is missing," the whimpering voice cackled.

"Shhs!" deep voice ordered. "Be quiet!"

"I know!" squeaky retorted. "I know!"

The two intruders came in the back door and started toward the front. They came abreast of where David was hiding. David reached out and grabbed the back one by the throat, as he reached down and pulled the man's gun out of his holster.

"What – "

"Now, what would you boys be up too?" David asked in a menacing voice, pulling the hammer back on his gun and pointing at the one in front, who had whirled around to see his partner held by a stranger. This man had a gun thrust unceremoniously under his partner's ear. The barrel of this gun never wavered, nor did the hand that held it.

The hostage David was holding immediately wet his trousers and fainted. David threw this one to the floor in disgust. Still pointing the weapon, he looked at the one still standing.

"Okay you! Drop your gun!" David said, while moving toward the man. "Talk quickly or so help me, I'll decorate the walls with your tiny brains."

One of the men had a pockmarked weasel face, with a livid purple scar coursing down the left cheek. A dirty gray slicker covered a thin body. He had on a pair of boots with the heels run down and a brown felt hat, whose brim was broken and was always falling down. The brim hid dishwater hair that threatened to peek out from under the hat. He had four front teeth: one gold, two were black tarry stained and one completely black. Tobacco juice had dribbled down his chin to stain the front of his gray slicker. When the wind shifted in the room, David would swear that he could smell the fear that emanated from this filthy person.

"There's no need in that," the man said, his voice trembling. Dropping his gun to the floor and shifting from one side to he other and back again. He looked at David, tried smiling and with a pleading voice told in a shrill voice of his mission.

"My name's J.O. Jensen. My partner here is Clovis Hardesty. Me and him were planning to make an early withdrawal from this here bank. Course you being here first, we'll just mosey along."

As he was saying this, he began to crab sideways toward the back door. Clovis started to regain consciousness, evident by his eyes starting to flicker open. He started to arise when David hastily thrust him back to the floor. He then looked at J.O., who had suddenly stopped his progress and was standing quite still. J.O.'s eyes were locked onto the barrel of the gun pointed at him. The longer he looked, the bigger the bore seemed. In just a moment, he black hole of the barrel seemed to him to encompass everything.

"Hold it right there," David ordered, motioning with the gun. "You sit right down there and make yourself comfy, I'll tend to your compadre."

The semiconscious man had on bib overalls, one strap hanging onto dear life by a thread. Worn-out boots with holes in both soles were on his feet. A flour print shirt torn at the collar was loosely draped on his thin frame. His crumpled filthy black felt hat lay on the floor beside him. David took wire coat hangers, parts of twine from the desk and tied up Hardesty tighter than a Christmas turkey. Then as an afterthought, he pulled Hardesty's filthy bandanna from the dirt-encrusted neck and stuffed it in the prone man's mouth.

The old man was starting to gag a bit, but quickly quit, as he stared at the unfeeling face of the man who had him covered and now tied up. He immediately saw that his captor was without any feeling of good will toward him and Jensen.

"Look, maybe we can be friends," J.O. whined, unconsciously scratching under his right arm. "You know after all, I'm sure you're a right nice fellow."

David watched this poor excuse for a human and almost got sick to his stomach. But, who knew?

"They might just be useful to me," he thought. "Think, David, think!"

"These two just might be the solution to my problems," he thought, suddenly smiling as he came upon a new plan. He began to take a fresher interest in them. David grinned as he pondered these latest developments. Rob this bank and leave two bodies behind. A fitting present to the town for giving him the money he needed in his escape. He smiled, his lips pulled back evilly to show his yellowed teeth.

"J.O. had the dynamite, so I'll need him. However, what would I do with the other?"

As if to answer him, Hardesty rolled on his back and brought his hands up to his chest. He started to squirm on the floor and breathe heavily. His nostrils were quivering as if in pain and his eyes were starting to get wider. Quickly, J.O. rushed to the squirming man, heedless of David and removed the gag from Hardesty's mouth. Hardesty quivered, his eyes starting to roll upwards in their sockets. A thin line of gray dribble began to form at the corners of his mouth. His emancipated body was starting to twitch horribly.

"Say!" J.O. exclaimed, looking up at David. "I think ole Clovis is having another one of his spells. Wait here and I'll run out to our horses and get his medicine. Be quicker than a wink. Won't be a minute?"

"You seem to forget," David said, motioning with his gun. "You're covered. You're not going anywhere unless I say so. You catch my drift?"

J.O. was alternating the looks being given between David and his fallen companion. Beads of sweat were starting to form on his forehead. He began to rock as he shifted his weight from one side to the other. J.O. was busy wringing his hands and looking dejectedly down at Hardesty. He remembered Hardesty was his only friend, but this man had a gun pointing at him and it was not wavering any.

"Sort of damned if I do and damned if I don't," he thought. Then he looked at David again, stopped swaying on his feet and hurriedly decided, "I'd better do what this fella says to do right now," he thought. J.O. nodded to David.

"All right," David tiredly said, as he motioned with his gun. "Go and get the medicine, but remember one thing. You take longer than one minute and your friend here will have three eyes instead of two. Know what I mean?"

Nodding his understanding, J.O. hurried out the back door. J.O. had just closed the door, when David looked down at Hardesty and smiled at him coldly. David hovered over the tied victim.

"What has to be done, has to be done," he thought. He relished what he was going to be doing. "Good bye, friend," David said, as he squatted next to Hardesty and placed his hands on Hardesty's throat. He began to squeeze his hands. The veins on the back of his hands stood out in stark relief. Hardesty's eyeballs began to protrude, as his face took on a sickly, gray pallor. He raised his hands to grasp David's arms, only to just as quickly let go as he moved them to the hands at his throat. His tongue began to hang out of his mouth obscenely and his feet began to beat a tattoo the floor. David squeezed harder and put his full weight on top of the poor derelict.

Once this task was finished, David quickly grasped Hardesty's hand and just as he had expected the door opened. In rushed J.O. breathing hard. He looked at the body, gulped audibly and turned to David.

"Is he . . . ?" J.O. whimpered, dejectedly sitting on the sofa, his eyes were widening in disbelief. "Clovis and I went back some ways to our childhood. Now Clovis was dead and it was my fault I guess," J.O. thought resignedly.

"Yep," David said, trying his best to look sincere. "He told me that if you'd only hurry. He knew that this's going to be the big one. I was afraid to run out and get you. Besides, he was holding my hands awfully tight."

J.O. looked forlorn and lost as he sat on the sofa. Presently a tear meandered down his wrinkled face. He reached up and wiped his eyes with the back of a leathery hand. The novice robber looked at David and asked what he was going to do now.

"I need someone to lead me and this one was just that someone to do that, lead me," he thought, reaching up to wipe a stray tear from his eyes.

"Tell you what we need to do now," David said, as he arose from beside the body of Hardesty, speaking with an air of authority and headed toward the door of the office that led into the front of the bank. He knew that the other man would obey him without any question. "We're going to blow that vault, get the money and hightail it out of here. Follow me!"

J.O. followed David meekly into the room with the bank's vault. He had brightened up considerably, for he now had a leader. He was happy, so happy he began to softly hum to himself. His long friendship with Hardesty almost forgotten, but he remembered that Hardesty was dead and he was alive. That was all that mattered to him now. Shrugging his shoulders, he docilely followed David.

They went into the front room and J.O. placed his tools down in front of the vault. He took a few sticks of dynamite from his satchel, taking care not to move too quickly. Assuming an air of some importance, he looked at David.

"Get behind that desk and don't move until the big bang's over."

J.O. dragged a stinker across the back of his pants and applied the flame to the end of a four-foot fuse. While the fuse was sparking as it raced to the dynamite, J.O. hurried and hid the other side of the teller's cage. He quickly placed his hands over his ears.

David had already thought of the untimely end of J.O. Jensen. His criminal brain had previously conjured up a decent number of scenarios. When the townspeople found the bodies of these two vagrants, they'd wonder at the identity of the bodies and possibly mill around for a while. Then the townspeople would form a posse and start a heavy pursuit. David figured on being long gone from the scene.

"I'll take the money and other valuables and scatter a few trinkets on the floor. By the time the money's counted, I'll be so far away the bank people would have to chalk up the robbery to fate," he thought. J.O. placed his fingers in his ears and watched the fuse sparkle as it raced toward its end at the vault's lock. David had crawled behind the sofa and turned his back to the sofa as he braced himself.

"I sure hope the old codger knows what's he doing," David pondered, while trying to make himself as small as possible behind the piece of furniture. He tucked his feet under him and covered his head with his hands. "If he don't know, then this'll be an added excuse to kill him. As if I needed a reason to kill anyone or anything.

Sometimes I think I kill for the simple reason that I like to," he thought, grinning to the dark.

The explosion was terrific. It seemed as if a small earthquake rocked the building. The walls vibrated, the windows were blown out and smoke covered everything. Through the smoke David could barely discern the outline of J.O. weaving on his feet. He arose from his hiding place, waved his hands to clear the smoke and rushed to J.O.'s side.

"All right, friend?" David asked. Not because of concern over J.O.'s welfare, but worry that J.O. might not be in any condition to complete the plan he had devised. David wanted help in loading the horses with his reward. Then he would eliminate J.O. according to the time table he had set up, not before.

"Just shook up a little," J.O. answered, taking his bandanna off to wipe the powder from his face. He was thrilled to think that David really cared about him. "Being part of his gang might not be so bad after all," he thought, as he hurriedly dusted off his pants.

He looked up to see David move to the blown vault. The doors were askew and David noticed the sacks of currency and a few gold bars and some silver that gleamed dimly where they stacked them on the vault's shelves.

"Not a bad haul," he thought. Chuckling to himself, David figured himself as a rich man. "Let's load up then," David said, hurrying toward the damaged vault. He had already taken three cotton bags from the back office to cache his loot safely. "Two for me and maybe one for J.O." Then David thought again and considered, "Why share at all? It's three bags for me alone," his greedy mind coming to the forefront again.

The outlaws started to fill their bags with the silver, gold and currency deposited in the vault. David loaded the bags, while J.O. took them outside to lash them to the

51

horses. J.O. had carried the last bag out and was headed back into the bank when he heard a strange voice come from inside the bank.

"Put your hands up!" Noel Green ordered, pointing a scattergun at David. He had heard the explosion as he was walking home after closing the stagecoach office. Noel knew beyond any doubt, that the bank was being robbed.

The stage manager hurried back to his office, unlocked the door and retrieved a shotgun from the place where it was hanging on the wall. Then he turned and quickly ran to the bank. Noel had peered through the window of the bank and saw the dust from the explosion plus the culprit loading the loot from the bank vault. He tried the front door and was happy to find it unlocked. Now he was standing holding a shotgun on the robber!

"Where's the sheriff or his deputy?" Noel wondered, as he was holding the shotgun on the robber. "No matter," he smiled. *'Won't* the town be surprised to hear of *my* heroic action? Even Kenny would be in awe. No longer would he be looked on as a mere clubfooted stagecoach manager. Wells, Fargo may even offer me a substantial bonus for this daring arrest," he thought, smiling at the success of his apprehension. Visions of the glory clouded his mind.

It was while Noel was thinking of these things that J.O. slowly slid up behind the stage manager. He was within two feet when he shoved his gun in the back of Noel. Noel stiffened and dropped the shotgun. It clattered on the hardwood floor.

"Should of set the hammer on the shotgun," Noel thought. "It'd surely have discharged itself from the impact of hitting the floor," He knew the sound of the explosion had probably already alerted half the town.

"*You* put your hands up!" J.O. said, pushing the gun harder into Noel's back. He grinned at David over Noel's shoulder. "I bet you're happy to have someone like me," he thought, feeling elated at being able to help his new boss.

David was inwardly cursing his capture by this man, but was relieved when J.O. showed up. Thinking fast, David was elated. His problem of getting rid of J.O. was here.

"The gods must be smiling at me today," he thought, happy at the latest development.

David waited until Noel had turned toward J.O., then he pulled out his gun. David squeezed the trigger and a slug went crashing through Noel's skull. After the man fell, J.O. came rushing over to David's side. He had a perplexed look on his features. David was calm looking as he glanced at the body of the stage manager.

"What'd you go and do a fool thing like that fer?" J.O. whined, jittering in place. "We could of tied him up and left. There weren't any call for that."

"Sure we could of, but we didn't," David said, emptying the spent shell casing on the floor. He replaced the spent cartridge and holstered his gun. "'Sides, he'd been able to describe us to the law. I thought we'd already decided who's going to be running this gang. *Me*, am I right? Or maybe you're having second thoughts?"

J.O. shook his head no, then began to scratch his head. He turned away from David and headed toward the back door. He was still scratching his head and thinking of the latest happening, when David pulled the scatter gun from the cold hands of Noel's. He pointed the shotgun at the back of J.O.'s head and pulled the trigger. The blast from the weapon took off the top of J.O.'s head. David drug the corpse to lay beside the other two.

The front door was ajar from the blast. David thought of how amiss he had been in going through the window. The door still had the key in the lock.

"Looks like someone was in a hurry and forgot to lock the door. Could of simply opened the door," he smiled ruefully. Quickly he hurried over and locked the door.

A short time later, David could hear the clamor of voices and the pounding at the front door. The bank robber glanced up to make sure it was securely locked. He even had gone so far as to move a desk to sit in front of the door.

"If I'd time," he thought. "I'd have wedged a piece of lumber under the door knob. Almost a perfect picture," he thought, "sort of neat and tidy,"

David took one last look at the two bodies and grinned at his efforts. He smiled as he went to a coal oil lantern lying on the floor. The globe was broken, but it was otherwise undamaged. He picked this lamp up and quickly unscrewed the cap on it.

"Dummies, never thought to go around the back way," David said, as he splashed coal oil from the lantern on the bodies and around the floor. Then he reached into his pocket and brought out a match that he drug across the back of his trousers. He threw the flaming article on the floor and the resulting blaze started quickly. After throwing down some papers to feed the blaze, he got the fire going good. He gave a quick glance at his handiwork, ran to the back door and slipped out. David jumped astride his victim's horse and waved his hat to spook the other horse to run in front of him. He galloped out of the alley, dodging a low-hanging sign as he rode out of town. Skillfully, he skirted the horses tied to the hitch rails as he urged his mount faster down the street. The flying steeds' hooves hurled pieces of dirt. He was fast disappearing from town headed to the south.

FOUR

"There he goes!" Big Tim Mastenbrook, shouted, as he pointed a scattergun at the fleeing bandit and fired the weapon. The shot peppered the side of the bank and blew out a window in the leather goods shop in the process. Before he could fire again, David had galloped around the corner of the nearest house and vanished. That was the last the townspeople saw of their bank robber.

"Somebody get a bucket brigade going, or we're all going to be without a town!" Gary Sandusky yelled, replacing his gun. "We can always trail the crook after the fire is put out."

Gary had other plans about the expedition to capture the outlaw. He wanted to perform this deed alone. Thoughts of glory clouded his mind, as he envisioned heaps of praise laid on him, by the thankful populace. He would again be the center of adulation and the admiring glances' he got from the women would not hurt any either.

Then, sheriff Lee Wildman rode back into the town after talking to the cowboys involved and making them promise to pay for any damages. He rushed to join the throng of people at the front of the bank. Lee talked to Gary and was appraised of the happenings.

Lee thought to ask Gary of his whereabouts. Gary spoke of being asleep in the jail and did not fail to mention that he was among the first on the scene. Lee knew that tracking down this criminal was going to take time and preparation. Therefore, he bent to the task of fighting the fire. He joined the volunteers in passing the buckets of water.

The fire seemed to be a dry and thirsty monster as it drank each bucket of water poured on it. They dipped into a nearby horse trough, then passed buckets to another man who threw the quenching water on the raging inferno. The fire was unquenchable. It savored each drop as it yearned for more.

The clanging of a bell announced the arrival of the volunteer fire department and the water wagon. Tom Schellenburg was also the fire chief and he began to shout at his men. The roar of the fire made his commands next to useless. No matter how hard he shouted, the volunteers would look at him, make a cupping motion with their hands to their ears and finally give up. In frustration, they simply heeded their own commands.

As the townspeople took turns at pumping the water carriage, the flames appeared to get higher and hotter. It seemed as if the fire absorbed every drop of the precious liquid, like a blotter soaks up an ink spill.

The front of the bank was now engulfed in flames reaching to the heavens. A leather shop sent billows of smoke to invade the general store next door. The firefighters directed their hoses to the front of the store and saved it. However, water and smoke damaged the contents. They could not save the bank so they let her burn herself out. Finally, just the walls and part of the roof were standing, but still smoldering. The blackened vault stood amid the debris with its doors blown off and the interior bare.

The townspeople fought the fire all night. When morning arrived, they were dropping in their tracks. Some sat on the boardwalk, while others lay at the side of the street. Their blackened faces gave evidence of their nighttime activities.

The town had lost the biggest part of the bank, along with the leather goods shop and part of the general store. The bank would have to be rebuilt, as would be the leather shop. Hershey's Emporium was more smoke damaged than burnt. It would have to be cleaned up to make it more presentable. The gutted buildings cast a death pallor over the entire town.

"Say, Lee! Over here!" a townsman hollered, while poking at some smoking scraps.

Lee went to the fire-gutted debris that was the bank. He stepped through the smoldering bits. Gingerly, he skirted the edge of the mesh wire cages, which were now hot twisted pieces of metal. Lee walked to the person who had called him. Stopped and then raised his eyebrows. He looked quizzically at the townsman.

The speaker was Damien Dickerson, owner of the now burnt leather shop. He was black with soot from head to toe. His large hands were covered with blisters and the right side of his face. His forehead looked as if someone had tried to put a fire out on it with a damp ice pick. It was puffy and red looking. He would have looked funny, was it not so serious.

"What's going on Damien?" Lee asked. He knew that except for Kenny King, Damien Dickerson was the best tracker in town. Some towns have one tracker, but Clearwater could openly boast of having the two best in the Territory.

"See for yourself," Damien said, pointing to the charred remains of the three bodies. The corpse's were burned so bad that identifying two burnt humans would be difficult.

"One's Noel Green," Damien said, pointing to the body closest to Lee. "At least, he's the only one I knew hereabouts that had a clubfoot. As far as the other two, the fire burned them up very badly. I can't recollect any new people in town. You?"

"Come to think of it," Lee replied, a light going off inside his head. He pushed his hat up on his forehead. "There were two strangers at the saloon one day last week. I'll ask Big Tim. Maybe he knows something about them. They presented no problem so they did not call upon me to check them out. Still, as far as Noel, it looks like he heard the explosion first, grabbed his shotgun and ran over here. He must have got the drop on the bank robbers. Seems he was careless and let them turn the tables on him. He was able to blow one's head off with his greener, before the other one got to him. Two were killed outright by the blast and the other one skedaddled. Got clean away."

"Gary," Lee said, turning away from the bodies. He walked with Gary to the front of the smouldering bank. The duo stood out in the middle of the street. The air was almost overpowering them with the stench of burnt flesh. With their scarfs pulled up over their noses, their eyes showed their weariness and they spoke through the cloths. "Tell everyone you can get a hold of or that's available. They're to meet at my office in two hours to form a posse."

"I think," Gary responded, giving his gun belt an extra tug. "We can handle this ourselves, sir." Gary wanted to show everyone he could track and use his gun, even if he had to share the glory with the sheriff. He knew that with his quick mind, it would be easy to have all the glory to himself.

"After all, Lee's getting up there in years," he thought. Gary could think of no one better suited for Lee's job than himself. "It'd also get me off the hook, so to speak, for not being the very first upon the scene." He thought that he had checked every door, but evidently he had missed the bank.

"Can't cry over spilt milk, it's happened," Gary thought, as he was already devising a plan to foster the blame on someone else.

"*No*," Lee said softly, as if he were speaking to a small child, but forcefully. "Just get everyone like I said." He was also thinking, "Nonetheless, Gary could get his glory another way, not at the expense of the town," He knew that Gary wanted to have a grandstand play. "Not with my town!"

David rode south out of town at a brisk gallop, struggling to hold onto the ropes of the other horse laden down with riches. Pulling back on the reins for a moment, he stopped his mounts. Looping the reins over the pommel, he looked back. He knew that he should have ridden southeast toward the Red River, but he also knew that was the direction the posse would head first.

"At least that's the way I'd head after me," he thought. "Can always turn in the opposite direction later," he spoke to his horse. "Once I'm sure of the direction of the pursuit."

Eventually the sun rose before him. David laughed out loud to himself as he knew the glowing orb would shine in the eyes of the posse, making it that much harder to track him. He also knew the townspeople would spend the biggest part, if not all of the night fighting the fire he had started in the bank.

"If my luck holds up," he thought, "then the whole town will burn." There was no remorse in his actions. He started to slow his escape, since he knew the pursuit would be a long time coming. "If they come at all," he thought, his criminal brain trying to devise all kinds of escape to him.

David rode for a spell, then pulled his mounts up. He dismounted and began to walk his horses. Specks of foam were commencing to appear at the horses' mouths; their sides were going in and out at an alarming rate and spots of blood began to mingle along with the foam at their muzzles. One horse breathing heavily, lay down to one side of the road. The other horse took a few staggered steps then collapsed. It lay on its side by a gnarled tree at the side of the road. They were both extremely dead.

"Just my luck," he said in disgust, kicking the dead animal in the ribs. "Here I go and beat those people and my transportation falls down. Must of picked the only two horses in town that were like their owners, deadbeats, that's for sure!"

The killer looked behind him and saw no dust trails. The posse was not behind him, or at least not close enough to matter. He drugged the saddlebags from the carcasses, cast them by the rocks and surveyed his new surroundings.

David spied a fallen tree at the edge of the rocks by the hillside. He walked to the tree and tore a small branch from it. Once at the rocks, he dropped on his knees and thrust the stick into the hole at the base of the largest boulder. In just a moment, he felt a slight tug on the branch. He carefully pulled the limb from the hole. He smiled as he saw attached firmly to the end of the stick! Some sort of lizard! The jaws of the diminutive dinosaur were clamped firmly like a vise around the end of the stick. He stood with his dangling prize as if he were a person fishing holding his trophy.

"Sure would not want to get my fingers stuck in those jaws," David thought, being extra careful in his handling of the lively lizard.

David cautiously took another stick and guardedly pried loose the squirming denizen attached to the end of his thrusting limb. Once freed, the saurian scurried back to the haven of his hole, nudged aside a few rocks and quickly vanished.

"That'll make a safe place for *my* money," he thought out loud, standing up and placing his hands on his hips in satisfaction. He had already determined the money to be his instead of the rightful owners. "After all," he thought. "Possession is nine tenths of the law. It's my property now and by rights of ownership it is all mine. Of course I'll need all I can get to help me out in Mexico."

"It seemed so easy," David thought. He figured on paying that town another visit soon. Of course, he would be on the look out for any local yokels he could use. From experience, he knew he could recruit others easily. There was always someone in search of a fast buck. Someone, he hoped that would follow his orders to the letter.

"After all, I'm the mastermind behind any gang of cutthroats I can round up. Like taking candy from a baby," he chuckled to himself, taking out a handkerchief and wiping the sweat from his brow.

"Got to get me a hat," he spoke, knowing he had spent the last three days out in the hot sun without any sort of headgear. He had forgotten the hats of the sodbusters, in his haste to get as far away from prison and the two vagrants back at the bank. Still, to console himself, he remembered being too busy to worry about such things.

Though now it looked as if he would die of sunstroke with the hot sun bearing its rays down on the top of his head. He had already discarded the grass hat he had braided earlier. Now, he regretted that careless decision. Chuckling at remembrance of what, he had learned a long time ago at his father's knee,

"I never make a mistake. I thought that I once had done it, but was badly mistaken in that!"

David knew that plans could be changed. "So what," he thought, as he hurriedly took the bags to the rocks. After taking the biggest part of the paper currency, a few pieces of silver and a small sliver of gold, he shoved the rest of his valuables into the hole as far as possible. David felt the lizard as it attacked his hidden hoard. He quickly placed a small boulder at the entrance to the hole, but large enough for his guard to get in and out.

The outlaw took the canteens, one .44.40 Winchester rifle, a .44 Remington New Army Model revolver and a blanket. Then he started walking toward the mountains in the distance. These mountains were covered with snow down to the dew line. He smiled as he trudged to this apparent sanctuary of safety.

FIVE

"*You what?*" Lee Wildman asked, as he sat behind his desk and looked at Gary Sandusky incredulously.

"I said," Gary spoke softly, wincing at the tone of Lee's voice. "All I could muster was five men on such short notice."

The two had been discussing the formation of a posse. Lee had sent Gary out to round up all the able-bodied men he could find. Gary had returned to the office in less than an hour. He informed Lee of his failure in not getting more than five men. He got a cup of coffee and sat across from the sheriff. Slowly he sipped the hot brew.

"All right," Lee said, calming down and getting a cup of coffee. He sat behind his desk and asked Gary whom he had scoured up in the time allocated. He was desperately hoping that these men could probably join in this pursuit.

"Good men at that," he prayed silently.

Gary sat and looked at Lee for a long time. Lee was starting to get impatient, so he cleared his throat. Gary looked up at Lee and blurted out the names, wincing as he spoke them.

"Gale Loughmiller, Tom Schellenburg, Chris Barker, Kenny King and . . . Cooty Brown."

"*Cooty Brown!*" Lee exclaimed, sitting straight up in his chair and almost spilling his coffee. He looked incredulously at Gary. "The town drunk?"

"Well sheriff, he was willing to do and I quote, *"his civic duty,"* end quote. Besides, he's been sober for at least a week, I think."

"Cooty has never seen the day he was sober for a week. More like a half-day, no more. He'll even drink coal oil or Bay Rum!"

"Anyway, he'll be part of our posse. At least, he will be one more person," Gary said, knowing of Lee's feelings in this matter.

Inwardly, these men elated him. He knew that there was very much difference in tracking a man and say, being mayor, counting money, or sweeping out saloons, but the choice of these men would slow the sheriff some, he hoped. Enough time, for him to recapture the bank robber and reap all of the glory!

"You mean one more body," Lee said as he scooted back in his chair and placed his callused hands on the desk. He arose from the desk and suddenly groaned inside. "I'm getting way too old for this job," he thought. "Now, I'm to be saddled with babysitting the town drunk also!"

Sighing, Lee arose from his chair and went to the office window. He was busy thinking. "Gale Loughmiller, as the bank president and is involved in this posse more than anyone else, except him. After all, he was elected to uphold the law and a law had been broken," he reasoned to himself. "Tom Schellenburg's at least good with horses and a crack rifleman. Kenny King's an ex-Indian scout for the army, so he would be helpful in tracking down the robber. A man who would follow orders. Also someone he could count on when the going got tough. Chris Barker's the town's blacksmith. His immense size and survival savvy will come in very handily. Of course, Gary and I are quite handy with our guns and after all, *I am the sheriff!* It's too bad that I heard Damien Dickerson is possibly going to move. He could help Kenny and Gary with their tracking. As for Cooty Brown, time would tell."

A man walked into the office then. He stood and looked at the back of the sheriff. Gary directed him to sit and made a motion to the coffee pot. He received a nod from the man and poured an extra cup of java. The undersheriff placed the hot liquid on the edge of the desk. He cleared his throat.

"Sheriff?" Gary said, while nodding toward the stranger.

Lee turned from the window and saw the stranger. A frown crossed his features as he went to his desk and sat down. He took a sip of coffee, thinking, "I'm the welcome wagon? I have a bank robbery on my hands and now this." Then scolding himself for not being hospitable, he smiled at the man.

"Can I be of service to you?" Lee asked, remembering he was a public servant also. He then sat.

"Bob Davis, sir," replied the medium size man sitting in the chair, who quickly got to his feet and doffed his hat.

"The stranger might not have much going for him as a hard case," Lee thought, instantly liking this young man. "But at least he was mannerly. He'd stood up, removed his hat and had said sir. Yes, I think I will like this fine upstanding member of a community. Yet whose?"

"Sit, young man," Lee said, pulling his chair closer to the desk. "What can I or we do for you?"

Bob Davis was of medium build, dark haired and starting to get paunchy in the middle. He had been sitting at an office desk too long. He smiled and informed them he was new to the area. Bob also was moving his family here from back East. He had arrived on the stagecoach this morning. His family, wife and two children would be following him soon. Possibly within a week or two at the outside.

"Upon my arrival," Bob said, blowing gently on his coffee. "I noticed several people standing in front of a few burnt buildings."

He went to the men at the front of the blackened ruins where they informed him of the robbery. Bob knew he would be by himself for a few days, so he thought it best to offer his services to the sheriff. He had been a

Pinkerton operative for thirteen years, the last two at home office, 191-193 Fifth Avenue, Chicago, Illinois. Due to his health, he was forced to settle elsewhere, preferably in the West.

"You're health?" Lee asked. "I don't want a frail or sick person in the posse. Cooty Brown's bad enough, but to have to play doctor or take it easy with someone else was a bit too much," he thought.

"A bronchial disorder," Bob laughed. "Mainly my asthma. The doctors thought - and I heartedly agreed - that the change in a climate would do the trick. I've only been in the West for three days and already my breathing is the best it has ever been!"

This last was proved to Lee's satisfaction, when Bob jumped to his feet and thrust his arms out to the side. He breathed heavily for a few minutes. Then he even went so far as to go to where Gary was sitting and before Gary could object, placed his arms around him and picked him up. Bob shouldered his burden and without any effort at all walked across the room. Turning around, he brought the hapless Gary back to his seat. Bob deposited Gary, turned to Lee and grinned. He was not breathing heavy at all, nor was his face red from the exertion.

"You certainly have the strength," Lee said, chuckling at the look on Gary's face. "You and your smarty pant ways," Lee thought, as he inwardly chuckled. That stranger catching Gary off guard amused Lee. "I for one, welcome you aboard. Right now, we've five others to round up."

Lee asked Bob if he were sure he wanted to go along with the posse. Bob nodded an affirmative and looked at Lee with a straightforward glance. His eyes seemed to pierce Lee, who would like to have this polite person along after all. So Lee pulled out the drawer to his desk. He rummaged through the contents, then he came up with a set of keys. Taking the keys to a gun rack on the wall, he unlocked the chain at the side of the case. He slid back the chain and took five rifles from their enclosure. Lee handed Gary one, Bob one and placed the rest plus three boxes of cartridges on his desk.

Gary took two bedrolls and a large sack of foodstuffs. He gave Lee and Bob a nod, then went out the door to the waiting horses.

"He may be upset about something," Lee thought, smiling. "Wonder if it relates to the antics that just happened?"

Lee blew out the lamp, motioned Bob to the door and followed him outside. Bob patiently waited until the sheriff had locked the door. He followed the sheriff as he began to walk toward the members of the posse.

"I'd best offer some words of explanation about the members of our posse," Lee said, as he walked with Bob toward the others. Lee explained the make-up of the newly formed posse. He took special care to point out the hazards of having Cooty Brown along, but saw theirs was no other alternative. They were in luck having Kenny King and Gary Sandusky with them as they could track. Gary was also good with guns. Tom Schellenburg would keep an eye out for their mounts and provide additional firepower. Gale Loughmiller would be with them primarily to make sure all of the missing money was accounted for, down to the last penny. Chris Barker would provide strength and survival techniques.

When they reached the stable, the men were milling around waiting for the sheriff's appearance. Once Lee arrived, Gale hurried up to him and in a wavering voice expressed his concern over Cooty joining the posse.

"I don't know why he has to go," Gale whispered with vexation, taking a handkerchief from his inside vest pocket to wipe his bald head of perspiration. It was only midmorning and he was already sweating profusely. He looked nervous with his eyes darting around the town. Gale tried in vain to speak in a low voice to Lee.

"For the simple reason I said so," Lee stated with conviction. He was not one to be bamboozled by the bank president. "Now you'll gather around. You too, Cooty. First off, *I and I alone* am in charge of this posse. If anyone wants to complain, do so now. It'll be too late once we get on the trail."

Lee looked hard at Gale and saw the banker had accepted Lee's assessment of the situation. Gale still scowled but looked away into the distance. Lee noted this latest circumstance.

"If I didn't know better," Lee thought, "I'd swear that Gale's as guilty as sin. Of what, I don't know, but something's not right."

"You're probably aware I've a new addition to our posse," Lee said, while pointing to Bob Davis. "You'll also notice that this is a newcomer to our fair community. Allow me to introduce Bob Davis. He's a Pinkerton agent."

"Retired," Bob said, smiling at everyone. He doffed his hat and shook hands all around. When he had finished with the pleasantries, he replaced his derby back on his head, grinning at everyone.

"Anyway, this man's going to help us in the pursuit of the vermin that done this deed," Lee said with feeling. Pausing long enough to cast a glance around his posse.

As each man gathered around the new arrival, Lee saw out of the corner of his eye that Cooty was placing something in his saddlebags. Not to alarm anyone, Lee walked to the side of Cooty. He glanced around and was pleased to find that no one else was looking at the him and the drunk.

"That's not whiskey is it?" Lee asked in a whisper, as he stood directly behind the town drunk. "Or so help me, Cooty, I'll see you locked up in my jail so far back that you'll have to have sunshine piped into you, or beans shot to you with a cannon."

"Oh! No Siree Bob," Cooty whined. "This's my snake-bite medicine. However, I'll tell you what I'm going to do." With that, he reached in his saddlebag and brought out a small jar of colorless liquid. Cooty whirled on his heels and threw his concoction into a nearby vacant lot, praying it would not break. "I can always come back later for it," Cooty thought, already having figured on being back before nightfall or at the least in the early hours of the morning. "Time enough for me to find that jar, take a quick drink and hurry over to the saloon."

Lee grinned at this latest happening, scratched the back of his neck and called everyone to gather about him. When they had all assembled in front of the sheriff, he had them raise their right hand and deputized them. Then Lee pinned a badge on each man's breast pocket.

Cooty was all smiles as he looked down at the gleaming piece of metal pinned to the front of his shirt. He reached up and wiped his dirty sleeve across the badge, polishing it to shine brightly in the morning sunlight.

"Now, I feel as if I'm somebody important," he thought. He stood straighter and glanced about to the others. Cooty winked to one barmaid standing on the porch of the saloon. Seeing her wink back made his day.

After this little ceremony, Lee told the posse, he was going to inspect their hardware. He checked everyone's weapons and smiled.

"These men are definitely not going to a church social," he thought. "They seem to be ready for bear or, at the least and Indian uprising!" For a moment, he pitied the killer, but only for a moment.

Lee listed the firepower: two .44.40 Winchester rifles, two 1866 Model Winchester rifles, one 1873 Winchester, three Schofield revolvers, three .45 Colt Peacemakers and a twelve-gauge shotgun. The .44.40's with their 21-inch barrels were all right for long range, but the scattergun would equalize things up close.

"Say Bob," Lee said. "What're you going to be carrying? I saw the Smith and Wesson .45 and my rifle. Anything else?"

"Well, sheriff to be truthful," Bob replied, walking up to the sheriff. *"This* always comes in handy."

Bob's hand moved too quickly for the eye to follow and in his hand appeared a small derringer. The sheriff looked down the barrel of a nickel-plated weapon that was mere inches from his nose. He audibly gulped and ran his finger nervously around his neck collar.

"Huh?" Lee said, stepping quickly back a step. "What's that?"

"That, my friend," Bob said with pride in his voice. "Is my little insurance. It's a .41 Colt derringer. I keep it in my vest pocket for any emergencies that should arise. And believe me there's been a few."

The others stared at the man with the tiny gun. The sheriff gulped again. Bob Davis smiled and returned the weapon to his vest. The rest of the posse looked with admiration at this latest development. Kenny inwardly chuckled, Tom stood amazed, Cooty seemed in awe, Gale seemed worried, Gary was impressed and Chris laughed out loud.

"Let's go and get our man!" Bob shouted, as he wheeled around to the others who were staring open mouthed, as Lee had been previously.

The tension was broken. Each man mounted his horse and they started out of town. They raised tendrils of dust as they slowly rode through town. There were few people out this morning.

"I hope, I didn't upset you too much, sheriff," Bob said aside to Lee.

"Nope you didn't. However, to tell you the truth, I was a mite uncertain," Lee said, glad that Bob was on their side. "I'm getting too old for these types of shenanigans," he thought, as they continued out of the town.

Eight silent and somber men, a collection of the citizenry of Clearwater, Indian Territory comprised the posse that rode past the livery and turned south on June 29, 1879. The townspeople watched this procession of lawmen. Some cheered while others looked on passively. Even a stray mongrel stopped wagging his tail and hurried underneath the boardwalk at the saloon.

"South," Lee thought, "was where the killer would head. At least, that's the direction I'd be headed. South through Texas, toward Mexico and freedom." He knew that he had no jurisdiction across the Red River, but he headed that way anyway. "I'm the sheriff and he's the lawbreaker. It's up to me to catch him," he thought, setting his face in a determined look.

SIX

David had stashed his booty in the dangerous lizard's home and was walking toward the mountains in the distance. He had begun his reckoned long trek to the base of the mountains. Suddenly he heard the sound of hooves coming fast down the trail. David quickly looked around and spied a large boulder to his right. He ran and hid behind this rock. In just a moment, a stagecoach pulled by four horses came around the bend. To him this was a gift from heaven.

"Here were horses, possibly supplies and more money!" he thought, as he busily looked around his area.

The stage would be upon him shortly. David had enough time to pull a dead limb across the trail. Rocks on one side and a deep canyon hedged a passageway for the stage on the other. It was a perfect place for a hold-up.

The stage driver upon seeing the obstacle, pulled hard on the reins and quickly reached for the brake. This action caused the coach to come to a shuddering halt. The jehu wrapped the reins around the brake handle, cursed his luck and climbed down from his perch. He went to the limb, reached down to tug it to the side and grasped the limb with both hands.

"That'll be far enough," David said, pointing his rifle at the driver's mid-section. "Try to grab a piece of sky! Good. Now what would've for a poor wayfarer down on his luck?"

The driver made a quick grab for his gun. David squeezed the trigger. A slug from David's rifle slammed into the driver's breastbone, knocking its victim backwards. The body rolled into the ditch at the side of the road. David ran quickly over to where the body had fallen. He placed his foot at the driver's side and rolled the body over on its back. The driver was staring at the sky with vacant eyes. David reached down and removed the gun from the driver's holster. He clicked open the cylinder and saw that it was full of cartridges. Smiling to himself he tucked the weapon in his belt. Then he grabbed the man's hat and placed on his head.

"A snug enough fit," he thought, pulling the black felt hat down farther on his head. David reached up and slowly ran his hand along the brim to crease it just right. Satisfied with the hat the hat, he looked up the trail.

A brief noise caused him to whirl and raise his rifle. David glanced at the stage and was surprised to see a man stumble out of the coach. The passenger missed the first step and fell into the dust. The traveler hurriedly got up and quickly brushed the dust from his clothes.

David saw a man in his late twenties, black short-cropped hair parted down the middle and a small frame. He had on a plaid suit, green vest and high water shoes. The man seemed busy providing a death-hold on a small bottle of whiskey.

"A drummer," David muttered, stepping closer to the man.

"Sir," the drunk said slowly, his voice slurring. "Please let me introduce myself. Name's Cromwell Crothers. I'm the only representative of *Lilith's Little Liver Pills*. The one and only pill guaranteed to get your day off to a glorious start, or your money back. For only one thin dime, one-tenth of a dollar, I'll be forced to part with a bottle of this wonderful marvel of the ages."

David smiled at this funny sight. He began to guffaw. With tears streaming down his cheeks, he tightened his finger on the trigger. He placed a neat third eye smack in the middle of the salesman's forehead. David ambled to the body and placed two more slugs in the quivering corpse for good measure.

"Looks like your boots are now my boots," David said, thinking how it was funny, the way the salesman's body twitched each time a slug entered it. "Just wish I'd more bullets and time," he thought.

David's shots were spooking the horses. They began to prance and move away. He ran to the horses and grabbed their cheek straps and pulled down on the straps.

"Whoa! Whoa," he yelled, straining to hold the animals still. His boots were making small furrows in the dust.

David finally calmed the horses down and he walked back to the stage cautiously. He hefted his rifle at the port because he did not know if there more passengers or not. David gave a cursory glance into the stagecoach. He was making sure of no one else would make an impromptu appearance.

He went to the salesman's body and quickly searched it. A billfold in the inside pocket of the jacket revealed little currency, but the pocket also contained a small flask of whiskey. The whiskey's sister was lying by the outstretched hand of the drummer. Rolling the body over on it's back, David straddled the dead man's legs and quickly pulled off the salesman's boots. These he tossed aside.

David crawled on top of the stage. Looking under the driver's seat, he was satisfied to find a strongbox. Throwing the box to the ground, he jumped down and walked to the box. Drawing his gun, he shot twice to break the lock. Bullets were ricocheting off the lock to go screaming off in the distance. The lock shattered. David dropped on his knees and grunted with an effort as he raised the lid.

As he was rifling the contents, he grinned with satisfaction. He found stacks of currency and a small pouch of gold dust. He removed these items and sat on the grass and started to count his newfound wealth. There were more than ten thousand dollars in currency and he did not know how much the dust was worth. Nevertheless, he figured it to be substantial.

"Well, bust my britches and call me one-hung low, but I think my ship's came in to port. I thought I had waited so long for my ship to dock hat my pier must have collapsed!" he chortled aloud, causing a hungry coyote to quickly devour its meal of a rabbit and scurry away into the brush.

David went to the boot of the stage and flipped up the canvas cover. He discovered a veritable cache of items. One carpet bag, one trunk and two suitcases tied with ropes were lying there. He tugged these items out of the boot and tossed them to the ground.

Like a child at Christmas, he went eagerly through his new found treasure. As the child would do, he squealed with delight at each discovery. His hands started to move fast as he gleefully tore open his prizes.

The trunk was bound for San Angles to a millinery shop. It was full of pins and needles and dress making material and one complete dress. Small swatches of material lay at the bottom of the trunk, along with various pieces of wool.

The carpet bag held legal papers, a sheaf of writing materials and two hundred dollars. He could use the currency, but discarded the rest as nonessential. David pitched the bag into the bushes at the side of the road.

One suitcase comprised a variety of household needs, a suit, one ruffled and an off-white shirt. The other suitcase had a white shirt and string tie and underneath was the best surprise of all; for there nestled at the bottom was *a pair of pearl handled gleaming Colt .45's in a handmade smooth leather holster*! David promptly forgot the rest of the presents for the time being.

He could now get out of these prison clothes. David stood, threw the hat to arc gracefully into the bushes and started to remove his prison clothing. He was all the time looking over his shoulder because he did not know how far behind was the posse. Yet he was used to taking chances and this seemed about as good a chance as was available now. Knowing this, he began to hurry. David rushed to the stream at the side of the road and waded into the cold stream. David quickly plunged his head under the water. The coldness of the water made him draw his breath in sharply. He returned to the edge of the stream and splashed water over his emancipated body.

After finishing his absolutions, he headed back to the shore. Once on the bank, he took bunches of grass and by rubbing briskly he dried himself.

"Now," he thought, "I'm dry enough to try on them clothes."

David was pleased at the almost perfect fit. It was as if the owners knew his size and shape. Though, he would have to roll up the trousers a little, loosen a shirt button or two and tighten the belt up a notch. When this was finished, he retrieved his hat from the bushes and looked down. He thought that the clothes fitted him well enough to pass a muster. The boots of the dead drummer were a tad large but, after all, *"beggars can't be choosers,"* he thought. Stuffing some of the legal papers in the shoe to make his feet feel more secure, he flexed his feet in the boots and took a few steps.

His eyes sparkled as he looked fondly on the twin revolvers. David reverently removed them from their resting place in the holster. After performing this rite, he loaded the guns and spun the chambers. He placed the holster around his waist and tied the leather thongs around his legs. He smiled as he saw how smooth the guns slid from the holster as he made several quick draws. Not caring about being overheard, he took another chance that the posse would not be near.

He went into a crouch and rapidly drew, pulled back the hammers and squeezed the triggers simultaneously.

The guns bucked in his hands. David's ears were ringing and his eyes smarting from the explosion and the gun smoke. When the smoke cleared he went to an old rusted tin-can which served as his target. He picked the can up and was pleased at the results. Two bullet holes were an inch apart and about an inch from the top of the can.

"Not bad," he spoke to himself as he replaced the spent cartridges with new ones from the belt on the holster.

"Son, you're not only fast with a gun," David's father had once told him, as the two shared a dusty bottle of whiskey. "But you're accurate as all get out. The best I've seen in many a moon."

. "What does my father know?" he thought. David shrugged the compliment off as the vain muttering of a drunken fool Nevertheless, as the saying goes, *'seeing is believing'*. Now, he had the proof right before his eyes.

"Not bad shooting for a man who'd spent the last year in prison," he reasoned to himself as he returned to the stagecoach.

Then remembering the top of the stagecoach, he scrambled up to see if there was any more booty for him. He made sure the leather straps were secured tightly across the top of the guns.

"Wouldn't want them to fall out and get damaged any?" he thought.

Like an anxious child, he couldn't wait before opening another surprise. He pulled back the tarpaulin covering the cargo. A Mexican saddle studded with small silver stars lay atop a mail pouch and a horse blanket. A coffee mill, roll of newspapers and a stack of magazines was the rest of the shipment. He pitched the saddle and mail pouch to the ground and quickly but carefully jumped down beside them.

"Not worrying any though," he thought, "finders' are keepers, I always say," as he moved the mail pouch to one side. David was surprised that no shotgun guard was with the stage with all of this freight. "Their loss, my gain."

He took his gun and shot the lock of the mailbag. David turned the bag upside down and spilled the contents on the ground. He dropped to his knees as he began to rifle the contents. Aware of time being of the essence, he took what he thought might be of some worth to him and let the wind disperse the rest.

David went to the horses and selected two. It took him awhile to free the animals from the traces. They were still skittish. He finally got them calmed down enough to be led to where he had his loot. He would have to retrieve his cache from it's hiding place also. He chose a sorrel with a white star in the middle of its forehead. David threw the blanket on its back, then he saddled the horse. He made a bridle from the leather reins. He made a loop of the rope and swung it over the other horse. David loaded his keep and went for the money in the lizard's abode.

"A small detour, but a necessary one," David said, as he was riding to where his other money was deposited.

Once he had his treasures, he took a last look around the Indian Territory. David swung up into the saddle and clicking his tongue. He turned his mounts toward the south. The outlaw put his heels to the side of the horse and headed toward Mexico. David did not see the trail of dust that marked the progress of the posse only two miles behind him.

Yet Kenny King saw him. The sheriff had sent out Kenny to reconnoiter. Lee had figured that maybe Kenny could pick up the tracks of the fugitive quicker than the slow-moving posse could. Kenny had been riding close to the stream when he heard gunshots. He quickly ground tied his mount, dismounted and went up a knoll. Kenny peered over the rim and watched David calm the horses down. Then he saw David go into the stream.

Kenny thought of how easy capturing the criminal would be. He almost went down the hill. It would have been children's play in making this apprehension. He could have the prisoner tied tightly to a tree and be all smiles when the posse rode up. Then he would strut around and tell everyone just how hard it had been to corner this criminal.

"I'll not lie, only stretch the truth a little," he reasoned to himself.

Kenny arose, but then stopped. He remembered Lee's admonition, no matter how trivial, to report to him anything. Kenny turned back toward his mount. After slipping and sliding down the hillside, he swung up in the saddle and headed back to the posse. He was going to report to Lee and no one else!

He quickly swung up into the saddle and clicking his tongue. He urged his mount back toward the posse. Trails of dust were quickly hiding the horseback rider as he rode swiftly to the place where he thought the posse to be found.

SEVEN

"How much further?" Gale complained, as he was raising his legs in the stirrups to take the pressure off his feet. "These boots are killing me."

"At the top of that hill," Lee answered, turning in his saddle to look at his posse. "There's an old line shack up there I think. We'll stop and rest."

Gale had started to complain before they had gone one mile. His boots were getting tight on his swollen feet. Especially after they received a drenching crossing the Red River. Now the sun's rays were drying out the soft pliant leather. The boots began to shrink causing his feet to feel miserable as they were squeezing them. He had questioned Lee about the advisability of crossing the Red River.

"Look, Gale," Lee had answered, staring Gale in the eye and making sure everyone else heard him. "I know that I've no jurisdiction here in Texas. Nevertheless, I want to bring the killer back to justice. We'll just have to cross that bridge when we get to it. Of course, each of you can go back, but I aim to continue. Anyone care to complain?"

"How else can I be sure that I cover my tracks unless I make the capture or kill, preferably the *kill*," Gale thought, he wanted to catch the killer also. "It's up to me to make sure of that happening and *no one* else."

Gary wanted to stay abreast of things as well as Gale. He wanted to be on the capture, to be able to tell others of his involvement. And just possibly turned things his way as to make him the one who did the capturing. He was ever the opportunist.

Tom smiled and nodded yes to Lee's plan. As Clearwater's mayor, he felt that he had a responsibility to the citizens in recovering their money. Besides, he was the chief officer of the town. He wanted to keep his campaign promises of having a safe and secure town to raise a man's family in and to prosper.

"May have too many irons in the fire," he thought. "Newspaperman, helping out at the livery and being mayor also." Tom made a promise to himself that once this hunt was over, he was going to see about sprucing up the town a bit. "I'll have to replace that sign at the edge of town," he thought, remembering that it was in a sorry shape.

"Torn and disfigured, a bad state of disrepair," one citizen complained.

"Yep," he thought, after riding out to check on the sign, "it does need repairing or replacing. I'll just have to get on with it someday." And like the loose boards at the livery, the thoughts promptly vanished, whisked from his mind as the air stirs dust.

Bob felt a sort of exhilaration at being able to help his new town. He had jumped at the opportunity of helping his adopted town out and the thrill of doing what he did best help.

"Only this time, I'll not only be after a lawbreaker, but one who has personally hurt me through *my town*!" In his mind's eye, he had already adopted the town.

Kenny had said that he was in for the long haul. He also got a thrill out of the pursuit of the killer. He was finally doing what he liked best and was good at, tracking. The admiration of his fellow men made him sit straighter in his saddle. That, and him wanting to see the robber dead too.

"A lark," Cooty first thought of joining the posse, but now he wanted a drink in the worst way. At first, he seemed to thrive on the respect the others had shown him. Yet now, he was having second thoughts and those thoughts were having second ones too. "Sure could use a drink about now," Cooty mumbled aloud, wiping his forehead of the perspiration that had formed there and pulling his hat down lower on his head.

"Just bet you could," Gary laughed, turning to Cooty. "One drink and you wouldn't know when to stop!"

Cooty had ridden out with the understanding that they wouldn't be gone for more than a few hours. The few hours stretched into a day, then another. Already they had been gone for two days.

"Two long and hard days and nights, not to mention very dry ones at that," Cooty thought, as he was busily trying to massage his throat.

The first day, he had a hankering for some whiskey. The second one, he was starting to see delusions and the delusions continued. He could swear that he saw a cool lake up ahead and mentioned this to Lee.

"Only a mirage," Lee said, starting to feel sorry for Cooty somewhat.

"Now, on top of all the other troubles I've had to bear, my stomach muscles were beginning to cramp and my throat was slowly starting to constrict," Cooty thought, as the temperature was getting drier and drier, hotter and hotter.

The sun's scorching rays began to bear down on him relentlessly. Sweat began to gush down his face as if he were crying. His bandana was thoroughly drenched as was his sweat-stained shirt which clung to his back like a second skin.

"Boy, I'm sure enough hot," Cooty muttered to the wind, still massaging his throat. "My spit would probably hang a rabbit. Or at the very least, certainly strangle one!"

Gary had grown impatient with the slow progress of the posse. He had been the one who wanted to scout ahead and maybe capture their quarry. Visions of glory that would be heaped upon him at his return with the robber, danced in his head. However, Lee had sent

Kenny ahead to do the scouting. No matter how much he tried to hurry them, the posse seemed to take their sweet time. Gary figured he would die of old age, before they would track down the killer and make the capture.

Tom had seen to the welfare of the horses. He made sure they were not being rode too hard, slowed when they got sweaty, rubbed down often and given enough oats and water. Tom was not only a good sharpshooter, but he was also kind to the animals. He seemed to have a feeling when it came to the well being of livestock.

The posse had crossed the Red River and was now deep inside the Texas border. They were looking around as if they were the hunted instead of the hunter. Each looked furtively around the countryside, expecting a threat at any minute. Heedless of the dangers, Lee forced the posse forward.

Lee had finally sent Chris back to town for more supplies, when he became aware of the pursuit taking longer than he had anticipated. Already, the men were starting to grumble, Gale being number one. Of course, Cooty wasn't too far behind Gale in the complaining department either. Lee knew the men were hungry. His stomach was starting to grumble also. He saw the indirect looks pass between the men as they watched each wolf down their meager fare.

"My stomach thinks my throat's been cut," Gale whined again, taking a swig of tepid water from his canteen. "No food down there in quite sometime."

Gale replaced the lid on his canteen. Then he raised his bandana to wipe his face. Beads of sweat were running down his face making his collar get as black as his mood. His scowl seemed to get bigger as the corners of his mouth turned down more. It was no secret. He did not like Cooty Brown. He had ridden up behind Lee, leaving Cooty to bring up the rear. Gale wanted to put as much distance between the town drunk and himself as possible. Yet at the same time he did not want to alienate Lee or Cooty. He might need them later. Gale was all the time careful to keep his options open.

The posse arrived at the line camp shortly. The wooden shed was falling apart, windows missing and the roof had holes in it. Lee observed all this as he rode into the clearing. This building was definitely not going to provide any shelter to them.

"Oh well," Lee thought, "it's at least worthy of a stop for a rest. The men and the horses needed that as well."

Cooty," Lee said, as he was pulling his horse to a halt. "Why don't you and Bob gather some firewood? Gary and I'll try to scare up some small game. Gale, when the men get back with the wood, will you please make a fire. That way, Chris and Kenny will have something to hone in on."

As the men started in all directions, Lee saw Tom look at him expectantly. Lee had also noticed the backward glances Tom had cast toward the direction the posse had already traveled. First, it had been the trouble with Gale and Cooty. Now there may be another concern slowly creeping upon him.

"Problem?" Lee asked Tom, puling his horse closer to the lanky townsman, who seemed to be fidgeting in his saddle.

"Well, sheriff," Tom replied, tugging at his shirt collar. "There is and there isn't."

"Oh?" Lee looked at him questionably, stopping his mount and turning in the saddle to gaze upon Tom. "What might that be?"

Tom explained his dilemma. The lanky cowboy hated to be gone so long and leave the stable unattended. He went further and mentioned his father being gone and Chris was on the posse too. Tom felt derelict in his duty to his father. Tom was left in charge of the stable and now not only the other owner but himself was in a posse.

The stable was left unattended. It was the only livelihood his father had and his father was depending on him to watch it.

"Besides all of that," Tom said unfortunately, but hopefully, shoving his hat up further on his head. "Miss Thomas has asked me personally to watch over the foaling of her filly."

Lee smiled as he knew of the sweetness Miss Thomas and Tom shared. He remembered the shy looks passing between the two at the last church social. They were all gooey eyed. He sort of envied them.

"Look, Tom," Lee said, with an understanding smile in his voice. "Why don't you go back to town? After all, we may all be returning to town soon."

Tom in his haste to be gone, didn't bother with asking Lee of the last remark. He waved his good-byes to the rest and hurriedly wheeled his horse. Applying his heels to the side of the horse. He started to gallop back to town.

Lee looked at Tom's receding back and wistfully wished he were a tad younger. That Miss Thomas was a fine-looking woman. Then catching himself, he called out for Gary to lead out in their hunt for game.

"I'm the president of the bank and now I'm reduced to making a fire," Gale was fuming as the men left the camp. A menial job, beneath his dignity, but a necessary one, the sheriff told him. Only to Gale was it time consuming; time that took away from the capture of the bank robber.

He wanted to be the first to catch up with the robber. Then the bank president would calmly shoot the miscreant, claiming self-defense. He would make an accurate account of the money, except ten thousand dollars. The bank had not lost that much money, but he needed the extra to make up for his speculating in the stock market!

Everyone had said it was a *Bull Market*. People in the know, were eagerly telling one another of the great possibilities involved and the untold wealth. Why even the man at the railroad depot in Oklahoma Station, had said in a confidential tone of voice.

"Only wish I'd the money to invest in the market now. Just between you and me, ole Jay Gould and them other robber barons aren't going to be twiddling their thumbs and let that prime real estate in Kansas go to waste. Gould and the Union Pacific, right now control the railroads in Kansas. They'll surely be buying up all the options they can. Well, I wish I could but," he said, taking Gale aside and whispering with conspiratorial feelings.

Gale immediately headed back to Clearwater and rushed into the bank. He alighted from the stage and hurried across the street to the bank. Once inside the bank he nodded at a customer and rushed to his office where he slammed the door after telling the startled clerk, he did not want disturbed, for any reason whatever. The bank president wanted to get his business over with fast.

"I don't want anyone to bother me. If I am, *you'll* be hunting another job come morning!" Gale had said, as he stormed into his office and quickly sat at his desk.

Gale pulled out the desk drawer to reveal the deeds to over half the farms in a fifty-mile radius of Clearwater. All these farms, because of the recent drought, were way past due on their accounts. Many owners were men he had grown up with, dated with and helped in the birthing of two of their sons.

He could use these deeds as collateral, when he *borrowed* the money from the bank in Fort Worth. As the president of a bank, no one questioned him. After he made a killing in the stock market, he would replace the deeds and no one would be the wiser. Gale had it all thought out nicely. Invest wisely in the market and, like a farmer waiting for his crops to mature, he would watch his money evolve to wealth beyond his wildest imagination.

It would take two days of hard riding to get there. Gale had a good thoroughbred that needed to stretch its legs. Now would be the good time to do that very thing. He did not want anyone to know his whereabouts, nor what was happening, that ruled out the stagecoach as it was too slow. He would need a faster mode of transportation, thus his horse. Of course, he could take the railroad, but again, the need for secrecy prevailed.

One day to complete his transaction and maybe take in a sight or two. Then he would start back home for the return trip of two days. Only this time, he would leisurely ride back to town. He might stop by the Bar de Har and see his old friends' Jeff and Judy Corey. Overall, he would only be absent from the bank five days.

"Well, I've been working hard lately and I'm a widower," he thought to justify his actions. Gale would tell everyone he needed a vacation. The stress of the job and the responsibilities involved, he needed a respite. However, he would be gone from his duties. Gale would make it his top priority to remind them he was *their* president. He would only be gone from *their* bank for five days.

Naturally, Gale would remind everyone, that because he took the business of their money seriously, he would not be absent from the bank any longer. He could envision himself relaxing in Europe, spending the money he had shrewdly invested. The liquor helped to make-up his mind to borrow the deeds, worth almost sixty-five hundred dollars.

That had been over two weeks ago. Now, he received a telegram from his broker in Oklahoma Station that read:

MONEY GONE STOP
HIGGINS ABSCONDED WITH MONEY STOP

WHEREABOUTS UNKNOWN STOP
DID NOT BUY STOCK STOP
ADVISE ON OPTIONS STOP

MERCER

"All's lost!" Gale had read the telegram with trembling fingers. "How can I make the payment to the bank in Fort Worth now? What'll the bank directors think? For that matter, what will my friends think? The poor people that I have played God with their trust? What can I do? To think that I trusted Oliver Higgins with the money. HA! *My money*? Now Higgins's gone and with *my* money!"

While Gale was having his own pity party, David White was in the process of making plans to escape prison. He escaped the next day. Three days later the bank was robbed. A day after the robbery, Gale was in the posse to bring back the perpetrator to be tried and surely be executed.

Gale saw the chance to redeem himself. The robber dead and the money recovered, except for ten thousand dollars, sixty-five hundred to the bank and thirty-five hundred to him!

"I need the money," he muttered to himself. "Besides, I'm the one who took chances. It's only right that they should pay me for all the anguish I've been through."

He used this line of reasoning as he started to gather armloads of firewood Cooty and Bob had brought to camp. Gale dug out a place in the middle of the camp and made a small fire at the center of the clearing. Once the fire was going good, he sat back on his saddle to rest a moment.

He lay for a while, then strained as he arose to a sitting position that way he could probably pull off his offending boots. Gale groaned with an effort to pull the boots off, they were still tight on his feet. Finally, he could extricate his swollen feet. He wiggled his toes in an attempt at getting the blood to circulate. Once this was done, he breathed a sigh of relief. He reclined back on the saddle and closed his eyes. Momentarily, he dropped off to sleep, dreaming of the quick end of the bank robber. A slight smile made his mouth seem almost relaxed.

Cooty had quickly crawled into his bedroll after nodding to Gale. Once he was settled, Cooty quickly dropped off to sleep and began to saw logs. Gale was not aware of Cooty, as he was sleeping the rest of the wicked and weary. Bob had already left, saying he was going to check on the rock formations and the possibilities of the ancient abode of cliff dwellers. These motifs he had seen earlier in the in the day.

"I'll be back before the others," Bob said, to the two men at the campfire, as he rode his horse in the direction of the far ruins.

A deadly reptile of the desert, a diamondback rattlesnake, started to crawl toward the campfire, as the snake felt the heat from the fire penetrate its scaly skin. The reptilian eyes took in the sleeping form by the fire. The viper's long tongue darted in and out of its mouth, as it tested the air for vibrations and smell. Slower and slower, inch by inch, this harbinger of death slithered closer and closer to the fire and the warm sleeping body.

Another set of eyes watched the sleeping shape besides the obsidian eyes of the viper. These eyes were as cold as ice and as hard as granite. The dark eyes belonged to an outcast from the missionary group camped twenty miles to the west. They had accused him of making improper advances to the wife of the leader of the group. The group made him leave their camp and vowed to go the authorities if he did not do so.

He was a man with long matted hair, speckled with gray and encrusted with lice. Crooked teeth filled his mouth and patches of gray stubble surrounded it. During the fight after being discovered they had torn one eye out leaving him with a hideously empty socket. This unsavory character had an ugly purple scar that laced the side of his hollow face. The kind of face nightmares are made of to scare children, make women faint and strong men hastily check their guns strapped to their sides.

This ghoul had on an old burial shroud, which he had torn hurriedly off the body of a decaying body of a recently buried settler. He had no problem with disturbing the dead. "After all," he thought, "they're dead and will not be needing them anyway." His present clothing having been torn to shreds by the angry missionaries, were in tatters. He promised them that he would some day return and pay them back for their treatment of him. On his feet were moccasins that were threads bare and fastened to his feet with strips of the same shroud.

"John Jacob Jinklehymer Smith's no one's slave," he muttered to the darkness, as he slowly began to move toward Gale. Then he stopped and the reptile stopped. The snake started to move forward, so did John. In his hand was a large piece of wood he had hardened by roasting it in a fire. John squatted still, watching the snake and the reposing form, making for a macabre tableau.

The diamondback slid closer, its muscles undulating in the semi-darkness. John also started again to move forward stealthily. And, unlike the snake, had eyes not only on the reclining figure, but also the serpent. He was ready to make his move any minute, either to the human or to the snake. John was prepared to do battle with one or the other or maybe both, it did not matter to him. He had no fear for the simple reason, one has to have a mind and his had completely left him. John was no babbling idiot; he was death incarnate.

John stopped and watched warily for a moment. Then he crept closer toward the man and reptile. The snake, sensing trouble, rapidly curled up into a coiled, deadly and silent weapon.

The vibrating viper opened its mouth to reveal two long fangs that glistened as the light of the fire reflected off them. They were dripping with mucous looking venom, as its tongue quickly darted in and out. It started to quiver, its tail vibrating, making for an almost inaudible rattling sound.

Gale slept on, the sleep of the exhausted. Once, he gave a quick snort and then resumed his snoring. He was not aware of the dangers so close to him.

John sat back on his haunches and guardedly watched his adversary. His fingers tightened on the club. Suddenly, Gale rolled over in his sleep and thrust an arm out toward the snake. Quickly the snake struck as if was a coiled spring quickly untangled. Its body had straightened out as it's opened mouth with the hypodermic fangs sought the warm flesh, it knew was waiting in the man's unprotected arm.

Just as the snake was about to strike its mark, John brought the club crashing down on the reptile's head. At the same time, John reached out with his other hand and grasped the snake behind the head. He held this struggling serpent away from him. John squeezed harder and harder, repeatedly. When he had finished this grisly task, he smiled evilly and threw the dead rattlesnake into the bushes. Then he turned back toward Gale, squatted a few feet from the sleeping banker and patiently waited.

They had fought this seemingly endless battle between natural enemies quietly. So silent, they never disturbed Gale. John sat near the sleeping man and observed. The other person was not moving.

"I'll deal with him later," John thought to himself. He had patience, he could spend all night if it that is what i took.   Interminable minutes went by before Gale stirred. He rolled onto his back and opened his eyes.

Gale awoke to find John hovering over him.   At first, Gale started to quickly sit upright.   John pushed him back down with the club.   He grinned at Gale with a wicked smile and pointed to his mouth.

"Sure," Gale whispered, misunderstanding the man as to being quiet.   Gale tried to sit up again   "Just let me get my saddlebags here closer to the fire.   I've all of the food you could possibly want in my saddlebags."

The screwy stranger allowed Gale to scurry toward the saddlebags.   Gale hurriedly picked the saddlebags and carried them back to the fire.   Then pushing Gale to the side, he immediately went through them, dumping the contents on the bare earth.   There were strips of beef jerky, some dried corn, a small coffee can and a pouch of tobacco.

While John was ransacking the saddlebags, Gale was quietly moving to where the shovel he had used in making the campfire lay against a rock.   He picked the shovel up and turned toward John.   Gale raised his means of salvation above his head.   John heard the sound of movement behind him and he looked up.   He quickly rolled to the side just in time for Gale to miss his head by scant inches.

As John was rolling, he reached into the piece of rope that was his belt and drew out a homemade knife.   Gale wheeled about and started to advance on John, swinging the shovel before him.   John dropped into a crouch and waited until Gale was closer.   Gale moved to within striking distance of John and swinging the shovel as hard as he could, took a swipe at John's head.   Gale missed, but John didn't.

John plunged the knife up to its hilt in the lower groin of Gale.   He then twisted the knife and drug it upward slowly.   Gale's life giving blood gushed over John's knuckles.   The crimson blood dripped upon the barren earth, which absorbed the blood as a type of offering to the sand god.

Gale's eyes began to bulge from their sockets, became glassy and surprised registered on his face.   His mouth opened, but nothing came from it.   A look of disbelief washed across his features as he slowly toppled to the ground.   Once on the ground, he rolled on his back and stared at the stars for the last time.   Finally, he quivered for a moment, bok a deep breath and became still.   John pulled the knife from Gale's chest and wiped the bloody blade clean on Gale's trouser leg.

The sudden noise of the scuffle caused Cooty to stir from his bedroll and see two shadows by the campfire.

"They must be dancing," Cooty thought.   He began to wonder if it was another of his hallucinations.   Then shrugging his shoulders reached down and pulled the blanket back over his head and went fitfully to sleep.

Cooty did not see Gale's death, nor one of the shadows move toward him.   He was not aware of anything amiss, until he felt the cold steel of the knife blade as it was slid quickly across his throat.   Then it was too late.   He was dead.

John wiped the bloody blade on Cooty's blanket.   The killer replaced the knife in the rope at his waist and went through the victim's pockets.   The outcast found nothing important.   Then he drug the bodies to the concealment behind a sand dune.

Once the bodies were hidden, he returned to the fire and started to go through the remaining saddlebags.   The sound of hoof beats caused him to scamper off into the distance.   Far enough to be safely hidden, but still close enough to be able to see.

"More victims for me," John chuckled into the night air, as he subconsciously moved his knife up and down. He was preparing for more prey.   The light of the moon made his eyes gleam and his hideous mouth broke into a smile.

EIGHT

Lee Wildman and Gary Sandusky were busy hunting small game for the camp's larder. They had ridden a mile from their campsite when suddenly Gary pointed with his rifle to the sky west of them. He reined his mount in and Lee did likewise. They looked up at the ominous darkening sky.

The sky had become darker and flashes of lightning streaked across the horizon. The inevitable thunder quickly followed, seemingly making echoes in the sky. The wind was brisker, causing tumbleweeds to race across their paths. Rabbits had scurried to their burrows, as had all animals seeking shelter from the approaching holocaust.

"Looks like the making of a sandstorm," Gary had shouted. The wind was starting to shriek like a banshee. "We'd better be heading back."

"You're right, Gary," said Lee, busy wheeling his mount around and pointing its head toward the campsite. "Let's move!"

They started to ride hard toward the camp. As they drew close to the camp, Lee motioned for Gary to halt. Lee quickly jumped from his mount and turned to see Gary dismount also. The men almost collided as they sought some sort of refuge.

Taking their horses to a small hillock, they waited. Lee and Gary tried their best at holding on to their hats and at the same time the reins to the horses. Lee finally crouched down on the far side of his horse. Gary struggled to hold on to the rains of his mount, which was starting to rear as it became more skittish. He finally got the animal to calm down. Then, he squinted to look down the hillside.

"The camp's there," Gary hollered against the howling wind, as he was pointing down the hill to the outline of the shed.

"I know," Lee replied. "But I think, we'd better take care of our horses. We can walk to the camp from here."

"I suppose," Gary yelled, as he was taking the saddle off his mount. "We'll unload the horses first. They can fend for themselves. They know how to survive the storm better than we do."

Quickly they pulled the saddles from the horses and hurled them to the ground. Then the horses, relieved of their burdens, quickly bolted. They started toward the wilds. Gary started to protest, but was told by Lee that they could always find them later. He knew the horses would soon return to the campsite. Gary looked at the departing back of the horses, shrugged his shoulders and followed Lee.

The wind had died down a little as the two men walked to where the campsite was found. When they arrived there was no one around. Both men started to search the empty campsite.

"Where's Gale?" Gary asked. "Or Cooty and that new man Bob Davis?"

"Got me," Lee answered, still looking around the area. "It's not like Gale to wander off by himself. Especially without his boots. I just checked the shed and he's not in there. As far as the other two, I simply don't know."

"Look here," Gary said, as he was walking to where the contents of the saddlebags were strewn about as if someone had searched them.

"Gary," Lee cautioned, pulling his gun from the holster. "We'd best be on the lookout for anything and everything. I'm not hankering for any surprises."

They went to Gale's blanket spread on the ground. The wind had rearranged it to resemble a body. Lee squatted down and traced the bloodstains on the blanket with his gun. He stood still and looked around the campfire. He thought that he heard something. He made a motion for Gary to be quiet. Treading softly, he walked to a small sand dune. Gary followed him and pulled his weapon from its holster. Lee motioned for Gary to go around the opposite side of the sand dune to wait for his signal. They were to leap out and catch the unwary suspect.

"Now," Lee yelled, jumping around the edge of the sand dune and pointing his gun.

Both men were looking at each other and Lee smiled sheepishly. They holstered their weapons and advanced on the still shapes by the sand dune. They were staring at the huddled forms of Gale and Cooty. Lee rushed to Gale and grabbed his right shoulder. He turned Gale over slowly. The body rolled to its side. Staring up at them with forever vacant eyes was Gale Loughmiller!

Meanwhile, Gary had checked on the remains of Cooty. Gary noticed that Cooty's throat had been slashed from ear to ear. He then walked to where Lee was examining the body of Gale.

"Cooty's throat's been cut," Gary said, then motioning toward the corpse of Gale. "Look at the size of that wound?"

"Yes," Lee said, bending over the inert form of Gale for a closer look. "It seems that whoever did this wasn't satisfied with simply sticking poor ole Gale, but enjoyed it too. Gale has been cut from breadbasket to brisket. From the appearance of that wound, the killer twisted the knife on its upward journey. A bad way to die. Of course anyway's bad to a person who has to do the dying."

"I don't want to sound a pessimist or b be a worry wart," Gary said, while casting his gaze skyward. "We'd be safer to get to some sort of cover before long. The storm's getting worse and it's not going to spare us any.

Besides, these two are not planning going anywhere soon."

The wind had picked up in force and started to blow harder. The men hunkered down as the wind blew tiny pieces of sand at them. These fine particles of sand were hitting their bodies hard enough to make them feel as if minuscule shards of glass were pounding their skin. The men pulled their bandanas up to cover more of their mouth and noses.

They made it to the side of the camp, Lee glanced around. He saw no other way, so he grabbed Gary by the arm and struggling against the wind pulled him to an arroyo. Both went falling into the gully. At the bottom of the ravine, they buried their faces to the wall of dirt. As Gary was burying his face, he drew his bandana up to cover his mouth and nose again. Lee did the same. The sheriff and his deputy burrowed in the side of the gulch as if they were moles seeking the protection of Mother Earth.

The storm seemed to last for a long time, or so it seemed to the two huddled figures. Soon it was over and then the stars appeared to sparkle brightly as some silver nuggets in the night sky. The moon was full and hung in the sky as if suspended by an invisible thread. A shooting star streaked across the horizon making its long journey through the heavens. Lee could tell by the position of the stars. Morning would not be long arriving.

Lee and Gary started to the top of the bank, sand and dirt falling behind them, as if they were prairie dogs seeking the bright warmth of the coming day. Lee reached out and secured a hold on a scrub pine at the edge of the ravine. He strained to pull himself over the rim. Once he was safely on the edge, he turned around and stuck out a hand for Gary to grasp.

After much tugging, grunting and patience Lee was able to get Gary over the hump. They looked at what was left of their camp. Their only light was from the full moon. The men were able to make out the various shapes of things. The line shack was gone, only a few boards were left sticking up from the side of a sand dune to remind them of its existence. Most of their equipment was gone too.

"Think we'll check on the bodies," Lee said as he started toward a sand dune.

"Know what you mean," Gary replied. "Or at least what's left of 'em."

The two stanchions of the law went behind the dune to inspect Gale's and Cooty's bodies. The corpses were almost covered completely by the sand. Only the stocking feet of Gale protruded from the pile of sand. Cooty's body was almost completely covered with sand and he had one black boot that seemed to be thrust up through the sand.

"Go and get a blanket," Lee said, as he dropped to his knees beside the still form. "I'll uncover him. Then we'll get Cooty and tie the bodies to the horses. Once that's done, then we'll head back to town for a Christian burial."

Lee was inspecting the remains of the men, when he caught the glimmer of a blade out of the corner of his eyes. The knife was in a stranger's hand and it was aimed for Gary's unprotected back!

Lee drew faster than he thought possible from his crouched position and fired at this apparition. Gary whirled to see what all of the commotion was about.

"*What the . . .*" Gary exclaimed, drawing his weapon, weaving it around and looking about for further trouble.

"Don't know," Lee answered, arising from beside Gale's body and warily walking to the prone person. He still had his gun out and was looking for further trouble. Lee wanted to be prepared.

While Gary replaced his gun, Lee reached out with the toe of his boot and rolled the body over on its back. He holstered his weapon, then squatted to begin a cursory examination of the receiver of his bullet. Lee's bullet had torn out the upper right side of the face and most of the nose.

John Jacob Jinklehymer Smith stared back at them with one eye widened with surprise and a sort of a melancholy smile on what was left of his lips. He looked somewhat less fierce in death than real life, but was still able to make Gary unconsciously cross himself. Lee looked down at the corpse with distaste in his mouth.

"Looks like we caught up to the killer of Gale and Cooty," Lee said, reaching down to close the one eye of the body.

"But what about that new man?" Gary asked, surveying the campsite once again.

"Got me there," Lee answered, rubbing his hand over his chin. "But let's get on with the task before us."

They went back to where to the campfire, which had burned itself out, leaving only smouldering ashes. Lee started to retrieve Gale, as Gary tried to place Cooty on the back of a horse. The horse was skittish at the smell of blood and the burden Gary attempted to place on its back. Gary spoke soothingly to the animal and finally got the horse to become calmer. After the horse got still, he hefted the gruesome burden to the horse's back and lashed it securely to the animal's back.

Lee appeared with the remains of Gale slung on his back. He placed the body down beside the fire. Lee noticed Gary finishing the lashing of his burden. Nodding to Gary, Lee placed Gale on the back of a horse, securing it also.

"I'll check the area one more time for Bob," Lee said, as he started to inspect the area for the last time. He wanted to make sure that he did not forget things. "Lately," he thought to himself, "I've been forgetting too much. Oh well," he pondered, "must be getting old after all." Smiling ruefully, he began his search, only this time he made a more careful inspection of the surrounding locale.

"I'll help you too," Gary spoke softly, for he did not want left out of anything. "You never know what is happening, about to happen and had already happened if you don't include yourself," he thought, as he tagged after Lee.

NINE

Chris rode into Clearwater late at night. The town lights were out except the ones in the saloon. He could hear the noises that emitted from the batwing doors of the saloon as he rode abreast of them. It sounded as if someone or ones were having a good time.

The light from the saloon shed an unearthly glow on the buildings across the street. Their false fronts loomed at him as their shadows seemed to make the structures move of their own inclination. Chris felt a need for a drink.

"A whisky would sure help me out now," he thought, as he turned aside his mount. The blacksmith rode up to the hitch rail in front of the saloon. Getting tiredly off his horse, he wrapped the reins around the hitch rail and walked slowly up the steps. He could hear someone giving the piano keys all sorts of trouble, as if they were mad at the world and wanted to take their anger out on the piano. "Must be a new piano player in town," he thought, smiling to himself. "Or maybe the old one learning new songs!"

Chris looked over the bat wings and spied Big Tim Mastenbrook polishing the bar with a rag that had seen better days.

"It must be his Sunday rag," Chris thought smiling, it has so many holes in it. He saw there was a new barmaid carrying drinks to a group of miners, their occupation evident by the dirty overalls, hobnailed boots and sweaty bodies. The smell permeated the saloon. Filthy or not, they spent their money spent as anyone else.

Chris could see a cowboy in the far corner that had passed out. The cowboy's hat was pulled down on his head and his feet splayed out in front of him. His three companions were busy at the poker table. Two had their hats tilted back on their heads as the other one had a bandana tied around his head.

Two with the hats were the brother's Deckard, Mike and Herman. One with a bandana was Dan Ramos, a half-bred Mexican. The other half was Chiricahua Apache. A bad mix in any one's eyes. They were all whooping it up a bit. There were two half empty bottles of whiskey and four dirty glasses on their table.

Chris noticed they were all armed. The brothers had .45 Colts slid into their holsters tied down to their legs. Ramos had .44 Remington revolver, evident by the reinforced rib that ran on the underside of the gun. This made the weapon still serviceable after being banged around all day out on the open range and the scrub brush.

"Bartender!" Ramos shouted, throwing back another drink. "Bring us another bottle and don't take forever about it either."

Big Tim placed a bottle of whiskey on the new barmaid's tray and she walked to the table. She placed it down quickly. However, she was not quick enough, for Mike suddenly reached out and grasped her by the arm. It seemed the more she struggled the tighter his grip became. She looked with imploring eyes at Big Tim for help.

"All right, men," Big Tim said ominously. "Let her go."

"Sure, Big Tim," Mike replied, in a hurtful tone. He did not want to get Big Tim mad at him or his brother. Up to now, because of all of their hell raising, the Green Parrot was the only place that Mr. Hadley had said it was all right to visit.

"Visit," Mr. Hadley said, looking hard at them. "I do mean visit. Now you boys don't want to know what it is to get on my bad side!"

Mike was drunk, but not too drunk. He did not want to raise the ire of either Mr. Hadley or Big Tim, but at the same time wanted to take his anger out on someone, because the new woman was rejecting him. He began to sulk and drink more quickly, as if he could drown his misfortunes. His black mood caused him to drink harder. It wasn't too long before he had drunk more than he could properly handle. The cowboy was almost falling down drunk.

"Lookee there," Herman said, since Mike was despondent and wanted to bring his brother out of the pit of despair. He nudged Mike in the ribs and pointing to the drunk cowboy lying sprawled out in the corner.

"Whoee!" Mike exclaimed, apparently coming out of his ugly mood. "Thomas is sure enough going to have a big hangover tomorrow."

"Well," Herman intoned in a mock somber voice and sneaking the half-full bottle of whiskey inside his shirt. "We'll just have to take care of that problem really quick like, won't we boys?"

"Yep," Mike replied, dragging his sleeve across his mouth. "A little hair of the dawg. Don't you think?"

They were all grinning and taking turns at passing another bottle. Herman was by far the drunkest of the trio. Each time he raised the bottle to his lips for a swig, he missed his mouth and poured the whiskey down the front of his already dirty shirt. He wiped his mouth with the back of his hand and passed the bottle to Mike.

This was the scene Chris walked into as he swung open the saloon doors and walked to the bar. He didn't pay any attention to the drunken revelers. Instead he walked to the bar and ordered whiskey.

"Come on, Chris," Ramos waved and pulled out a chair. "Have a drink with us."

Chris looked at the cowboys and gave them a hard stare. He was here on business not to lollygag around. He turned his back on the cowboys and continued to drink his whiskey. The smithy heard a chair scrape on the sawdust floor. In a moment, a drunken cowboy was standing behind him. Chris hoped he did not get too close, his fetid breath was bad enough.

"A man could just get drunk from smelling him," Chris thought. He also figured, ignoring the cowboy would do the trick.

"What's the matter? You too good to have a friendly drink with us boys?" Mike said in a slurred voice, his tongue tripping over his crooked teeth. He had drunk his bottle and was quickly depleting Herman's. Mike had a grudge and wished to take it out on someone. That someone was evidently standing before him. All thoughts of the threats made by Mr. Hadley vanished from his drunken head. He arose from his table and started to stagger toward the hulking shape of the town's blacksmith joining his drunken brother.

"Nope," Chris said softly, tilting his glass up and swallowing the whiskey down fast. He placed the glass down on the bar, looked at Big Tim and nodded another. Chris still had not turned to face the inebriated cowboys. "Prefer to drink alone."

"Well, maybe we don't want you to drink all by lonesome self, do we boys?" Mike said, his voice raising in volume and drunkenly looking over his shoulder at his fellow drinkers. He was full of instant courage.

Standing behind Chris, Mike suddenly reached out and placed a gnarled hand upon Chris's shoulder squeezing it hard. The veins on the back of his hand started to pop. He squeezed with all of his might and it did not seem to faze this giant.

"Friend," Chris said patiently, shrugging the hand off his shoulder. He glanced up in the long bar mirror and noticed the cowboy was weaving a little on his feet. "Like I told you. I want to drink my drink alone. Thank you kindly though."

"You don't seem to catch my drift, Big Man," Mike said, winking at his brother and their friend still sitting at their table. He felt like David in the Bible, in that he was determined to tackle this Goliath. Only one thing, this Goliath did not taunt him, or for that matter, pay him any mind, he was just standing alone and did not want to be bothered. Mike spun Chris around and threw a roundhouse punch at Chris's face.

Chris watched the blow coming, leaned to the side and at the last minute reached out with his calloused hand, engulfing the smaller one. He brought the hand down quickly against the edge of the bar. Everyone in the saloon could hear the bone breaking in Mike's hand.

The miners quickly put their money on the table and hurriedly left the premises with the new piano player following suit. They began to exit the saloon so quickly that the swinging doors were scarcely still behind the backs of the miners. The patrons of the bar knew when trouble was around and they did not want any part of it. They planed on returning after the brawl was over. Later, much later.

The miners had enough to do, swinging their picks all day long, without having to swing their fists at nighttime too. The piano pounder, though too much of his delicate hands to want them, banged up, and the bar woman hurried to the backside of the bar. She had seen enough fights and wasn't hankering to be hit by any flying glass or otherwise hurling chairs.

Herman and Dan had placed themselves to either side of Chris, as the mass exodus began. Herman quickly threw a punch that connected to the side of Chris's face. The contact between cheek and fist made Chris see stars for a moment.

Ramos leaned back and kicked out with his right leg to connect with Chris's side. Chris reeled and fell against the bar with his broad back, sending glasses clattering to the floor, as the bar stools swayed on the brink of falling over, but stayed up righted after all.

Chris raised his hands to his head, where he pressed them against his temples in an attempt to clear it. Shaking his head to clear it, Chris lashed out and hit Herman with one of his humongous fists, as he backhanded Ramos with the other.

Then Chris grabbed Mike's injured arm and saw Mike wince with pain. Chris grunted and with no apparent effort, he threw Mike through the air to crash against the table next to the piano. The bottle and glasses from the recently vacated miners, teetered for a moment, then went crashing to the floor.

"All right!" Big Tim growled, reaching under the counter. He raised a shotgun and leveling the scattergun across the top of the bar. Its barrel pointing ominously at everyone, the cowboys in particular.

The bartender figured that he would fire the greener over their heads and if that did not do the trick, his next volley would turn more deadly. His knuckles were beginning to whiten from the pressure he applied to the trigger of the sawed off shotgun. He was ready to commence firing, only seeing the outcome of the fight stayed his finger. The color was slowly returning to his hand.

Chris stood shaken on one side of the room, while Herman and Dan were breathing heavily and had taken positions on the other. The Deckard brothers had momentarily stopped their advance on Chris, but they were in a sort of stalemate. The stopped their forward progress, while looking warily at the barrel of the shotgun. They knew of the shotguns' apparent range and decided that they were too close for comfort.

Herman had seen the damage a greener could do once in a bar in Arkansas. The poor victim had been cut completely in two. Another had lain in the sawdust with just a stump for a head, the blast from the shotgun having took it off. When he had returned to the ranch, he spoke of it in awe to his brother and friends.

Mike was lying unconscious by the bar, while Thomas was oblivious to what had taken place while he was out. He was in a comatose state underneath a large Regulator wall clock. The clock chose that time to chime then. The time was eleven in the evening.

"Now, you boys." Big Tim slowly spoke in somber tones. He did not want any further damage or the off chance someone could get hurt badly. "Pick up your friends and get on out of here, but remember to pay me what you owe. Sober up some, then come back and I'll personally buy you all a drink. If you don't see it that way, then the undertaker is going to be doing a tolerable amount of business tonight!"

"Thanks," Chris said, as he was busy rubbing his bruised knuckles. He reached down and picked his crumpled hat from the floor. Brushing the sawdust from it, he beat it against the side of his leg. Then he placed the hat squarely on his head, wincing where the hatband applied pressure to his bruises.

Chris turned to face the cowboys, who were busy picking one another up from the floor. They got the drunk cowboy by the clock to his feet. Then Herman walked to the bar and slapped down a few coins. He then turned, glared at Chris and walked around the bar to help his brother. Mike staggered out from behind the bar holding his injured arm, with his brother's arm helping him to stay upright.

"You won't be hearing the last of this, Blacksmith!" Herman said, as he helped the crippled party to the saloon doors.

"Let's hope so," Chris said, shrugging his shoulders. He knew that it could have been worse, especially if it were one on one. The big, burly and large smithy was

111

afraid of his own strength and rage, in particular, when riled.

Herman dragged the back of his hand across his bloodied lips as he went out the doors. The drunks stomped across the boardwalk and down to the hitching rail. Chris could hear them get on their horses and the sudden sound of their horses hooves fade into the night as they rode out of Clearwater. Turning back to Big Tim, he reached into his back pocket and asked what it cost for the damage.

"Nothing to you!" Big Tim said vehemently, waving his hand in the air in dismissal. "A few broken glasses and a chair that are repairable. Besides, if there were any at all, I know how to get hold of the owner of the ranch where them boys are employed. Old Man Hadley will be happy to pay and then if I know him, be only too happy to have them boys work extra hard to make up the difference in their paychecks.

"I can just see them now," Big Tim thought. "Once Hadley gets through tearing them a new posterior. He'll go through them like a dose of salts' work on a body. I wouldn't give any odds, but them boys will be a long time coming before they go to hooraying you or anyone else."

Chris could only smile as he watched Big Tim wipe the bar of an imaginary spot. Big Tim was grinning ear-to-ear and chuckling. Finally, unable to hold it in any longer, Chris started to laugh. Big Tim looked at Chris and started to guffaw mightily too.

The two laughed so hard that tears began to course down Big Tim's cheeks, while Chris tried his best at holding on to the edge of the bar. He lost his grip and slowly slid down the side of the bar. He ended on the sawdust floor with his legs spread.

Big Tim asked of the posse after they had calmed down. He helped Chris to his feet as Chris told him that the posse was still out on the range. The sheriff sent him back to town to get more supplies. Once the supplies were in hand, he would be headed back to rejoin them.

"How's that new dude doing?" Big Tim asked, as he was pouring another drink for Chris.

"Thanks," Chris said, throwing his head back and letting the fiery liquid rush down his throat. Then holding his hand over the glass declined Big Tim's offer of another drink. "You must mean Bob Davis," Chris replied. "Let me tell you. Just wish we had more of his caliber with us, instead of Gale Loughmiller. That man's a blessing in disguise. Loughmiller is a royal pain in the butt. Pardon my French."

Chris spent the next few moments extolling the virtues of Bob. Big Tim let him talk, as he got busy wiping the bar again for the umpteenth time. Then he remembered Chris was a loner. The kids said he was all the time talking to himself. A real loner - maybe too lonely.

"You boys all right?" the new barmaid asked, after sweeping the debris left by the broken bottles and glasses and placing a tray of empty beer mugs on the bar. She turned around and started to trim the lamps at the sides of the saloon.

"Just fine, Kim," Big Tim laughed, wiping the bar again. He was so nervous that he seemed to have an unconscious urge built into his subconscious, in that he was fidgety all the time.

"Kim? Please come here for a minute." Then thinking of Chris's situation, literally smacked himself in the forehead. Here is my answer staring in the face. "Tim, you're a big dummy," he thought.

Kim stopped her trimming of the lamps and came back to stand beside Chris. She looked at Big Tim with a question in her eyes, as if to say, "well, here I am, fire away."

"Oh, Chris," Big Tim said, as he looked at Kim. "This's my new barmaid, Kim Temple. Kim, this is Chris

Barker, our town blacksmith and part owner of the livery. Also, one of my best friends."

As they were saying their pleased to meet you, Big Tim. was busy looking and thinking. Chris was a bachelor and Kim was sort of unattached, if you count being attached to that no-account Bart Temple as a marriage. He was inclined to believe shackled was the proper word. There was word that Bart up and left for parts unknown with one of the town whores. It was a good riddance to bad rubbish folks would say.

Kim had tried to hold her head up, as she walked by the townspeople, but that was hard to do. The old biddies in town loved to gossip about everyone, it seemed to Big Tim. The juicer the news, the better their stories got, as with each retelling, the fables became bigger, bolder and bawdier. This went on in town continually for so long that people would start to look at one another and wonder if it were true.

One day last week, she marched into the saloon with her head held up high and asked for a job. Tim admired her spunk and hired her on the spot. The bar owner had not regretted making that decision. He only wished there were more of her kind around.

"However," he knew, "if wishes were beer, he would be forever passing it out."

Big Tim could see something was going on between the two. Sparks seemed to fly in the air as the two looked at each other. They were gooey eyed as they glanced at one another, never mindful of the rest of the world. Chris would sip his beer and look at Kim over the rim, his eyes seemed to be dancing with merriment. Kim, on the other hand looked at the big smithy and her eyes seemed to be lively and vibrant.

"May I walk you home, Miss Temple?" Chris asked, quickly doffing his hat and shuffling his feet as a young swain would be tempted to do. He was also blushing, as his cheeks were becoming flushed and his ears began to redden.

"Well, I don't know?" she said, as she looked questionably at Big Tim. She was hoping to be alone with this courteous man, if nothing more than to talk with. For since Bart left, she had been very lonely. The people in town shunned her. They were afraid that her misfortune would befall them, so they did their best in avoiding her. As if by mere association, her anguish would affect them also.

"Sure thing," Big Tim replied, taking off his apron. "You go on. All I've to do is finish putting out the lamps and locking the doors."

He turned toward Kim and winked at her. Then with his head, he motioned for her to leave. Big Tim walked with them to the saloon doors. Then he shooed them out the doors, grinning all the time. He smiled when he saw Chris extend his arm for Kim to grasp. The bartender smiled even more, when he saw her comply. Arm in arm. They went down the dark street.

"Ah," Big Tim breathed softly. "What young love will do to you."

Sighing, he walked back into the saloon. In a moment, the lights flickered and went out. Big Tim closed the front door, then he locked it and started the stairs to his quarters. He was more than half way up the stairs, when he stopped and returned downstairs to check on the windows. After taking care of the windows, he ascended the stairs.

TEN

The stars were gleaming in the night sky like the sunlight glistens, as it sparkles of the calm waters of a placid lake. The breeze, laced with the fragrant smell of lilacs, flowed gently across the street, as Kim and Chris walked in the bright moonlight. They were headed toward the boardinghouse she now called home.

The boardinghouse was at the far end of town. It was a two-story building, made of lumber carted in from the upper part of the Territory. The building had a new coat of whitewash that had been painted over the aged lumber. A large porch surrounded the front of the structure to end midway down the evening side with a porch swing was on it. New wicker chairs were placed like sentinels on either side of the front door. Light in the parlor window glowed faintly through the stained-glass window casting it light on the porch and pathway. The house had a white picket fence at the front with a gate barring entrance.

"Here we are," Chris said, as he opened the gate for her. "After you, ma'am."

"So we are," Kim replied, wishing the night would go on forever. She hesitantly started the path. Then she stopped, turned toward Chris and asked if he would like to join her sitting in the swing.

"I promise not to bite," she laughed, thinking this big man could not possibly be scared of her. After all, she had seen the way that he handled himself tonight in the fracas at the saloon. She noticed the irony of the situation; a big man who's fearless in the face of outnumbered odds and tough cowboys, but was gentle to her. "I'll just bet," she thought, "this big man is kind to children too."

"I don't know," Chris responded, quickly removing his hat and looking sheepishly at her. He was just going to walk her to the door as a proper person would do, but now he had to decide. "What do you think Miss Purdy might say?"

Kim was glad it was dimly lighted on the pathway. Chris could not see her smile as such gallantry. They had only known each other for such a short time and already she was smitten with him. They say that love is blind, but in her case, it was also deaf and mute. After all, she was a barmaid and he was worried about her reputation. Such concern was evident in his virile face. Here, this brawny man was evidently afraid of him being with her, would affect her reputation with the so-called respectable people of town.

"Hah!" she said. "I don't rightly care what anyone thinks. All I do care is what I think and right now I am not concerned with the gossips in town. The devil with them! Where were they when my fine upstanding husband took off to Lord knows where? Did anyone offer any help? A job? Some sympathy!"

She said all of this in a rush, then stopped. The tiny, dark-haired woman reached up and started to twist a tendril of hair around her fingers. She became lost in thought and her mind was far away.

"Kim," Chris asked. "You all right?"

"Huh?" Kim replied, startled. "Oh, I'm just fine now. I was thinking about the *good* help I've received from the town since my troubles began to surface."

"Yep," Chris said, misunderstanding her last statement. "Know what you mean. People will help out in any way they can."

Kim did not want to correct him, especially as she had just met him.

"Let him think the best of the townspeople," she thought. "Only I know better!"

Arm in arm they walked up the pathway to the porch. Chris brushed off the seat with his hat and motioned for

Kim to sit. She sat, moved over, patted the seat and asked if he were going to sit also?

The two sat in the swing with Chris pushing the swing to make it glide smoothly back and forth. He moved his arm up to rest on the back of the swing. Kim placed her head back against his arm. They rocked for a while, neither saying anything, just enjoying the evening, the stars sparkling, crickets making their nightly noise and the gentle breeze.

Then as Chris gently turned Kim's head toward his, their lips brushed against each other. At first she was withdrawn, then she pressed her lips hard against his lips. Finally, she broke the embrace.

"Oh, Chris," she gasped. "What will *you* think of me?"

"Look here, Little Lady," he said, staring at her hard. "I think, no, I know, you're the best thing that has happened to me in a long time. Mercy, if I wasn't an old man, I would say I'm taken with you."

"But, you're not old," she said, looking at him with pride in her eyes. "You're in your prime. Tell me of another man who could have managed himself as well as you did tonight with them cowboys."

Chris did not want to tell her that if the fight had gone on any longer, he would have been too tuckered out to finish it. He was lucky, but the cowboys had not counted on his strength.

"Funny how you get all muscle-bound blacksmithing every day," he thought. "The many hours spent swinging the hammer and hammering on the anvil in shoeing horses and the added time working the bellows up and down gave me the exercises. My strength, from lifting anvils, plows and lugging the carriage wheels from one location to the other, was an added benefit that certainly came in handy tonight!"

119

Chris grinned to himself as he remembered the look of disbelief on the cowboy's face as he grabbed the cowboy's fist and the utter amazement as he effortlessly pitched the cowboy over the bar. He noticed also the awe in the eyes of the other cowboys and Big Tim.

"Maybe so," Chris said, turning to stare out in the darkness. "But you seem to forget one very important matter. The reason I'm alone. I like it. You promise not to tell a soul and I'll let you in on a secret?"

"Oh?"

"Yes. I say I like it. But liking it and keeping warm on cold nights or eating a good home cooked meal doesn't always seem like a good deal. Just being able to have someone to talk to and more important, having someone to care is. "

Then quick as a fleeting shadow, Chris arose and hurried to the gate. He reached the gate and stopped. The blacksmith turned and looked back at her. Then he doffed his hat and said with a conviction in his voice.

"You go to bed and sleep on what is happening. When I get back to town, we'll sit and have us a long talk. I promise you that!"

Kim watched the big man go down the street with a purposeful stride to his demeanor. Funny how things work out, she mused. Then she remembered fondly her mother saying how all things work out for the good. His sudden departure brought back painful memories to her. The disappearing acts of her husband.

"Was this the same?" she questioned herself. "I certainly hope not!" Kim gathered her shawl about her shoulders and opened the door of the boardinghouse.

Chris remembered what he was in town for and he felt bad at this diversion. He decided not to let this little setback bother him again. The big man walked determinedly toward the general store. Nothing or nobody was going to stop him now, he vowed, as he climbed the wooden steps of the general store.

"Here I was in town to get supplies for the men and was enjoying myself instead. I'll not let the men down again," he spoke to the night air, as he began to pound on the door of Abner Hershey's Emporium.

"Open the door, Abner," Chris said loudly, at once glancing around to see if anyone else was out tonight. He did not want to bother anyone's else's night sleep.

In a moment, he heard chains on the door clink noisily and slide back. The door opened a crack. A small chain was still in place keeping the door from opening fully. Chris could barely make out the frightened face of Abner Hershey.

"Lord a mercy!" Chris muttered to the night air. "Abner, you don't have to worry about anyone shooting you. They would probably grow a long gray beard and get long in the tooth before they could gain entrance."

"Whatcha want?" Abner asked, in a meekly sounding voice.

"It's me, Abner. Chris Barker, open up. I need some supplies."

Chris patiently explained the circumstances of him being here at this late hour. Seeing the look of doubt on Abner's face, Chris told of the posse running out of supplies. The sheriff had sent him back for more staples.

Abner scratched his bald head, mumbled to himself, unlocked the door and allowed Chris to enter the premises. Chris walked past Abner to stand in front of the counter. He asked Abner if he could hurry some, Abner just snorted and took his sweet time. He raised the globe of a coal oil lamp and brought it to life. Then, he adjusted the wick higher to cast more light on the premises. Abner placed this lamp on the counter.

Hershey's Emporium was a one story wooden structure with a false facade that made it appear larger. It was found next to the burnt leather shop and two doors down from the sheriff's office. As it was, the store was thirty by fifty feet, wooden floors, or what you could see of them. Merchandise, barrels and various racks of men and women clothing. These racks were topped with hats of various shapes and sizes. In front of the counter about three feet away, a large wooden pedestal housed various catalogues.

"Grandma was slow, but she was old too," Chris said heatedly, wishing the storekeeper could hurry up. He wanted to make good time to apologize for his apparent tardiness to the posse.

"Yeah, yeah," Abner rejoined, but going slow as a snail pace. "What happened to your face - a horse kick you?"

"Never mind," Chris said. "Just get the supplies for me, please." He did not want Abner to know of his fight. Abner was worse than a town crier, besides, he was also a notorious gossiper. Chris did not want the news of his fight broadcast to the world. He did not mind any mention of the fight, but his resulting relationship with the new barmaid was his own private business. Chris knew that Abner, once he got a hold of the least little bit of gossip, was like trying to take a tasty morsel out of a pit bull dog's mouth. Abner would worm around and Chris did not want it known about Kim Temple just yet.

"Maybe when I get back to town, but certainly not before!" Chris thought.

Abner took off his white nightcap and replaced it with a green storekeeper's shade. He then removed a pair of spectacles from the pocket of his brown night robe and placed them gently on his bulbous nose. His beige shawl was still loosely draped over his shoulders. On his feet were a pair of house slippers so large, he had a hard time keeping them on. He finally got busy and started to fill Chris's order for the supplies.

Abner got a small wooden ladder and placed it against the wall, he slowly, but methodically, started the rungs. He reached the top shelf and got a bag of dried beans off the shelf. Slowly, he started down the ladder. Then he moved to stand in front of the same wall, while busily scratching his head as if he could get his brain in to gear faster.

He placed the beans on the counter. Abner stooped and reached under the counter to come up with a pound of Arbuckle coffee, which he placed beside the beans.

The storekeeper looked up and pulled his spectacles down lower on his fleshy nose, evidently thinking of something else he could pawn on the blacksmith. He smiled when he noticed Chris was turning the pages of the latest mail order catalogue. Grinning to himself, Abner shook his head and shuffled his feet to where he had strategically placed a few barrels. He removed the lids of the barrels and then turned back to Chris, who was still leafing through the catalog.

"You think that the posse would like some fruit?" Abner said, hoping that it would, as he needed to get rid of some fruit that ripened too quickly. The bananas had the start of brown streaks on their skins, the apples were getting extremely soft and the pears were becoming too mushy for the average populace.

Getting no answer from Chris, he replaced the lids on the barrels and went to the back of the store. There he moved another ladder to the side. Once he was at the top of this ladder, he got down from the rafters a bag of dried apples and a sheaf of over ripe bananas. He descended the ladder and replaced it by the side of the back door. Abner went to where he kept the meat and raised the lid on a barrel. The grocer reached in the barrel and secured a slab of bacon. Abner wheeled and brought out a packet of hardtack from the shelf behind the counter. Placing this in a burlap sack, he turned back to Chris.

"Say, Abner. I could sure use some of your hard pieces of candy," said Chris, grinning at Abner. "Seems my horse and I have developed a sweet tooth lately."

"The sheriff's going to pay for all of this?" Abner asked, as he was going around Chris to walk down the aisle. He knew that the sheriff was going to pay, but wanted confirmation from the big blacksmith.

"Of course he's going to pay," Chris replied hotly. Then seeing the skeptical look on Abner's face as he stopped and turned around to gaze at the blacksmith again, said. "I'm going to pay for the candy myself. All right with you?"

"Sure thing, Chris," Abner smiling in justification, as he was waddling to the front of the store. He stopped, then leaned over the counter and retrieved a small sack of candy from under the counter. Abner placed the supplies in the sack and handed them to the patiently waiting blacksmith. He stood back and gave Chris an imperious glance. Then he went on to explain to the blacksmith of his plight.

"A lot of this merchandise has been smoke damaged, but I'm taking a loss by letting you have these goods at a greatly reduced price," Abner said, sighing. "I'm selling them to you below cost."

"Thank you kindly," Chris said, knowing that Abner was going to charge the sheriff a pretty penny for these damaged supplies. He knew that all of the town businesses, well most of them, thought it wasn't robbery to place their snouts in the town's trough.

"After all," some said. "It's not as if we're stealing, just getting our fair share out of the town's coffers."

"The sheriff said to put all of this on his tab. I think I'd best be going now. I've a far piece to travel tonight," Chris said, looking outside the store's front window. "If I hurry, then maybe I can reach them before it gets any worse. The sky is starting to flash and it looks uglier than Old Man Moses prize Berkshire sow."

Chris went to the door, walked through and down the steps to the hitch rail. He tied the burlap sack to the leather thongs of the saddle. Then swinging up into the saddle, he touched his heels to the horse's flanks. Pointing the horse in the direction of the posse, Chris rode at a canter out of the sleepy town. Once, outside the city limits and away from sleeping people, he urged his mount into a gallop. Chris planned on being able to reach the posse before it got daylight.

"That's some gal," he thought, as he rode through the countryside. He could not help but smile at his recollection of Kim Temple while gingerly reaching up and touching the bruise on his cheek. Thinking of her caused him to be more careful in his riding.

ELEVEN

Bob Davis was born June 21, 1844 at a farm in the middle of Indiana on the first day of summer. According to his mother and the other women in town, it was the longest and hottest; most certainly the hardest to her. He was seventeen when he joined the Grand Army of the Republic or the Union Army, depending on whom you were talking to at the time, in 1861 as part of the Chicago Dragoons.

The Army had stationed Bob at Fort Belvior in Virginia. He was there when Abraham Lincoln was assassinated. Bob had been walking near the Ford Theater, when a group of people rushed by him shouting, "the President's been shot!"

He could still remember as if it were yesterday, the hustle and bustle of the crowd in its confusion, jostling him along the street. They pushed, elbowed Bob and almost trampled to death in the mob's fury. The mob began to wander around the streets aimlessly. Suspiciously looking at each other. Only later, did he find out that John Wiles Booth, a noted Shakespearean actor was the assassin.

When the war was over in '65, he had seen enough of life's hard and often cruel realities, to ever return to the small farming community where he grew to manhood. He was now twenty-one - twenty-two in two months - and a grown man. Some say, he was more mature than the other twenty-three-year-old men in the nation's Capitol, in '65, be they union or confederate.

Bob returned to Chicago and joined the Pinkerton Detective Agency. He quickly advanced to an operative after having successfully apprehended the notorious Bill Walker in a shootout on the city's south side. In this gunplay; two operatives plus one civilian were killed and two civilians were badly injured. The grateful citizens of Chicago gave him an award. Allan Pinkerton, in his Scottish ways, only snorted at him. Yet to give Pinkerton his due, after that incident, he included Bob in more discussions and jobs.

Then, after many years of exemplary service, he was forced to retire. Bob had to move to a drier climate because of his health. He had difficulty breathing, almost like tuberculosis. Only thing was, he did not spit up blood, just a hacking cough. Keeping his family awake for hours was troublesome enough.

"Ever had trouble breathing, Bob?" a doctor had asked, sitting back in his chair at his office in Chicago.

At first, Bob shook his head no, then he remembered as a child he had the customary diseases that afflict most children; chicken pox, measles, mumps and once, a severe case of the whooping cough. He mentioned this to the doctor, who began to shake his head no. Then as if a shot of brilliance interred his head, the doctor looked intently at Bob and asked if he were ever bothered with asthma or any other bronchial disorder.

"When I was a tiny infant, my mother said I had a lung disorder. Gripe, she called it," Bob said, mystified he could recall that event so long ago.

"Well, my friend," the doctor said, pleased with his impromptu diagnosis. "It seems as if it's back again."

When Bob informed his employers of the results from his doctor, they were all very solicitous toward him. Allan Pinkerton offered him a substantial severance allowance, although one could see the Scotsman in him rise to the forefront. Pinkerton paid Bob with a small amount of currency and tried to get Bob to take markers or vouchers for the rest. He was thinking that Bob would not live long enough to collect them. How wrong Pinkerton was to believe everything the doctors told Bob. He later proved them all wrong.

Then Bob moved his family back to Indiana. There he tried to make a success of farming, but his heart wasn't in it. He uprooted his brood again and he had operated a small newspaper in Arizona. This venture failed miserably, so he tried to be a speculator and land developer. Bob was a success, but his health began to deteriorate so badly that his wife suggested they move again.

Bob thought the world of his wife and not only to please her but thinking about his health, had chosen the town of Clearwater, Indian Territory. He had done some checking with various people and found that Clearwater was a town similar to the one he had grown to manhood in. It was small enough to be friendly, but simultaneously large enough to grow on you.

Now, he was in a posse hunting a vicious killer. He had thought at the time of the bank robbery. "Here's not only a chance to get back to what I like best, detective work, but perform a good deed for my adopted town."

Bob helped Cooty with gathering the firewood and was now busy heading toward the cliff dwellings he had spotted earlier in the day. He dabbled in archaeology, and the rock formations at the base of the cliffs seemed to beckon to him right now; that and a chance to be out of earshot of Gale and his constant complaining.

"He'd complain if he were hung with a new rope," Bob thought, as he was riding toward the old Indian cliff dwellings.

When he'd mentioned to Gale his interest in the dwellings, Gale looked askance at Bob and muttered into the distance.

"It's a fool thing to do," Gale said pompously. "Rocks are just rocks, if you ask me."

"Well, no one is asking, you old windbag," Bob muttered to himself, turning back to his horse and finishing packing his saddlebags. He believed in being as diplomatic as humanly possible to his fellow man. But there is a far cry between being kind to people and letting them roughshod you.

Bob noticed Cooty was starting to stretch out in his bedroll. Out of the corner of his eye, he saw Gale do the same thing. The former Pinkerton man saddled up and waving good-bye to the men started toward the rocks. Being as he was a former city dweller, he gave no heed to the changing sky, the brisker wind, or the sudden drop in temperature.

A little under an hour later, Bob was starting to reconsider his decision of the visitation. He was not one to do things rashly, but the opportunity presented itself and he had decided to follow his inkling. The wind was getting brisker and there was a chill in the air. He was at the base of the mountain. He looked about him and saw steps that had been cut into the face of the cliff. These steps led upward to the abode of the ancient Indians. Bob figured on some sort of shelter up there. The lone adventurer quickly started to ascend.

"I can just see myself," he spoke to the wind. "Fall down these steps, break a leg and be caught out here in God knows where."

Bob had reached the top of the steps when the wind started to wail. Pieces of sand began to assail his unprotected skin. These fine particles seemed to enter his clothing at will. He pulled the collar of his coat up and his hat down tighter on his head.

He hurried into the furthest reaches of the cave. Bob rushed to a corner where he sat and waited for the storm to unleash its fury. He felt safe, secure and sheltered in the interior of the cave.

"It must be an underground hot spring in here," he thought, as he went deeper into the dimly lit opening.

Outside, the wind was picking up in intensity. Bob felt drawn to investigate the storm. He immediately went back to the front entrance. As Bob looked out the opening and down the side of the cliff, the wind almost bowled him over. He reached out and grasped a protruding rock and held onto it securely.

Down at the base of the cliff, he could see; deer, antelope, coyotes and wild cattle rush to the base and huddle together, heedless of their animosity in some calmer surroundings. He could see where his horse had been tied to a small sapling. The wind uprooted the sapling. Bob saw that his horse was no longer tethered there. He figured on finding his mount once the storm was abated.

"Too bad men can't be hat way," Bob said aloud to the wind, sitting with his back to the wall. He took a deep breath and continued his vigil. Bob was going to wait out the storm. He hoped the storm would take all day, as that would give him ample time to examine the dwellings. He was an optimist, or one who could make lemonade out of a nothing

TWELVE

The sky was still dark, but the wind had died down as Lee and Gary started back toward town. They had tied the bodies to the backs of the horses, they were worried about the newcomer, Bob Davis. But as Lee had suggested, they had another concern. The lawmen better get the bodies back to town.

"The bodies being out here in the open with the sun bearing down, they will not be pleasant after while," Lee spoke judiciously.

"But, what about Bob?" Gary asked, not really caring, but it sounded good. Besides, he had to think about himself, didn't he? The town could only afford one hero in his eyes.

"When we get to town and dispose of the bodies, we'll come back here to find out what can be done. By that time Chris and Kenny will be here to help us in the search. Speak of an angel and you will hear the flutter of wings. Isn't that Chris riding up ahead?"

They reined in their mounts. Lee placed his hand on his forehead and peered into the distance. Gary had crooked his leg upon the saddle pommel. He also looked into the vast remoteness.

"I believe it is, Lee," Gary answered, pushing his hat back on his head.

The lawmen sat astride their mounts and waited for Chris to come up to them. When he arrived, they noticed at once, the cuts and bruises on Chris's face. The knuckles of both hands were badly bruised also. His right cheek was swollen, as was his right eye. The eye was starting to turn black from the deep purple it had been earlier. Before that, it was a sickly looking yellow at the general store.

"What happened to you?" Lee asked, alarmed. "You look like someone has chewed you up and spit you out in pieces."

"More like three someones," Chris said. "If you think I look bad, you ought to see them other fellows."

The big blacksmith laughed, then winced. He reached up and gingerly touched his cheek. Chris took notice of his creaking bones as he shifted in the saddle. The pommel of the saddle seemed to be pushing in extra hard at his stomach. Leaning back in the saddle, he started to tell them of his recent adventure to take his mind off his injuries. Chris spoke of the fight in the saloon. He also recanted the story Big Tim had told him about Old Man Hadley. He did not tell them about meeting the new barmaid, nor was he going to be so forthcoming.

"After all, a man's business is his and no one else," Chris thought, grinning to himself, despite the pain of moving his mouth afforded him.

Lee and Gary chuckled as Chris was telling of the fight. They knew the rumor of Old Man Hadley and they felt instantly sorry for the cowboys.

"I wouldn't want to be in the same country as them boys, let alone in the same area," Lee said, starting to laugh harder.

Gary could just envision the boys having themselves took to task by Mr. Hadley. He figured Hadley to line them up and dress them down like he was still a captain in the Grand Army of the Republic. All spit and polish, with an over bearing manners to boot. Hadley could give one the cold shoulder so bad, you thought that you were going to freeze to death in the middle of August.

"When he gets through chewing them, a new . . . Well, anyway, they'll end up looking like warmed-over death. Their lives won't be worth spit. They'll think again before they go picking on someone or tearing up a business," Gary said laughing at the vision conjured up in his mind's eye.

The three cowboys laughed at each other's recollection. Gary pushed his hat up on his head, while Chris started to grin self-consciously. He was not proud of having to rely on his brawny stature.

Then on a somber note, Lee explained about the untimely end of Cooty and Gale and the disappearance of Bob Davis. He also told of having to take the bodies to town for a proper burial. Then they would go after the killer.

Lee turned to Gary and nodded, as he clicked his tongue and started to town with his freakish freight in tow. The two deputies wheeled their mounts and began to follow the sheriff back to town.

"Hold up, men," Lee said, after they had ridden a spell. The sheriff reined in and swung around in his saddle. He had seen a dust cloud off in the south, as if someone was riding hard to overtake them. In a moment, Kenny rode up to them.

Kenny reined in his horse and nodded to the men. He looked at the tarpaulin-covered bodies. Then he glanced at Lee with a question in his eyes.

Lee told of going hunting with Gary, the return to the campsite, the subsequent finding of Cooty and Gale and shooting the outcast. He did not mention his burning desire to bring the robber and killer in to face the justice a court of law would surely be meting out to him. Lee was not a vindictive man, but couldn't help to smile at the thought of seeing the criminal swing from the business end of a rope.

Kenny relayed the news about his quarry and suggested that he return and follow the trail more. He planned to bring the culprit to his just reward in any way possible. "Preferably dead," he thought, smiling at doing that very thing.

Lee thought the latest revelation over and told Kenny, he would have to wait. There was a more pressing need, mainly get the bodies to town.

"What about that new man, Bob Davis?" Kenny asked, having found a kindred spirit in the dude from back East.

"I'll tell you more about our plans on the way," Lee said, urging his horse forward. "These bodies are going to start smelling to high heaven in a little while."

The remaining members of the posse rode into town with the grim reminders of a failed expedition lashed to the backs of two horses. Townspeople came out of the stores and stood on the boardwalk as they grimly watched the solemn procession heading down the dusty street to the sheriff's office.

A few openly stared, while others averted their eyes, seemingly staring off into space. One woman clutched her throat; another placed her hands over her mouth. The children stopped playing and huddled together as they looked, all thoughts of play whisked from their little heads as the wind drives a dust cloud out on the prairie. The town cur stopped wagging his tail and slunk off to his hiding spot underneath the boardwalk.

"All became quiet, as if the town were mourning too."

Once at the office, three of the four dismounted. Lee handed the reins of his horse to a waiting townsman. No one said anything, all were deep in thought, as the people sorrowfully looked at the bodies wrapped in tarpaulins.

"Here, get these men to the undertaker," Lee said to one townsman. "I'll be over later to fill out the paperwork on them."

As the townsman led away the horses with their burdens lashed to their backs, Lee resolved never to take anything for granted. He had led the men out on what may be a seemingly short chase. So far, he had accomplished nothing.

He had ridden out in hot pursuit of the bank robber with eight hardy men. Two he had sent back to Clearwater. Now, he rode back into town with only five and then two were dead on top of that. He had succeeded in nothing except, two men killed, a third missing and the trail of the fugitive becoming further remote. He felt he had failed and, like a failure, walked to his office with his shoulders slumped and downcast eyes.

Gary was contemplating. He felt a personal slam to the happenings. "I'm supposed to be a tracker, but I'd lost the trail. Of course, Kenny had found it. But that was Kenny, not me." In retrospect, he could always shift the blame to the sheriff. If they had not been hunting food for the men, none of this would have happened.

"There were too many ifs. It was like the old saying, 'if the dog hadn't stop to take a . . . ' then it would have caught the rabbit'."

Kenny was fond of this saying, when things did not go to suit him. Dog, rabbit, be that as it may, Gary knew that he was as much at fault as anyone else. Next time, if there was going to be a next time. Throwing his shoulders back, he promised to himself, "there'll be a next time, nothing's going to stop me."

Kenny was remembering how close he had been to capturing the killer. He had been tempted to make the apprehension but no, Lee said to report to him. As a former Indian scout, he had learned over a long period, you did not question orders, you only did them to the best of your ability. He was also perplexed at the savagery he had seen in this latest quest for justice, Gale cleaned and gutted like a fish and Cooty's throat slashed horribly. Cooty never knew what was happening, only that it was final.

Chris was the only one of the remaining hunters to have a barely discernable smile on his face. He was smiling at the opportunity of seeing Kim Temple again.

Outwardly, he was in a somber mood, but inwardly rejoicing at the prospect of finally having a lifetime partner.

The blacksmith turned his horse in the direction of the livery and raised small puffs of dust as he leisurely rode to the stable. When he had reached the entrance of the stable, he dismounted. Pulling his bedroll and possibles from the horse, he started to his office.

"Chris?" a soft voice spoke from out of the shadows cast by the waning sun.

Chris turned toward the voice. Surprise and pleasure registered on his features as he saw that the speaker was Kim. She immediately rushed from the building and threw her arms around him showering kisses on his lips. His giant arms went automatically around her shoulders, he squeezed softly as if she were breakable.

Kim was also surprised at the way he gently held her. She gave him a reassuring hug and held her head back to gaze on the face of this gentle giant. Kim knew, he could crush her easily, but no, he held her as if she were a glass figurine.

"Chris," she said softly, hugging him more. "I'm not fragile and I'll not crumble."

Smiling, he clenched her harder and then he led her into his office. Once, inside the office, he turned and kissed her gently. She returned his kiss and started to tug him toward the cot. Her intentions suddenly became apparent to the large man. He stopped and she looked up at him with a question in her eyes.

"No!" Chris said, emphatically. "I don't want to sneak around like some kid caught with his hand in the cookie jar. It's not that I don't want you. I want you so bad, it is a deep burning within my very being, but I'm a little old fashioned."

Not only her own feelings took back Kim at first, but at the way this man seemed so gallant. She looked

138

lovingly up at him, then took his face in her hands and standing on tiptoe, she kissed him repeatedly.

When the embrace was over, Chris held her at arms' length and smiled. He did not say anything, nor was anything to be said. Then he wrapped his big arms lovingly around her and squeezed her harder this time.

"Chris, I'm what people would call damaged goods. I've already been married, so sex is not something new to me."

"They'd best not let me hear them say that to you," Chris said, heatedly. "Kim, it may not be new to you. Besides, I want it to be new for *us*. As I've already said, I am a bit old fashioned."

"Chris," Kim said in hushed tones, looking up at Chris with respect in her eyes and some awe and possibly a little disappointment. "You don't want me?"

"It's not that I don't want you. I want you very much. You see, Kim," Chris said with great feeling, holding her at arms length. "I don't want you hurt by anyone ever and want to take care of you myself. I know that we've just met and I don't know a thing about you, or you don't know a thing about me. Would you consider . . . if I, or we . . . could, you . . . would you? You know what I mean, don't you?"

"Chris Barker," she said, looking expectantly at him, unsure of his feelings in this matter, but willing to take the chance. "Are you asking me to marry you? Because if you are, my answer would be a resounding, '*Yes!*' "

When the news of the nuptials reached everyone's ears, people were delighted. The women at the Green Parrot were ecstatic. Big Tim was beaming so brightly that one would have thought that he was the one supposedly being married, especially after Kim asked him if he would do her the honor of giving her away at her wedding. Big Tim was very touched and while he couldn't help but feel more fatherly toward Kim in spite of him being only a few years older.

"She's the kid sister I never had," he thought, as he wiped the bar profusely.

Kenny and Gary slapped Chris on the back and offered him their congratulations. They returned to their table and their bottle of whiskey, which they almost depleted. Tom went to the telegraph office to wire his father in St. Louis the good news.

When Chris went to the Emporium for more supplies, Abner was all smiles. Heedless of the way he had treated the posse for supplies, Abner acted as if nothing had occurred.

Chris could only stare at the man in amazement. Forgiving the man, because Chris did not know of the troubles Abner possibly had. He went ahead with the business of getting a few nails and a sack of hard candy.

"When you're married," Abner said, sacking the nails and writing down on a green ledger Chris's purchases. "You two love birds, must come over and do your shopping. I might even throw in some good articles I've received from St. Louis."

"Oh," Chris thought, "all of this time you been pawning off your bad items on me." Yet not wanting to cause ill feelings, he said nothing. After paying for the nails and candy, Chris left the establishment.

"A glorious day," he thought, as he walked out on the boardwalk and thought of how thankful he was for his blessings. "I've my health and I've found Kim. What more could a man ask for?"

Then, Tom out of breath ran into Chris. Tom wrapped his lanky arms around Chris's massive torso and shouted.

"I'm going to have a new mother!"

"Whoa! Slow down and let me get this straight," Chris said, trying to relieve himself of Tom's sinewy arms. "You're getting a new mother?"

"Yep," Tom said, excited at the news. He was so thrilled that he bounced around the massive form of Chris. Tom's face glowed with the news, as he smiled at Chris.

Tom told Chris that Jasper had found a new bride in St. Louis. A spinster owner of the boardinghouse Tom's father was lodging with other bachelors. Tom thought it happened extremely fast, but at the same time, knew his father was no youngster himself. As the saying goes, 'there is no fool like an old fool'. Well, his father was almost certain proof of that.

When Tom had gone to the telegraph office to wire his father of Chris's wedding, the owner of the telegraph shop had grinned at Tom and handed him a wire he had just received. The wire announced the good news that Jasper was to be married on July 1.

"Say," Tom said, as he quit reading the telegraph again, looked up at Chris with a question in his eyes. "What day's this?"

"Think it is the 2nd," Chris replied, smiling at Tom's good news.

"Omigosh!" Tom exclaimed. "My father got married yesterday! Anyway, they're coming here after a short honeymoon. They'll be here on the 10th of the month. I'm sorry, Chris, but I can't keep on jawing with you. I have to rush home and give the house a good cleaning, get supplies, groceries and . . . "

The last was said as Tom quickly darted into the street and raised his arms. He reminded Chris of a town crier, which in essence, Tom was.

"Listen people!" Tom shouted at the top of his lungs. "My father's getting married, no strike that, got married yesterday. He's going to bring his new bride to our fair town in a little less than two weeks. I'm going to the Green Parrot and if anyone wants a free drink, they'd better hurry over there!"

Chris chuckled at Tom's antics and looked with amusement at this latest display from the mayor of the town of Clearwater. He pulled his hat lower on his head and started down the steps to the street and across in the wake of Tom toward the saloon.

Abner had come out of his shop upon hearing the uproar. He smiled, pulled off his apron and after locking the door, turned to join Chris. They walked side by side. The two men exact opposites, Chris gigantic, Abner diminutive.

Keeping up with the long strides Chris was taking was hard for Abner, but keep up he did, Abner's bantam-size legs pumping furiously to keep up with the stride of the Goliath size of Chris's massive legs.

The Green Parrot was the watering hole of the cattlemen, miners and townspeople. It was a large two-story wooden building with an equally large mahogany bar. The bar seated twenty people, attested by the stools sitting in front of it. Five tables and chairs were in front of the bar and a pool table stood at the back, next to a long hallway to the outside. Scattered spittoons added to the decor.

Back of the bar was a long mirror. The mirror had reflected many scenes, not all of them pleasant. A painting of a reclining nude was over the top of the mirror. The patrons would swill their brew and lust after the nude. Many a fistfight had broken out over the painting, each combatant vowing that the lady in question was someone they had either loved and lost or was someone they personally knew. A stairway next to the pool table led to the offices upstairs: Cattleman's Association, surveyor, lawyer and the living space of Big Tim.

The present crowd in the saloon was noisy, but otherwise well mannered. All the townspeople Big Tim could muster on such sort notice were attending.

Cowboys, miners, tradesmen and anyone else Big Tim could manage to latch on to were there. Many were raising their glasses in a toast to Chris and his new bride-to-be. The crowd also made a toast to Tom on the good news of his father's wedding. Another would hurriedly think of more toasts, which meant more drinking.

"What's the matter, sheriff?" Big Tim asked, while refilling another glass of champagne.

"I'm sorry, but I can't seem to get in a festive mood. Not with one of my deputies missing. You know, that new man, Bob Davis. I can't help but feel as if losing him was my fault."

"No, it wasn't," Chris replied vehemently, as he was sitting at the table with Lee. Looking up at Big Tim, he nodded and accepted a glass of champagne.

"No one forced him to go along with us. I'm surely glad he did, but at the same time I'm sorry he is missing. I don't believe he would begrudge us celebrating my wedding," Chris said, sipping the bubbly liquid. He crinkled his nose as the bubbles in the champagne tickled the hairs in it.

"Maybe not, but just the same," Lee said, emphatically. "I'm planning on making a return trip out there. It maybe a tad out of my jurisdiction, but I think I can find him. I know where the old Indian ruins are found."

"Count me in, I'll help you," Chris said, drinking the last of his champagne and calling out for Big Tim to bring more champagne and pretzels to the table.

"Me too!" Tom said, with enthusiasm, looking around the crowd and spying Kenny and Gary, motioned for them to join them.

As the others crowded around the table, Chris explained the newly founded task. Everyone said they would help in any way they could. They liked, even admired Lee, who at times could be really hard on a lawbreaker, but still compassionate enough to be called a friend. Tom mounted a table and announced to everyone within earshot of the decision of the group at the table. Lee and Chris were proud to be able to call Tom their friend.

"Listen up people. One of our townsmen is missing. Bob Davis. He's the stranger that moved to our town to start a new life. Citizens, he no sooner arrived than he swiftly volunteered to help us track down the varmint that robbed our bank."

When Tom got through explaining to the people, he stepped down and sat at the table with Lee and the others. It got very quiet for a moment, then it seemed as if an avalanche of people descended on the sheriff with offers of assistance.

Finally, Lee stood up and motioned with his hands for quiet. When the crowd had calmed down, Lee glanced at the crowd of ranchers, farmers and tradesmen, all his friends and sighed with pleasure. He cleared his throat and began.

"Thank you, but I only need two men to help me. The rest of you can help by staying good law-abiding citizens while I am gone. Gary's your undersheriff. I know each of you'll do your duty and help him out if the need arises. I've selected Chris and Kenny; Chris because of his strength. We may have to do some lifting and tugging, Kenny, because of his trail savvy. No telling of the trail that new man has left."

Lee told Chris and Kenny to meet him at his office the first thing in the morning. They would pack up and be gone at daybreak. Lee, having come out of his apparent slump, raised his glass and proposed a toast to the new betrothed.

The next morning the rooster was starting to crow on top of a fence by the livery. As the men rode out of town toward the Indian ruins, each had a determined look on his features. They were going to find Bob Davis or else!

THIRTEEN

Bob Davis was in the process of exploring the ruins. He had waited out the storm and was now going toward the back of the cave. After removing his shirt and ripping the material into pieces, he took the cloth and wrapped it around a piece of burnt wood. This stick he found by an abandoned fireplace. The remainder of the rags he placed in his pocket. Bob felt relief wash over his features as he took out a few of his waterproof matches. He dragged the matches against the rock surface of the cave and applied the flame to the torch. He cast a wary eye around his surroundings.

The sight appalled Bob. The cavern was immense. Its vastness reminded him of Grand Central Station in New York City. The only difference he could readily discern was the quietness. No steaming engines, no whistles, no clanking of iron wheels, or the escaping of steam from the engines and no noise made by the hurly-burly of people. The din of the station was missing. All was quiet, as still as the night.

The cave seemed to him as austere, cold and lifeless. The stalagmites seemed to tower above him, making him instantly aware of how small he was in comparison, while they festooned the stalactites hanging down from the cavern ceiling with bats. These creatures were immovable, as if they were anchored to the stalactites. The residue from the furry mammals was scattered on the floor of the den.

Bob walked to the edge of an enormous cavity in the floor. The opening seemed to have an indirect form of lighting. Peering toward the light, he grinned.

"A good thing," Bob thought, "as my torch is about to play out." His torch, as if it heard him, began to flicker and finally quit together. The spacious room was instantly plunged into darkness momentarily. The lighting from the yawning aperture gave him enough light to make out a series of steps leading downward into the dark chasm.

"Fear? I know no fear," he thought, as he started down, then hesitated. Bob began to pray in earnest anyway. "I don't believe in taking any undue chances either," as he began his perilous descent. "Better safe than sorry." Thrusting his shoulders back and his head held high, he continued downwards. He reached the floor of the fissure and began to look around.

"Why am I here? It's not to find buried artifacts, or to explore new rock formations," Bob was going to investigate any possibility of treasure, but stopped and thought. "I'm here to wait out the storm and go back to help *my* people in their time of trouble. Some neighbor you are," he chastised himself, as he decided to return to the posse.

Bob started to ascend the steps. He placed one foot on a step and immediately slipped. He tried again. Again he slipped. The moisture from the cavern and the bat guano made the going slippery. Now he was becoming worried.

"Without a rope, I'm trapped down here!" he thought, almost in a panic.

After a few minutes of trying to scale the cliff face, he turned and scanned his whereabouts. Light from a cut high in the wall face was the sunlight coming from a fissure in the chasm. The glow was now beginning to fade.

"The sun must be going down," he thought.

"I'll be found," he thought. "Don't get excited. Lie down and rest, you can always search later. Must conserve my energy while I can."

Bob had no way to tell how long he had slept. He woke up cold and hungry. It was now that he wished he had not tore his shirt up for the torch.

"Nevertheless, if wishes were nickels, I could retire a millionaire," he thought ruefully.

He knew he would be found. What he didn't know, was when, or in what condition. Bob had not thought to take any foodstuffs or a canteen with him, as he had not planned on being gone this long.

It was pitch dark in the cavern. He fumbled in his vest pocket and took out a match, which he struck. His eyes widen in expectation. Hurriedly, Bob made another torch to replace the one that had burned out on him minutes ago, or was it hours? He had lost all sense of timing. All he was aware of was the coldness and the hunger that seemed to assail his body. He also knew, that to make time go faster, he should stay busy. Bob shrugged his shoulders and started to the hidden hoard.

At the bottom of the fissure lay a vast amount of conquistador armor. Helmets, breastplates and antiquated swords and a myriad of other artifacts including a few pottery shards lay on the floor. The entire find was covered with dust and rusted almost beyond recognition.

Bob picked up a brass shield and by rubbing it briskly with a piece of rag made it shine brightly. He was able to cast more light forward by tilting the shield a little to pick up the light threw off by his torch that he stuck into the side of the wall. He used this reflecting light to continue his inspection. He stepped carefully as he began to walk carefully among the articles strew on the floor about him. Bob stopped ever so often to examine an artifact he had found in the dim light.

"A brass shield, rusty cutlasses and some relics left by maybe, Hernando De Soto, when he had explored parts of the Southwest," Bob pondered of his recent finds.

He picked up the cutlass again and swung it about. Bob could almost hear the shouts of the conquistadors as they clashed with their enemy. Dropping the sword, he picked up an hourglass figurine. It was while looking at a particular piece. Bob heard a familiar voice holler for him.

Quickly placing this figurine gently on the ground and hurried to the steps of the grotto. The ex-Pinkerton man looked up and was barely able to make out the dim figures of some men standing at the lip of the crevice. Relief seemed to flood his heart, as his smile got broader.

"Bob! Bob Davis!" Chris shouted down the dark abyss, his booming voice echoing off the walls of the chasm.

"Yo!" Bob yelled back. "Down here!"

"We've found him," Kenny said, as he was busy lighting a hastily made torch.

"Yeah!" Lee said, glad the man was not hurt, remembering the fate of Cooty and Gale. "I'd have a hard time accepting this thing, if I'd lost this one too!"

Chris found out through questioning that Bob could not make the ascent as easily as he made the descent. It was too slick, so Lee immediately reached to his side, where he removed a lariat and handed it to Chris.

The sudden movement and the noise of the men caused the bats to emit high shrieks and vacate their perches. Bats flew out the cavern's opening to fade away in the dusk. The cave opening was momentarily obscured as the winged mammals swarmed into the night in search of food.

Chris tossed the rope down to Bob. Then Chris wrapped the rope around his waist and started to tug on the lifeline. His boots started to slide forward toward the drop-off. Kenny and Lee placed themselves to either side of Chris. They grabbed Chris by the waist as they helped to anchor him. Together, the three men were able, after much slipping and sliding, to pull Bob up to the lip of the cavern.

In a moment, Bob stood on the edge of the crater. He heaved a sigh of relief and looked at his rescuers. Chris was out of breath from the recent exertion as were Kenny and Lee.

"Never in my life was I happier to see anyone as I'm right now this very minute!" Bob said, with emotion that made the others seemingly blush.

"Before we say anything," Lee said, moving toward the opening of the cavern. "I suggest that we at least get out of here!"

"I'm for that!" Kenny enthusiastically stated. "I'd feel a whole lot better being on the outside!"

The men made a quick descent to the base of the mountain. There they reached their horses and untied them. Lee looked around the area, as did Bob. Chris was grinning so much that Kenny nudged Bob and pointed at Chris. Bob walked over to where all the men was gathered.

"I want each of you to know," he said. "How very much I appreciate being part of the Clearwater citizenry. Can see by your faces that you're all waiting to tell me the latest news. So why not now?"

The men had gathered around Bob, each telling him of a different story. Lee was reporting not only the loss of Cooty and Gale, but of the fugitive's trail. Kenny was assuring him of coming back here another day. He was also an amateur archeologist. Together, they would make a field day of it. Chris was beaming with pleasure, as he told Bob of his upcoming marriage.

"Hold on a moment," Bob said, trying to disentangle himself from the hugs of the men. He was excited also at being rescued, but he could not make head nor tail of their conversations. "Please, one at a time. You first Chris, you're the one that seems most excited."

"Sorry about that, men," Chris said in a jovial tone of voice. "I certainly invite you to my wedding, I mean our wedding," Chris said, looking at Bob. Then, so not to be out of place, told everyone else they were invited too.

"There'll be free drinks, free food and anything else free that Kim and I can come up with," Chris said, with feeling. He was grinning with a smile that was hard to contain. It was so infectious that before long all the men were smiling.

"Until a little over a week ago, these men were all strangers to him. Now, they treated him as one of their own." Bob could barely take all of this information into his brain. "I know that I'm most definitely going to like living with them and the town."

"You lost the trail?" Bob asked the men, getting up in his saddle.

"Yep," Lee said, mounting his horse, "but it's a small setback. When we get to town and deliver you safely, I'm going out again!"

"He means," Chris said, getting on his horse. "We're all going out again. The same posse with the same plan, only this time, we will capture the vermin or die trying!"

"Right on!" Kenny said, as he started to curl his lariat around the pommel. Then he swung into the saddle also. His mount was a little skittish, it was anxious to return to town and the safety of the livery.

"These men have included me with them," Bob thought as he looked at the men and smiled. He was proud to be considered a friend to them. He had never had what one would call a close friend before. "Now, I have three and am considered one of them." The feeling made him smile as he looked at his newfound friends.

"Well, gentlemen," Bob said, starting to ride to town. "As I've already said once, but it's worth repeating, let's get our man!"

The dust was swirling around the four tired men as they rode into town. The dust-covered horses walked with a slowness that bespoke many a tired mile had gone under their hooves. The saddles creaked each time a man made a move and the jingle-jangle of the spurs added to the somber mood like bells tolling for the late departed.

A town person came out on the veranda of the saloon. He looked with disbelief at the men's appearance. Then he quickly ran back into the saloon and shouted of the presence of the new arrivals. In just a moment, the patrons of the saloon came spilling out the swinging doors. They ran to the men on horseback and expressed their happiness at seeing the men safe. Soon everyone in the small town of Clearwater was joyfully standing and waiting expectantly for the men to get off their horses.

"Hello, Lee" Tom said, holding the reins of Lee's horse as Lee slowly dismounted from his tired animal.

"What's this?" Lee questioned Tom, noticing the people milling around the four men. The crowd was all smiles as if they were the cats who swallowed the canary. Men grinned, women smiled and the children laughed out loud.

"It's a surprise!" Tom said, as he was busy handing the reins to another townsman. "We are not only going to celebrate the safe return of your men, but the 4th of July!"

Lee had noticed the bunting draped on the false fronts of the stores as he rode in but was too tired to pay any more attention to the festive mood of the town. He did take notice of the new paint splashed on many buildings.

Abner Hershey had gone all out in decorating. He had painted his store in red, white and blue to resemble the American flag. The red and white stripes ran horizontally, while the stars were on a field of blue at the northwest end of the Emporium. They positioned tiny flags in each window, while large flags and bunting were hanging from the porch.

"Whoa!" Chris exclaimed, trying to calm his horse down as a few of the children had set off fireworks near the horses. The children were chased away by some.

Chris began to smile as he remembered that 'kids will be kids'.

Then he saw Kim standing in front of the saloon. He quickly dismounted and handed the reins to another townsman. Kim had quickly run down the steps and rushed up to Chris. She then threw her arms about his neck and showered his face with kisses. All the time murmuring about how happy, she was that he returned safely.

The townspeople had gathered around Bob Davis, each clapping him on the back and saying how glad they were to have him safe. Kenny reached out and took Bob's reins out of his hand. Bob nodded thanks to him, then looked up and saw that his wife and children were at the edge of the crowd. They rushed to him and he got busy receiving hugs and kisses from his wife and children who had come in on the stage last night.

"I'm glad you made it back all right, Dear," Susie said, as she was hugging Bob hard. His two children had grasped him around the legs and were hugging him too.

"Susie, my love," Bob said, with great emotion. "I do think we've found us a home here. A place to put down solid roots. No more chasing something intangible."

Beaming, Bob surveyed the crowd of people that had formed a phalanx around his family. He was utterly amazed at the people of this town. He especially looked with fondness on the men who had rescued him.

"I'll never can pay them back for all they've done," he thought, as he returned his wife's hug.

"Looks like we are going to celebrate good tonight, folks," Big Tim said, as he picked a small child up and placed him on his huge shoulders. He carried the child to the porch and swung him down to sit with the other children who were raptly watching the older folks carry on. Big Tim turned and with outstretched arms making people hush and pay him attention. He motioned for Tom to join him on the veranda. After a hurried conversation, Tom smiled and turned toward the calmer crowd.

"Tonight," Tom began, then placed his hand over his mouth to hide the clearing of his throat, "we'll have an old-fashioned social at the Church of Christ building. That's if it's all right with the pastor. You know, ice cream and cake. We'll have tea for the ladies, sarsaparilla for the kids and of course," he turned and winked slyly at the menfolk. "Stronger drink for the men outside."

He then started to tell everyone within an earshot, of his plans for building up the town. While Tom was extolling the virtues of the town, Lee slipped quietly away to his office. He quickly opened the door to his office and slipped inside.

Once inside the safety of his domain, the door firmly shut and the shutters to the window closed, he relaxed. He leaned back and placed his boots upon the edge of his desk. Tilting his hat over his eyes and getting more comfortable, he drifted off to sleep with anticipation of the capture. This thought was foremost in his mind.

FOURTEEN

David had ridden south after the incident with the stagecoach. He had maneuvered his mounts across the Red River. Once during the crossing he had to place his arms around the throat of his horse and swim along beside him. He tied his lariat around the other horse's neck and to his saddle pommel, it docilely followed.

Finally he let go of his horse's mane and grabbed the pommel of the saddle and beginning to kick his legs stayed afloat. Twice he thought he was going to drown. He had swallowed so much water that he believed he had drank five gallons of it. The two wet creatures had wearily struggled up on the bank of the Texas side. The other mount was already on the bank and shaking the water from its hide.

David hurriedly looked back across the river and smiled as he saw no pursuit. He swung up into the saddle and applied his heels to the flanks. He started to canter his horses off across the bleak land. Now he was in west Texas. A land so scorching during the day and bitter cold at night, only a horny toad could survive.

"I'll either die of the heat, or die of the cold," he muttered to himself as he guided his horse through the arid landscape.

Clumps of cactus, desert flowers and occasional tumbleweed greeted him in his trek across Texas toward the land of freedom, flowing with milk and honey, or as in his case, tequila and señoritas. He stopped and uncapped his canteen. Raising the canteen to his lips, he let the lukewarm water flow down his parched throat. A lonely hawk flew in lazy circles above his head, catching the down drafts to make the flight last longer. David watched the flying creature for a moment. He admired the way the bird would dive at the earth, then suddenly veer upward again, borne aloft by the warm air currents and soaring in the sky seemingly effortlessly.

David raptly watched this avian of the air. "How I envy the freedom the bird has," he thought, as he raptly watched the hawk in its many maneuvers through the clear air of the Texas sky. The hawk would fly high in the air, then seemingly plummet toward the earth. At the last moment, it would veer up into the atmosphere again. The last time the hawk dove straight down but did not reappear. At first, David thought the hawk had misjudged his distance form the earth and crashed. However, he smiled when he saw the victor become airborne with his victim, a rabbit clutched tightly in its talons. The hunter of the heavens flew away to its lair to devour its feast.

"That's me," David thought, "slow to move and fast to catch the unwary. Might even change my name from David White to **'The Hawk'**." The more he pondered this new idea of a name change, the better he liked it. Visions of grandeur soared through his head, as he rode deeper into the Texas wilds. He was fast becoming a real legend in his own mind.

He rode for a mile, then saw a likely place to make camp. Stopping his horse, he dismounted and pulled off his saddlebags. David carried the bags to where he was going to make camp. He squatted to make a quick survey of the contents.

David began to rummage through the saddlebags. He came upon a can of beans and a jar of peaches. Searching deeper he found a can of Arbuckle coffee. He laid aside the peaches for his dessert. Then placed the beans by the campfire he had started, after gathering a few twigs and the limb of a downed Blackjack tree. Taking a beat-up coffee pot, he poured some water in it. He opened the coffee container with his knife. David threw in a handful of coffee grounds, after the water began to boil. As he was waiting for the coffee, David began to think if plans.

"So far, everything has worked out the way I've planned. I break out of prison, steal me a horse from those sodbusters and go to Clearwater. There I rob the bank, with a small amount of help from those two derelicts, which I should thank dearly. They not only provided a way for me to break into that vault, but afforded me the means to escape. Of course, they lost their lives in the process, but this is the way of life. Or in their case, death!" David thought. "When I ride south, I'll organize another gang. With my brains and their brawn, we can do anything our hearts, or to be more specific, my heart, desires. Nothing will be impossible for me!"

He grunted with an effort to rise from the saddle and went to the fire to check on the water. The slowness of the water to boil and the length of time spent in coming this far, he figured the posse to be so far away from him made David considers cleaning up a bit.

Taking a whore's bath, he began by wiping his neck and face and his armpits with the water from the canteen. It was after he had washed the last of his body that he saw the water was boiling nicely.

Grabbing a piece of the saddle blanket, he made potholders to touch the handle of the coffee pot, which had started to glow red. David gingerly removed the pot of coffee from the fire. He opened the beans with a rusty knife and was soon busy shoveling the beans into his mouth. Washing down the beans with a steaming cup of coffee, David lay back on the saddle and rolled a cigarette. Sighing as if he did not have a care in the world he watched the trails of smoke rise gently into the night air. He flicked the cigarette into the fire and got comfortable in his bedroll. Using his saddle as a pillow, he slowly drifted off to sleep confident of his plans for glory.

Upon rising David saddled his horse and headed south. He had reached the outskirts of a small town in west Texas as the sun was taking its nightly plunge behind the mountains.

"Town's no bigger than a whistle stop," he thought. "Three buildings, a livery and a few adobe houses." Twin strands of steel and a large water tower beside a broken corral showed the presence of a railroad. "Judging by the activity going on in this place, it's about as dead as I feel right now. Feel as if I have been drug in wet and lain out in a stiff wind to dry."

The dogs snarled at him as he made his way to the cantina. He kept a wary eye on the dogs, but all they did was snarls and the hair on their backs raised a notch or two. He walked to the opening. After brushing the dust from his clothes, David went to the cantina. He pushed aside the blanket used for a door and entered he dimly lighted bar.

Once inside he quickly moved to the right of the doorway to let his eyes become adjusted to the dimness. David blinked his eyes rapidly to adjust them from the harsh light outside to the almost imperceptible light inside. He swiftly took in all of the small place at a glance.

A fat bartender was sweating profusely. He looked bored with life as he half-heartedly wiped the bar. The barkeep was losing an uphill battle against trying to look busy at doing the job of wiping the bar. Two banditos sat at a table to one side with a partially filled bottle of tequila before them. A third person sat at a table in the back near a door. Flies seemed to buzz continually in the cantina's fetid air.

A young señorita waltzed up to David and asked if he wanted a drink. Nodding yes David walked to the only other unoccupied table in the establishment. He brushed a chicken off the table and smiled as it squawked toward the back door. David sat and pushed his hat up on his head as he looked at the other patrons in this bar.

"Five in all," he thought, after seeing the patrons. There were two banditos, an American, the bartender and the señorita. "My six-guns have ten shots. Ought to be enough in case anything out of the ordinary happens?" Like all the outlaws he knew. David kept the hammers of his guns resting on an empty chamber. "Only a fool would keep the hammer resting on a live shell," he laughed. "A fool or a one legged man."

The two Mexicans gave David a cursory stare and seeing no threat to them returned to their drinking again. They poured a drink, then quickly tossed it down their throats. One of the banditos drug a swarthy hand across his mouth and let out a loud belch. The other laughed uproariously.

One of the Mexicans had a buckskin shirt over filthy whipcord trousers. A tiny gold chain with a cross was around his neck. The cross was tarnished and one arm was broken off making the cross hang lopsided. He was forever twirling the chain. Light from a candle seemed to bounce off this relic.

His friend had a dirty green shirt, with a red bandana and white peon trousers. These trousers were tied with a piece of rope. Large gun belts with many filled cartridges were around his waist. The other had his gun belt doing double duty; one to hold his weapon and the other to help in holding up his trousers over and immense girth. He chuckled at his drinking companion. Both had well-oiled holsters filled with a .45 and a .38 respectively. The handle grips on the guns were shiny, showing much use. Cartridge belts criss-crossed their chests. The two Mexicans were missing a few teeth. One had a gap between his two front teeth, while the other's teeth were also in bad repair. They pushed up their sombreros on their foreheads revealing both had shocks of greasy black hair.

"Gooch eye," David thought, while looking at the American outlaw. This one had one green eye and the other was blue. The outlaw had a beard that was a sickly color of yellow, as was the straw looking hair that peeked out from under his filthy forage cap of the late Civil War. This head gear was so tattered and dirty, it would be hard to say which side of the recent skirmish was his side. By the looks of him, it did not matter any as he looked like he liked to switch sides at a moment's notice or whichever side would be more advantageous to him.

"I'm too smart to get involved in something that didn't pay," David thought. "Blue or Gray, it did not matter as I could have cared less." He had been too young for the war. Although the thought of killing someone else whetted his desire, he still had been too young.

"He don't look like much," the American reasoned, as he looked at David with a calculating eye. He thought of the many ways he could lord it over this stranger, while he was subconsciously reaching down and touching his gun. More of to reassure himself of its presence than anything else. A large Bowie knife was tucked into his waistband along aside the gun. The knife was tarnished evident by the rusty looking hilt.

The señorita brought David a bottle of tequila with a withered old lime. He was to squeeze the lime on his wrist, add salt to this, take a swig of the burning liquor and lick his wrist. He looked with distaste at this meager offering.

It was while David was doing this ritual of drinking, the American sauntered to David's table, pulled out a chair and sat. The smirk on the American's face immediately told David, "this was a hombre on the prowl." David was put out by the way the American made himself at home.

"Hey," the American said, extending his hand. "Name's Jeremy Small. Yours?"

David did not shake the proffered hand, nor say anything for a minute. The atmosphere seemed to change in the small cantina as it became very quiet. No one had moved. It was as if time were suspended. Then he looked Jeremy coldly in the eye.

"*White.*"

"White, huh," Jeremy responded. Then looking to the señorita as if to make points with her, puffed out his chest, drew his stomach in and paused long enough for the desired effect on the others.

"Say," Jeremy said, starting to finger his gun. "Didn't catch your first name."

Now, the chairs began to scrape on the dirt floor, as they were suddenly pushed backwards. The bartender had ducked behind the makeshift bar, the little señorita was sort of cowering in a corner with a fascinated gleam in her eyes. She had been friendly with Jeremy too long according to her reckoning.

"Must be a signal for the other two creeps to guard the door," David thought, as he slowly moved his hand down to inches from his gun. He had already decided to be the first to draw blood and now might be as good as any to him.

The Mexicans stood with their arms crossed like the dog *Cerberu*s of Greek mythology. They were guarding the door, as the dog guarded the entryway into the dark realms of the dead.

"Ugly as sin and twice as smelly," David thought, their looks reminded David of the dog too.

"What's the matter," Jeremy said, puffing out his chest more, glanced about to make sure he was being watched and to assure himself of the positions of his two compadre. "Cat got your tongue? I'm speaking to you."

"Mister to you," David said, as if Jeremy were something to be rid of soon, or an unsavory task to perform.

"This man's a big frog in a small pond down here south of the Red River," David thought. "Most definitely going to have to bring him down a peg or two." Quietly and slowly, David slid his gun from his holster. He hid it from view under the table. David grinned at Jeremy, as he watched out of the corners of his eyes the two at the door.

David knew he could place slugs in Jeremy and maybe one at the door. However, there were two at the door and that did not count the fat bartender nor the señorita. The bartender may be fat, but I imagine he can move fast when he has to move. As far as the señorita, David knew many men who were planted in the ground over mistaking a pretty young thing to be harmless. He had already figured out what to do in case of gunfire. David tensed and smiled again.

"I, Jeremy Small, am being made fun of again," he thought. Jeremy had a dumbfounded expression on his face. Then he glanced sideways at his followers, snarled, stood up and knocked his chair on its back. The American quickly drew his weapon, only to just as quickly replace it, as he stared down the barrel of David's gun.

Not wavering for a moment, David reached out and pulled Jeremy's gun from its resting place. He then placed the weapon on the table with the handle grips facing him. The two Mexicans had gone for their guns, but stopped, when they saw the outcome of Jeremy's actions.

"Sorry about our little misunderstanding," Jeremy said, trying to show a little bravado. "My name is Jeremy Small and yours is . . . Mister White. Right?"

"You got it, Ace," David said, still smiling. He motioned with his gun to the chair the outlaw had turned over in his haste to draw down on David. "Pick up that chair and sit. I figure you and I've something to discuss. Something, I believe that will put money into both our coffers."

Jeremy sat, David holstered his gun and the place returned to normal. The bartender stood up at the bar and began the wiping process again. Seeing as how the situation was, the two Mexicans went back to their table and sat. A little señorita came to David's table and placed her arms around Jeremy's shoulders. Jeremy ate this attention up. He reached up to his shoulder and gently began to rub the señorita's hand.

"See those two over there," Jeremy said, pointing to the two Dooby brothers. Jeremy saw David glance fleetingly at the two and nod. "They're two brothers who've ran afoul of the Federales in down in Mexico. Names are Ramon and Felipe."

Jeremy went on to tell of how the brothers and he were old compadre. The trio had been drifting around in west Texas for the last two months. They've even made forays up in the Territory. Small hold-ups, some cattle rustling and once they invaded an army outpost, but were quickly repelled by the soldiers.

"We're specialists, Mr. White," Jeremy stated, with pride in his voice. "Ramon there is a whiz at picking locks, knowing how to make a combination sing, blowing up safes and about any other dangerous job available. His brother Felipe's a little touched in the head, doesn't shuffle a full deck. His *Mamacita* dropped him on the head when he was a child. He's brave for the simple reason that he doesn't think too much or too often."

Jeremy turned in his chair and motioned for the Mexicans to join them. He grinned at David and playfully squeezed the señorita. David poured a glass of the fiery liquid, licked his wrist and squeezed the lime juice into his mouth. He then drained the glass in one big gulp. Licking the salt from his wrist, he wiped his mouth with the back of his hand. He poured another drink.

David saw the brothers hesitate, then he motioned for the brothers to come on over. The two burly men came to the table and at a nod from David, they pulled out chairs and sat. Both of them grinning like Cheshire cats. They were all smiles, but David noticed that they would not look you straight in the eye.

"A bad sign," he thought. "But bad for whom?"

As the four men sat in a circle at the dirty table in an even dirtier town in west, Texas, they discussed the various schemes they could probably carry out successfully. David had explained to them of his plans to form another gang of outlaws that would bring havoc to the Southwest.

"Of course," David said, in a more serious tone of voice. "You'll all and I do mean all, have to follow my plans to the letter. No hesitation on anyone's part or we'll all be caught, tried, convicted and hung!"

The three men looked at David and nodded in agreement to his assessment of their situation. Each man figured the different ways to spend his share of the money. They sat at the table warily looking at each one, while grinning evilly. They still did not trust each other.

"I can see," David said, while leaning back in his chair, polishing off his drink, with visions of glory and wealth appearing in his head. "*My* gang of cutthroats, being the best gang in the West!"

FIFTEEN

Lee was sitting at his desk with the members of his ill-fated posse scattered around his office. Gary and Bob were sitting in chairs in front of the desk. Kenny was leaning against the door leading to the cells and Chris was sitting on a cot by the window.

They had been discussing the various means of capturing the bank robber. So far, no one had come up with a viable plan, or one that all would agree would work. One or the other opposed each plan.

"I just can't go off and grab the man," Lee said, finishing his third cup of coffee. "Not if I still want to keep this and what it means."

He was pointing to the gleaming badge pinned on his vest. Lee had sworn to uphold the law and he was going to do that to the best of his ability. He felt as if he owed it to the people that elected him to office. Besides, he was a firm believer in fairness and the American way of justice.

"A man's handshake is his bond," Lee would say to people. "If you don't have that, then there is nothing to separate you from the common criminal."

"But we've go to do something," Gary said, moving about in his chair. He was getting restless. There had been too much delay according to him.

They all agreed, something must be done, but they were putting nothing yet forth as a remedy. They had reached an impasse. It was a matter of compromise. Who would give the best plan and who would take it? Lee and Bob were for doing everything by the book, while Kenny and Gary were for leaving town and tracking the killer down. If they were to cross state lines, then so be it. Chris was undecided. He had recently got married and he did not want to leave his new bride. He said he needed more time to think things out.

"More time!" Gary exploded, taken back by the amount of time already spent on this endeavor.

"Yes, more time," Chris said belligerently. Thrusting out his jaw with a fierce look of determination. He reminded one of the looks of a bulldog. He glared around the office at the men gathered there.

No one bothered looking at him directly, as they had their own problems to deal with now. The men were more worried, especially since they found out the dealings Gale had been up to in Oklahoma Station. How could he take their trust so lightly, they wondered?

It was almost a week after the rescue of Bob Davis that the town learned of the misdeeds of Gale. The bank examiner, Ferris Parsley, had made a visit to the bank after the death of Gale and examined the books. When he found a discrepancy in the books, he immediately came to Lee.

The sheriff and the examiner went over the books repeatedly. Upon further examination, Lee reported to Tom and expressed his feelings. Gale's bank account was depleted and the assets of the bank were in dire jeopardy. Mr. Parsley checked further back into Gale's dealings and came up with the banker's speculation in the stock market.

"We can seize all his property," Mr. Parsley said, shaking his head. "But him being a widower, the property alone cannot help at this time. I heard of his wife dying last year from tuberculosis. Now he's gone too. What surprises me more, a man of his position didn't have adequate assets? I think that he sank all of the bank's and his money in this stock market gamble."

"Not to mention ours too," Lee said, staring perplexed at the pile of bank papers. "But can we get any help at all?"

"I really don't know, Sir," Mr. Parsley said, in a final tone of voice. "There's a conglomerate back East that helps in these types of situations. I'll certainly approach them on this matter. They seem to target such happenings. It'll take me awhile to get in touch with these people."

"Hope that they can help," Lee said, rising to his feet and shaking Mr. Parsley's hand.

"I'm sure that they can," Parsley said, as he rose to his feet also.

Lee walked Mr. Parsley to the door and assured him as to the honesty of the people in town. Lee was also offered a reprieve, in that the man would not report to his superiors until the 1st of the month. Being as it was only the 8th right now, that amount of time would give Lee and the town government a little less than three weeks to come up with a better solution. Lee watched the back of Mr. Parsley fade down the boardwalk and hopefully walked out of the town's life.

"So I take it," Gary said, while answering a knock at the sheriff's door. "We've a shade under three weeks to make sure this town stays solvent."

"We don't want to forget the little guy, the farmers and us small businessmen either," Chris said, rising from the cot and sitting on the edge of the desk. He stopped glaring and looked around shamefacedly. "Only small children acted this way," he chided himself mentally.

"That's all right, Chris," Lee said, giving him a big wink. "We all blow up now and then."

"We sure do," Kenny chimed, nodding his head in understanding. "But back to our problem. The man said three weeks?"

"Yes. I know it doesn't give us much time, but that's all the man would allow us," Lee emphasized. "Three weeks."

Gary had opened the door in answer to the incessant knocking. Tom Schellenburg was standing outside with his arms full of newspapers. He rushed past Gary and dumped the papers on the desk.

"Excuse me," Tom said, his face lighting up, "for being so late, but I had to wait for these papers to arrive on the stage. By the way, Chris, it's going to need a repair done to the cheek straps of the lead horses."

Chris nodded and told Tom that he would take care of it before the stage pulled out in the morning. He, too, looked questionably at Tom and the papers. The others gathered around the stack of papers.

Tom had been somewhat despondent the last three days, ever since he had received a wire from his father, informing him of Jasper's decision to remain in St. Louis longer. It seems the spinster had more relatives for him to meet than he had previously anticipated. His father had expressed his condolences to Tom, but asked that Tom please help Chris with the duties of the livery a little while longer. Then Jasper would be bringing his new bride to Clearwater on the stage. That would be sometime in the near future, as Jasper was not aware of the time frame involved.

This morning, Tom had awakened to find himself thinking, "why worry over something you couldn't control." Therefore, he jumped from his soft feather bed, splashed water on his face and dragged a comb through his hair. Tom hurriedly got dressed and rushed to the newspaper office. Once there, he remembered what it was that he had been waiting on to come in on the stage. He sat at his desk and awaited the stagecoach. Tom did not have to wait long; he heard the stagecoach pull into the town. He rushed from his office to see if his surprise had made it all right. Tom was waiting for the newspapers and magazines, especially The Police Gazette.

After the papers arrived, he quickly thumbed through them. There at the bottom of the Police Gazette on a page near the back was the story he was hunting. He looked up at the wall clock and knew he was going to be late for the meeting at Lee's office. Tom figured the men at the sheriff's office to be as thrilled as he was at this very moment.

"What're these papers for, Tom?" Lee asked, busily spreading the papers out on the top of his desk. He placed the papers in such a way that all could readily read them.

"These papers may well be our and the town's salvation," Tom explained, as he stood back from the desk.

The papers had an announcement of a railroad running close to Clearwater. There were stories of the Indian Territory going to open lands previously held by the Federal Government to the settlers. The West, Indian Territory in particular was fast becoming a land of golden opportunity to the people back East.

"These stories are all mighty interesting, Tom, but where in the world is our salvation?" Kenny asked, while folding a paper he was holding.

"Right here!" Tom said, exuberantly. He pointed to a section near the back of the Police Gazette. He picked the paper up from the desk, opened it to the page and joyfully held it out for all to see.

"Let me see," Gary said, heedless to showing his impatience. He took the paper from Tom and gave it a quick glance.

TERROR OF THE WEST
by
Roderick Bockmiller
The West is terrorized by a gang of cutthroats
who have struck repeatedly. These ruffians have rustled,
robbed and pillaged throughout the West. The gang

has been responsible for untold atrocities committed against modern man. The authorities are confident of an early capture of this gang. An arrest is imminent. Details are forth coming . . .

"The story goes on to say, the leader of this gang is none other than our Mr. David White!" Tom explained to the expectant faces before him. He stood back with a satisfied smile on his face.

He had sent wires out to all mayors within a hundred-mile radius of Clearwater. A few had answered him with no luck, but one had the information that Tom sought. It seems there has been a rash of robberies, kidnaping and other violence near a town in West Texas. What piqued Tom's interest was a former gang member, after being caught had turned state's evidence. He informed the Texas Rangers that the gang leader had boasted of holding up a sleepy backwater town up in the Territory. This leader had laughed when he told of two derelicts helping him to blow the safe in the bank there. Tom had added two and two and came up with the sleepy little town. He was irked, when it was mentioned that Clearwater was not only a backwater town, but also a sleepy little town.

"Bob here," Lee said, turning his head toward the ex-Pinkerton operative, "has already informed us of the situation with White. But, as I've explained to all here, there's nothing I can do in an official capacity. It's a matter for the Texas Rangers now. It is out of my jurisdiction. I'm open to any and all suggestions."

This questioning of Tom's news caused him to be irritated with everyone. He calmed down when he saw the faces of the men seated around the desk.

"These are my friends," Tom thought, " like friends, they're to be helped too. And as Mayor, it is my duty to help out my fellow citizens in any way possible."

He looked at Lee and saw a man that time had etched many wrinkles on a weather-beaten face. He was the type of man who would go out on a limb to help you. But he was also a stickler to the letter of the law. Lee was a bachelor but was happy to be included on happenings within a family. Children were especially fond of him.

Chris had a worried look on his otherwise jovial face. His smiling face was replaced with a deep furrowed frown. Tom knew more than anyone else here Chris had all of his money deposited in the bank. The robbery was a devastating blow to the man. Chris was also worried about how everything that had happened would affect his new marriage.

Kenny was looking away deep in thought. His brow wrinkled in remembrance of the latest occurrences. The death of Noel affected him very much. Before Bob Davis, Noel Green was his closest friend. Noel and he had spent many a day hunting in the wilds of the surrounding territory. He was amazed at how well Noel could move quickly. Being club footed did not seem to slow him any.

"A man was handicapped only in the gray matter," Noel often boasted, he did not let his disability hinder him one bit.

Gary was happy go lucky as ever. To him, this was just another chance to show people how wonderful he was. He was not one to sit still and calmly let an opportunity pass him up.

"Seize the moment," he always was saying.

Bob was sitting back in his chair with his hands folded like a church steeple in front of him. He was contemplating the recent events. The man was the deep thinker of the group.

"David White's not only a killer, a horse thief, an escapee from prison, but our bank robber too!" Tom was enthusiastic, stopping long enough to get him a cup of coffee too. When Tom had finished getting a cup of coffee, he sat at the side of the desk. He had pulled off his hat to reveal a balding spot on the crown of his otherwise luxuriant hair. The mayor had placed his hat on the desk. "Also," Tom continued, looking about him. "This White gang has a sizable reward posted. I might also go on to mention, it says *dead or alive.*"

"Are you saying what I think you are?" Lee asked, sitting straighter in his chair.

"I think that Tom wants us to become bounty hunters," Bob said, letting his hands fall to the desk. "Isn't that right, Tom?" He cast his gaze upon the young editor. Then he looked at the others.

"Well, I wouldn't want to say that way," Tom answered, starting to feel uncomfortable under the stares from his friends. He began to pull at his shirt collar as a sign of nervousness. "I hate to be placed in this position," he thought.

"That's the name, friend," Kenny stated, looking at the newspaper man again. "Bounty Hunters. Anyway you want to cut it that's the name."

"I can't do that!" Lee said with vehemence, glaring at Tom for even coming up with the idea. It was as if he had been slapped in the face or had cold water splashed on him.

"Nor can I," Chris replied, who was a gentle man by nature, but could be nasty when prodded enough. He knew that the robbery had cleaned him out, along with some others. Chris was also worried the effect that this would have on his new marriage. But like his forefathers, he knew also that he would survive. "Might take a while longer, but it can be done," he thought, smiling at the other men.

"Count me out too," Gary said, figuring on using this new information himself. He had already been in a failed posse and he had no desire to be in another. Even if that one was called bounty hunting. But on the other side of the coin, he also knew that if a person was a bounty hunter then he would be his own boss, therefore he would hunt the robber alone. The proposition was sounding better to him after all.

"Well," Kenny spoke quietly, pausing to make sure that all could hear him. "I've done a lot of things in my life, not all of what you would call good, or take any pride in, but a bounty hunter? It might be something new to do, I say why not?"

"I'll tell you why not," Lee said. "All of you have families, with the exception of Kenny, Tom and myself and that may soon change for you, Tom. Be that as it may, you Tom, can't expect us to drop everything and go traipsing off into the wilds after this man?"

"Before Tom answers that question," Bob said, getting to his feet and pacing the floor. "I think we all and I do mean all, have to consider the options on this matter."

"Options?" Tom asked, hopefully, moving his chair closer to the desk and looking at Bob as a savior in this cause. Like a sailor lost at sea, Tom was willing to grasp onto anything to save himself and his town.

"As see it. We have three options," Bob said, halting his pacing and return to his seat by the desk. Then as a schoolmaster, he looked at the group of men and raised a finger. "One, we could forget this happening. Two, we could form a vigilance committee to study this more objectively. And three," he paused and looked hard at each man. "We could become bounty hunters."

"I can't believe this," Lee said, trying to stare down each man. "Here we are, grown men and calmly discussing hunting another man. Possibly kill him, which I would consider cold premeditated murder. Tom, do you seriously think we are cut out to be bounty hunters? Better yet, do you want us to become bounty hunters?"

"Yes on both counts," Tom said, this time more forcibly. "I see it's the only way out of this mess we seem to find ourselves in at this time. Well, can any of you all think of a better plan?"

The last was said as Tom sat heavily in his chair. He had given the idea his best shot. The mayor did not want the town to go belly up, but at the same time, there was turmoil in his heart. How would he ever hold his head up if he became a bounty hunter? He knew what his father thought of bounty hunters and it was not flattering at all. On one hand, he was trying his best at saving the town; on the other hand, he wasn't that keen on hunting another human being, no matter how much he detested him.

"Damn if you do and damn if you don't," Tom thought, "a no win situation." He did not want this dilemma decided by himself. "They were all in on it or they weren't. There's to be no other way."

"I can't think of one," Kenny responded, starting to warm up to the idea of becoming a bounty hunter. He had hunted Indians before, tracked them down and even executed a few. So he could see no big deal in this latest endeavor. He sort of relished the idea of tracking down the killer of Noel and Cooty, not to mention Gale.

"Me either," Gary said, changing his mind about objecting to the job. He had already figured on hunting this animal, even if it meant hunting him alone. "I'll show this town and everyone else what it means to cross paths with Gary Sandusky!"

"It's like I told you, Tom," Kenny replied to Tom's questioning look. "Or as they say in the army, I'm in for the duration."

"I'm most definitely not in," Lee said with fervor. "And I don't think you men should consider the proposition Tom has forwarded."

As each man sought to defend his position, Bob walked to a wall map of the southwestern United States.

Studying this map, he remained thoughtful. Then coming to a decision, he turned from the map and walked back to his seat. Bob sat and then as if a fire was place underneath him, jumped up and went back to the wall map. He peered close at the map.

"Do we even know where this White guy is at the moment?" Lee asked, leaning forward and making a steeple out of his hands. He hoped that no one did, as he still could not get over being asked to be a bounty hunter. "No matter, how badly I want to catch this vermin, I'm still the law!"

The rest of the men looked back at him with a blank countenance on their faces. Bob turned from the wall map and glanced at the sheriff. He nodded no. Chris made no comment, because all knew of Chris's feelings in this matter. Tom on the other hand, looked hopefully at Bob. Gary shrugged his shoulders and exchanged glimpses with Kenny. However, Kenny did smile and hitched his trousers up a bit.

"Need to know who's in on this hunt," Kenny asked, watching the other men closely. "And more importantly, who isn't?"

They all started to talk at the same time, but Lee silenced them with a look, that bespoke of his feeling on the subject. One by one, they left the office silently. Tom and Chris were the first out of the door, closely it softly behind them. Bob said that he would stay behind as he had a few things to discuss with Lee. Kenny and Gary did not say a thing, but left by the front door and headed toward the saloon. Everyone wished they knew the whereabouts of David White.

177

SIXTEEN

David White, or as he said to the members of his gang, for them to call him **The Hawk**, was in the process of robbing another bank sixty miles south of Clearwater in West Texas. He had been told that the bank there would be easier to rob than the one in Clearwater. There was no vault to consider this time, only a small combination safe. Small, as it was a freewheeling safe, tucked in the corner of the back of the room. It was supposedly full with the wages of the various farms and ranches; money that was to be paid later in the week. At least that is what David had learned from a patron at another bar.

His gang had ridden into the town at sunrise. The bright circle was rising over the mountaintops, casting shadows on the terrain, making the earth look spotted as a Poland China hog. It seemed as sleepy as the town of Clearwater to David. Inwardly, he laughed at the opportunity the small hamlet afforded him.

"It'll be easier than robbing the bank at Clearwater," he thought, mentally rubbing his hands.

The air was hot and humid on the outside of the wooden bank building. Inside the hot structure tempers were rising along with the temperature on the outside. Beads of perspiration ran down the sides of the heads of the robbers, as well as the heads of the victims. The victims in the small building, held their hands high above their heads.

There were two women and one man. Each was trying to outdo the other, as to see which of them could grab their little piece of heaven first. The women; a mother and her young teen-age daughter, each had on calico bonnets and were dressed in catalogue dresses made of durable cotton. The man had on clean bib overalls, clodhoppers, flour print shirt and a straw hat with the brim partly broken.

They were scared. The women had figured on doing a little banking before the heat got unbearable and the man was a new comer to the area. The man seemed bored with the robbery he actually hoped it succeeded. He had not made a deposit yet having just recently moved into this town. His money was secure in his right sock and that was where it was going to stay he figured. The farmer inwardly felt excited as well as scared for he had never seen a hold-up before. His eyes were gleaming almost as much as the hold-up men.

"All right. We can do this only one way," David said. "*My* way. I don't want any interruptions. Seeing as how the bank manager didn't think, we were serious in asking for the combination to the safe I had to shoot him." He glanced at his followers, smiled and said, "Now, boys, didn't I ask him real polite like?"

The two Mexicans nodded and smiled in agreement with David. They were worried about the noise of the gunshot, but David had told them that the sound was muffled because of the adobe walls. At the same time they weren't worried about having the combination to the safe. They had already counted on Ramon to do his job of making the combination warble open.

David motioned for the farmer to move a little to the side so he could see out the front window. He fleetingly pulled aside the curtain and looked outside. Everything was calm; evidently no one had heard the gunshot. A few businesses had opened and their owners were busily sweeping off the dust from the boardwalk in front of their stores.

He could see a few wagons. David felt exhilarated, for he had picked this place as only having a constable and his part-time assistant. Often this constable was drunk and David had found out the constable's assistant was down with the gripe. There was no one to guard the town! It was ripe for harvesting and David was the harvester.

"A sort of Grim Reaper at that!" David laughed, visioning himself in a black shroud holding a scythe.

Ramon and Felipe nimbly vaulted the low rail separating the safe from the rest of the room. Once in place, Ramon placed his bag of burglar tools on the floor. He rubbed the tips of his fingers against the roughness of the adobe wall, to make them more sensitive to the vibrations of the tumblers falling in the old lock of the ancient safe.

"Say Da . . . Hawk, why don't we take this pretty young thing along with us? I like the way her hair feels as if it is fine silk. It sort of reminds me of the color of the gold," Jeremy said, as he was standing beside the young woman and softly moving his hand over her bodice and down to her legs.

David could see the young woman was terrified of Jeremy's leering look and roaming hands. She stiffened each time Jeremy's hand moved over her body taking unwarranted liberties. Her mother's eyes widen with revulsion at this occurrence. David wanted to get this robbery over with and be gone before anyone got the wiser.

"Ha! I got it!" Ramon said, excited at his accomplishment. He swung open the safe's door to reveal three small bags of currency and one of coins.

David started toward the safe, while Felipe nervously pointed his gun at the hostages. Jeremy in the meantime, had worked his probing fingers around to the buttons at the back of the young woman's dress. The girl squirmed and looked at David with pleading eyes.

"Don't have time for that," David said, glaring at Jeremy. He did not want the apple cart upset.

"But Da . . . Hawk," Jeremy entreated, having undone the top button of the dress. He had been too long without a woman and this girl seemed handy. But he also knew the power David held over them.

Already, Ramon and Felipe were starting to like David and they followed him more than they ever did him. Jeremy knew how to bid time. The outlaw would just wait and see what is going to be happening before he made a move.

"A person can't be too careful," he thought, though he quit pawing the girl. Jeremy figured on better women, liquor and softer luxury later. He would be a rich man once this robbery was done.

Jeremy went to help the robbers clean out the safe. David grabbed one bag while the others took a bag a piece. They quickly started out the bank doors.

"Them?" Jeremy asked, motioning with his gun at the terrified hostages. He was all for killing them, or at least take the young girl as hostage. "Maybe David would relent and let me take the young woman," he thought, as he nervously started to slide toward the front door. He was ready at a moment's notice to sweep the girl up in his arms and exit the bank. His face was crestfallen when he heard what David said next.

"Leave 'em," David answered. "They're too scared to cause us any trouble." He did not want any encumbrances. "So far, everything was working out just well. Besides, he was going to make a point with Jeremy. Don't mess with me or face the consequences if you try."

The bank cashier suddenly reached under the counter and pulled out a gun. He was starting to raise the gun when David saw him out of the corner of his eyes. Wheeling, David shot the hapless teller in the head, spraying the wall behind the clerk a bright crimson color. The dead man fell across the counter.

The other hostages immediately dropped to the floor. The man scampered behind a desk and the mother placed her arms protectively around the shoulders of her daughter. Fear was making the women shake.

"Maybe this wasn't such a good idea after all," the man was thinking, as he tried to make himself as small as possible behind the desk.

"Let's move!" David shouted to the others, opening the door and starting out. He headed out the doors with a bag slung over his shoulders. It was this bundle that saved his life for suddenly a barrage of gunfire greeted him and his gang as they exited the bank. A slug tore into the side of the moneybag instead of him. Only the bag's denseness helped to absorb the impact. As it was, David could feel the bag as it jumped from the slug.

A group of private citizens opened fire on the bank robbers. Clerks, cowboys, farmers and anyone else who had access to a gun started to fire at the outlaws. Barrels, overturned wagons and horse troughs afforded the townspeople with enough cover so they could continue their shooting.

David and Jeremy got mounted and were wheeling their horses around to throw off the aim of the shooters. Both mounted outlaws began to fire at the people. David's round caught a cowboy in the arm as Jeremy shot another crouching in the doorway of a store.

"Hurry it up!" David shouted to the two remaining desperados as they were busy trying to reach their horses. The two were slowed by the loot they carried.

Ramon and Felipe had reached the safety of their cayuses, when a bespeckled store clerk stepped out of the shadows and cut loose with a greener. The force of the blast jerked the clerk backwards to the safety of the opened door of the general store. The onslaught of double ought buckshot in both barrels hit Felipe directly in the chest. He flung out his arms and fell heavily into a hitching rail. He somersaulted over the rail to lie in the dust of the street with his lifeblood being quickly absorbed by the sand.

Some of the townspeople started to emerge from their hiding places behind the various walls of safety. They seemed to increase their volley of gunfire toward the outlaws. Two storekeepers dropped on their knees and took careful aim. One was just starting to squeeze the trigger of his rifle when a slug from Jeremy caught him in the lower jaw. The others, seeing this fate, hurriedly ran back to their observation posts.

Ramon had ducked behind his horse and was leaning over the saddle returning fire. He had just pulled the trigger of his weapon, when a cowboy took that time to stand up at a watering trough. Ramon's slug caught the unlucky cowboy in the face, entering at the nose and exiting at the back of his head taking the biggest part of his skull with it. Hurriedly, Ramon leaped on the back of his horse. He followed David and Jeremy out of town.

SEVENTEEN

Kenny and Gary met at the Green Parrot and were discussing the information Bob Davis had given them. They were sitting at a table in the back with their voices lowered and seemed to be in a deep discussion. Kenny was doing the most talking while Gary sat back in his chair and smiled knowingly.

Big Tim had brought a bottle over and was starting to sit with them when one of the barmaids hollered for him to help her get a keg from the back storeroom. Sighing, he looked at the others with an apology and went to help her.

"Gotta get that keg before she throws a hissy fit," Big Tim thought, as he headed toward the storeroom.

"I'm glad he's gone," Kenny whispered to Gary. "Don't get me wrong, I like Big Tim, but there are some things I want to palaver over with you and you alone."

"Such as?" Gary asked, raising his eyebrows and pulling the bottle to him. He removed the cork and poured each a drink. Gary raised his drink, slowly sipped it and looked at Gary over the rim.

"Such as me being a bounty hunter," Kenny stated, while polishing off his whiskey. "The thought doesn't bother me any or make me loose sleep. You?"

Gary was thinking how he could turn this information to his betterment. He contemplated telling Kenny that he was having second thoughts about this business of bounty hunting. He was also elated at Lee's decision not to join in the hunt.

"That means," he thought, "I'll be head honcho. Kenny has already decided to go along and he was the one who wanted vengeance or his pound of flesh the most. I, on the other hand want to get the man who made a fool of me. How's I to know that he was in the bank that night? Or for the simple matter, I want to show the town people that I can do the job as well as the sheriff. Need to be careful when I approach Kenny with my ideas."

"The only thing that concerns me," Gary spoke slowly with a sly grin at Kenny, "is the idea of who is going to be in charge of our little expedition,"

"You, of course," Kenny replied, knowing Gary wanted to be in charge of everything. It didn't bother him, as he was used to seeing others take control in the army. It was like his Pappy used to say, "Son, let others take charge, but always be careful to keep your tracks clean."

"Why, thank you, Kenny," Gary said, happy at the direction everything was headed. "There's the matter of the others to worry about."

"Yeah," Kenny said, pouring another drink for them. "But they all decided they weren't going to help out any, least ways in the hunting department. It seems as if they don't want to get their hands any dirtier than necessary."

Gary knew better. It wasn't a matter of getting one's hands dirty; it was a simple matter of priorities. Lee had already bowed out because of his commitment to the law. Chris was busy with his new marriage. Tom was the mayor and had other duties to keep him tied down. Bob had just arrived in town, so he wouldn't want to go off running into the wilds in a search for the killer. He needed time to get his family settled comfortably in town. That just left Kenny and him.

"I think," Gary said, leaning back in his chair. "We ought to be making plans ourselves."

"Whatever rings your bell, then let's do it!" Kenny said, being interested, as he finished his drink.

"I do believe," Gary whispered, glancing around the saloon. "We'll be safer discussing this in another area. Don't you think?"

"Then, let's go to my digs," Kenny said, as he scraped his chair back from the table.

They waved good-bye to Big Tim and started for the doors. The two men went out the saloon after securing another bottle of the rotgut. They staggered toward Kenny's dwelling, heedless of the stares they were receiving from the people in the street.

Bob and Lee were sitting in the sheriff's office talking over the latest events. They were discussing the need to capture White and his gang of cutthroats.

"I am fully aware of our need to plan our work," Lee intoned, wiping his desktop of imaginary specks of dust. "And to work our plan. But how, is the pressing question before us now."

"You know," Bob said, sipping his coffee. "I'm somewhat in agreement with Tom and the other gentlemen."

"You mean about us becoming bounty hunters?" Lee asked, leaning back in his chair and propping his boots up on the desk.

"Yes, sir," Bob replied. "I think that's the only option open to us at this stage of the game. That's outside of us suddenly striking it rich in the gold fields."

They laughed at the utter absurdity of that happening. Bob was thinking also of how he and his family had been readily accepted by the town. No longer strangers, but now an integral part of the community. Already his wife had gone to various functions of the town and he had been invited by the town council to give a demonstration on the security of the new bank.

"Yes, I'm well liked and thought of in Clearwater, Indian Territory," he thought.

Lee was also reminiscing on the recent events; how the bank had been robbed and the senseless killing of Noel, Gale and Cooty. He remembered how the posse had lost the trail. Their subsequent return to town beaten and downhearted.

"I'm going to track down that outlaw and bring him back to justice, dead or alive," Lee called to mind, the silent vow he had made that day. "Preferably alive, but that call would be left up to the outlaw."

To be truthful, Bob," Lee said. "I've given it thought also. But as fast as it entered my head, I just as quickly let it exit."

Lee went on to explain to Bob his position on the matter. He was a duly elected public official. There was no way a person in his position could condone tracking anyone outside of their jurisdiction. Besides, the town of Clearwater and the surrounding area were his jurisdiction. Of course, he failed to mention that no one had defined his jurisdiction. All he could do was place out papers on the outlaws and hope someone brings them to him. However, he would try to think of something, but at this time didn't know what it was going to be.

"That aside," Lee said somberly. "I'd not be able to live with myself knowing I'd violated the people's trust."

"Well, sir," Bob asked, taking another sip of his coffee. "I certainly understand your stance, but at the same time another question comes to the forefront. How's the town to survive?"

Lee got to his feet and walked over to the door opening and looked out. Seeing no one, he closed the door. Then, he walked and looked out a side window. Satisfied, he returned to the desk. When he had sat, he looked over to Bob and began to speak in hushed tones.

"This morning, I received a wire from Mr. Parsley, the bank examiner. Anyway, it seems he has found for the town a group of people willing to underwrite the expenses of the town. In fact, one of those people's going to be coming in on the stage soon. As to their timetable, I am sorry but I'm not privy to that information. Mr. Parsley assured me they were going to bring enough money to tide us over until the bank can be restructured."

"Oh? Can you divulge the amount?" Bob asked while getting another cup of coffee.

"No, I can't. The reason being that even I don't know the exact amount, all I was told in the wire, it's to be quite substantial."

The two talked for half the afternoon. They spoke of the growth of the town and the coming to town of the prosperity upon the arrival of new businesses. Then Bob told Lee that he had to go and meet his wife to do some shopping for a house. He stood up and shook hands with the sheriff.

Lee walked Bob to the door and waved good-bye. He closed the door and sat back down. Lee crossed his hands behind his head and tried to think of some better way to help the town than having to beholden to outsiders. He hated to owe anyone anything.

"My strict upbringing," Lee thought, as he smiled at the reminiscing of his youthful days. It was while he was pondering these reminisces, an event happened that would solve all his and the town's problems.

EIGHTEEN

David White and his outlaw gang spurred their horses to achieve more speed as they quickly rode out of the sleepy little town. The small hamlet had suddenly become alive as if it was a hornet's nest violated. Citizens were busy laying down a fusillade. Bullets were flying fast and furious around the outlaws heads as if they were hornets buzzing by to hone in on their targets. Only thing, these insect's stings were quite deadly.

White and his gang dodged chickens in the roadway, jumped over a small cart and skirted mules laden down with sticks for the town's fires. White aimed back over his shoulder and emptied his gun at the defenders of the town. He smiled when he saw a person grab his chest and plummet from the top of a roof.

The townspeople watched as the man fell. The body bounced off the roof of a small shed and tumbled to the ground. It quivered once, then stopped moving all together. Seeing the outcome of the shot person caused the others to scatter like a covey of quail flushed from their hiding place to seek out better protection.

The bandits headed toward the safety of the Red River. David planned on hitting one side and when it tried to recover from this latest outrage, escape to the other side and vice-versa. He had grinned when he thought of this devious plan.

The only thing wrong about this hold-up was not the loss of Felipe, but the appearance of so many people.

"Where in the world, did they come from?" David wondered. "I'd figured that I'd it all worked out. I'd planned on there to be no one there to speak of in that little town."

Of course, he knew about the constable, but he was passed out from his night of drinking. David had noticed this earlier when he had reconnoitered the lay out. This was a piece of good news to the killer.

David reined in his horse at a small hill overlooking the place where he had his recent skirmish with the stagecoach. He turned in his saddle to watch Jeremy and Ramon ride up to him. In a swirl of dust, they dismounted. Jeremy threw down a moneybag to join the one Ramon had flung to the ground. The article was smeared with late Felipe's blood.

As the horses moved around nervously, David dismounted and walked to the plunder. He squatted down to inspect their haul. Eagerly, he opened a small bag of currency. Then he noticed the shadow of Jeremy as it crossed his bag. Looking up, he saw Jeremy dismount and look back to the town they had just robbed.

"We almost didn't get away," Jeremy breathed excitedly. Then he quit looking for any pursuit. He bent down and joined David sifting through the loot.

"But we did," David said in a controlled voice. "Get away. As long as *I* lead this gang, we will continue to get away. Right, Ramon?"

"Si Señor," Ramon whispered, fearful in the presence of David. "But we lost poor Felipe."

"Yeah," Jeremy said, looking up from his bag. He figured on getting back into favor with Ramon. "I thought you'd checked everything out before we made a move, *Mr. White?*"

David did not miss the latest remark by Jeremy. He knew that he had Ramon subdued, but Jeremy was something else.

"I may have to watch that one closer," he thought. He hated losing that dim-witted Felipe, but that was the breaks. "Win some, lose some," he thought, feeling no remorse over his loss.

"I did check out the town. Where all of those people came from is a mystery to me. Your guess is about as good as mine," David responded, noticing the movement of Jeremy to one side. Jeremy was fingering his gun. "That one's going to try me, sure as God made little green apples," he thought.

"Jeremy," David said, as he was busy figuring out his options, "I don't believe you'd better do that."

Jeremy had planned of taking over the gang anyway and now seemed to him to be a good time as any. Besides there was enough money in those saddle bags before him than he had ever seen in his life. Loot to last him a long time. He was tired of David all the time giving orders.

"Hah! I think it is past time to show Ramon and *Mr. White* who's the really hard case here."

Jeremy quickly made his decision and suddenly drew his gun. He fired hastily, too soon. David had been anticipating such a move and was already rolling sideways toward the horses. He had drawn his weapon and was firing from his position on the ground. Jeremy and he both missed.

Ramon was standing by the horses. He had a perplexed look on his face, as if he was trying to make up his mind as who to shoot. Ramon had been a friend with Jeremy for a long time, but at the same time Ramon knew which side of the bread his was buttered on. He whirled and fired at Jeremy also.

Jeremy had fired one shot at David. He looked with disbelief on his face at Ramon. Ramon had fired at him! Luckily both shots missed him as he crabbed sideways to a pile of rocks by the river's bank.

David cursed at missing Jeremy and was at the same time thankful Ramon had made a choice. He was pleased to see Ramon fire at Jeremy.

"Or had he? Maybe Ramon wanted all the riches for himself. I'll have to watch him also," David thought. He quickly ran to a place behind the horses and looked back in time to see Jeremy disappear into the rocks.

Ramon had moved to a safe spot in a grove of cottonwoods, away from David and Jeremy. A triangle of desperate men: Jeremy down by the river, Ramon to a stand of trees, and David to the safety of the carcass of Jeremy's horse, which had taken a bullet in the throat and was now lying on its side.

"Jeremy!" David shouted, moving about to be sure he had cover of the dead horse to rely on. "You're as good as dead!"

"Yeah," Jeremy replied tauntingly, reaching at the back of his belt for more cartridges and the spare weapon he kept there just in case. "Says who? You?"

David did not reply as he was quietly making tracks to a gully by the dead animal. He figured on Jeremy to talk himself to an early grave.

"Or at least long enough for me to get a clear shot." But he was also worried about Ramon. "Now where'd that Mexican go?"

As if in answer, Ramon fired at Jeremy's location. David could see little puffs of smoke fly in the air from Ramon's shots.

"Good, he's still firing at Jeremy," David thought. He could see Ramon still firing and running toward Jeremy's position. David started toward the rocks also.

David ran down the gully, stopping once to peer over the embankment. He saw that Ramon had reached the side of the rocks where Jeremy was hiding. Quickly David clambered up the side of the gully and moved to within a few feet of Ramon. He glanced toward Ramon and was relieved to see the swarthy Mexican breathing heavy.

"He can't fire at me in his shape, at least not accurately," David thought.

Ramon looked at David, raised his eyebrows and grinned. In his grin, David figured that Ramon had finally made the right decision on whose gang to be involved with. David motioned for him to go around the opposite side. Both would be in a position to catch Jeremy in a sort of crossfire.

Jeremy had accepted the inevitable. David and Ramon were going to kill him now. He checked his weapons to make sure they were loaded and took a deep breath. His nerves calmed down a little. He stepped out and fired his guns rapidly. He missed, but they didn't.

The weapons exploding at the same time were deafening to the ears. The roar of the guns echoed through the countryside. The slugs from Jeremy were wide of their mark. However, the bullets from David and Ramon found theirs. Jeremy now had three eyeholes instead of two. His mouth had widened considerably, as a round bored its way into the front teeth of his mouth. This slug took off pieces of teeth and part of his skull as it careened off into the distance.

NINETEEN

Kenny and Gary had drunk one bottle of whiskey and were now on their way through another. They had been up most of the night making plans for the bounty hunt. It had been decided by the two that Kenny would ride south of town on the desperado's trail and see if he could cut a sign. He was to keep going south, cross the river and stop once he was south of the Red River a few miles. Kenny was to make a bivouac there and wait. Gary would join him in a day or two.

"What am I supposed to do, twiddle my thumbs?" Kenny wondered about the day or two. Then he remembered, this delay would afford him ample time to sober up really well. "I'm going to throw a ring-tailed drunk tonight. Tomorrow is plenty of time to get my wits about me. I want to have as steady hand as possible when I tangle with those outlaws."

He had already decided that's what must be done. No questions , just catch up with them and shoot them down. The more he thought of this, the wider his smile became. Kenny tipped the bottle to his lips and swallowed more of the throat searing whiskey. The alcoholic drink was numbing the part of his brain used for reasoning and common sense.

"Sure that Lee doesn't know of this?" Kenny asked, replacing the bottle on the table. He was worried about Lee and did not want to ruffle anyone's feathers. Lee was his friend also and Lee had looked the other way when it came to a little poaching Kenny had done out in the Territory.

"Naw, he don't," Gary replied, pouring himself another drink. Part of his brave talk was coming from the whiskey. He poured another drink, polished it off and looked at Kenny shrewdly. "And even if he does, so what?"

Kenny grinned and shrugged his shoulders. He was trying his best to convince Gary that keeping Lee in the dark was best all around. The ex-Indian scout didn't want anyone to botch things up for him. He was willing to track down the scum and shoot them like the dogs they were.

"They killed without any thought, so why not him?"

Kenny also knew that Lee did not hold with summary executions. But, that was Lee, not him.

"After all, Noel was one of the best friends I had and now is the time to give Mr. White and his followers their comeuppance," Kenny thought, as he poured more of the amber liquid into his glass.

Gary was having similar thoughts about the untimely end of the killers himself. He had visions of praise heaped upon Kenny and him, when the townspeople saw them come into town with the bodies of the killers draped across the back of the horses.

Once again, Gary would be the hero. However, having to share the glory with Kenny was another matter itself; one that could be overcome in time. He smiled at the thought of Kenny turning over the lead to him without even a complaint. Gary dropped off to sleep in Kenny's bed with his boots hanging over the end, as his body became a tangled mess on the bedding.

Kenny had found a place on the floor next to a window. He let Gary have his own bed, laid out his blanket on the floor and was now comfortably snoring softly. After a while Kenny stirred and opened his eyes. He cast his gaze to the sleeping form of Gary, sighed to himself and rolled over on his back. Kenny went to sleep with a smile on his face, as he thought of tomorrow being another day closer to catching the killers of his good friends, Noel and Cooty.

Outside the wind began to pick up a little as the lights that had been blinking in the darkness slowly winked out one by one. Quietness enveloped the town. Out on the lonely prairie, a coyote begins to serenade the moon. A night owl made its customary screech as it sailed serenely over the roof of the livery. This aviator of the air was in search of its nightly meal.

The next morning, Kenny awakened to find Gary busy scrambling eggs. He didn't say anything, just got up from the hard foor and shuffled over to the washbasin. Kenny splashed water on his face. The coldness of the water wakened him instantly. He dried his face with an old rag. Then he turned to face Gary.

"Morning, Glory," Gary said, while spooning the eggs on two plates.

"Hrump," Kenny mumbled, pulling out a chair. "My head's splitting itself into two pieces. It feels as if two little blacksmiths with hammers are trying to plunk out a tune on anvils inside my skull. Believe they are somewhat off key at that!"

Gary chuckled and motioned to the platter of sourdough biscuits. He received a nod of thanks from Kenny, as he poured a cup of scalding coffee into a metal cup. He knew that Kenny was not an agreeable person until he had his first cup of coffee.

"Looks like it is going to be a bright and glorious day after all," Gary said, as he took a bite of the eggs.

Kenny just mumbled and started to tear into his breakfast like there was no tomorrow. He took a biscuit and sopped up the remainder of egg from his plate. He looked at Gary over the rim of his cup and smiled.

"Sure hit the spot," Kenny sighed and leaned back in his chair to scratch his belly. "I think I'll live after all."

"We'd best get started," Gary said, rising from his chair and pushing back his plate. Kenny did the same.

Kenny nodded, got to his feet and went out the door in the direction of the stable. He looked back and saw that Gary was headed across the street to the Emporium.

Kenny nodded to Chris as he saddled his mount. Not bothering talking, he headed out of Clearwater. Chris looked at the back of Kenny and wondered why he did not say anything. Shrugging his shoulders, the smithy returned to his labors at his forge.

Kenny went to where the posse had lost the tracks. He dismounted and began to look more closely at the ground. The ex-Indian scout bent over and carefully ran his hands over the faded tracks. He smiled as he looked up. Having made a quick decision, he swung up into the saddle and headed forward south of the Red River.

"I'm no longer in the posse," he thought, as he maneuvered his mount slowly forward. Kenny was not going to let anything stand in his way now. "I'm certainly going to get the killer of my two buddies."

He rode a short distance and stopped. Getting off of his horse, he walked over to where the tracks got more faint.

"These tracks may be almost faded, but I'm sure that by taking it slower, I can follow them to perdition if I have to," he thought, as he gently nudged his horse in the direction the tracks were pointing.

Gary in the meantime had left his Kenny's dwelling and walked to the Emporium. He wanted to get fresh supplies and ammunition. Then it was to the stable for his horse. The cowboy did not want to let onto anyone his destination, so he figured on not palavering with Chris. The less that knew his business the better off he was planning on being. Gary intended on finding Kenny and they would track down the robbers themselves.

"I figure to shoot first and ask questions later. That's if there are any later." The undersheriff had his agenda all planned out.

TWENTY

David and Ramon rolled the body of Jeremy on its back and started to rifle the pockets. Ramon wanted to take his knife and pry the gold fillings from the teeth of Jeremy. David did not. The outlaw leader didn't mind going through the pockets of the late departed, but he had a superstition at desecration of the dead.

"I'm a killer, not a ghoul," David thought, as he tugged at Jeremy's gun belt. "We'll get the money and vamoose."

David finally got the gun belt off the corpse and slung it over his shoulder. Then he bent to help Ramon as he was struggling with Jeremy's clothing.

"Si, Señor," Ramon spoke, after straining to pull off Jeremy's boots. Ramon sat on the grass and tried the boots on. The boots fitted perfectly. He grinned as he discarded his old ones by throwing them into an arroyo.

The outlaws stripped Jeremy of his clothes and walked to their horses. They mounted and without a backward glance rode to the other side of the sprawling river, leaving the naked body of Jeremy to the vultures. The unrelenting rays of the harsh desert sun would bleach out the bones, after the flesh had been picked clean by scavengers.

David rode steadily as Ramon would look back over his shoulder. This constant looking back by Ramon, prompted David to ask if anything was the matter. He wanted to keep abreast of all happenings.

"No, Señor," Ramon said with fear in his voice. "It's only I've a bad feeling about this latest robbery."

"Listen, Ramon," David replied, with fervor in his voice. "I believe you're forgetting one very important thing."

David saw the questioning look in Ramon's face. He explained as if to a small child. The killer's eyes became cold and the timbre of his voice had taken on a menacing sound. Ramon glanced at him with a sort of awe.

"*I* and *I* alone am in charge of things," Jeremy said, patiently, but tersely. "*I* thought we had that all settled back there with Jeremy? Maybe *I* was wrong?"

"Oh no, Señor," Ramon said, with resignation in his voice. "I know you're the leader. It is just . . . "

"Just what?" David asked, slowly moving his hand to the side, to make sure his weapon was free and clear in case he needed it. He inwardly sighed. "Am I forced to kill this one also? Well, if it must be, then so be it."

"Nothing, Señor," Ramon whispered. He missed Felipe bad, but again, Felipe was dead and he was alive. "If I'm to keep it that way, I'll follow this Gringo," he thought. "After all, I did see him shoot Jeremy and that fellow back at the town. He's a bad hombre for sure."

David suggested they make camp by the willows for the night. Ramon readily agreed. He quickly gathered small twigs and started a fire. When the fire was going good, he placed an iron skillet full of beans on the burning coals. Ramon took the coffee pot off the glowing embers and poured David a cup of the steaming brew.

"Ah, that's more like it," David said, blowing on his cup. Then he took out the makings for a cigarette and rolled one. He bent over the fire and retrieved a burning piece of wood and applied the flame to the end of his cigarette. Drawing the smoke into his lungs, he exhaled the smoke upwards into the night air.

After finishing his meal, Ramon took a piece of sagebrush, grass and some old rags to wipe the skillet free of the beans. He then reached for a cup of coffee himself. Ramon also enjoyed the quiet solitude of the night.

"I like the taste of beans cooked over a campfire better than the ones served me at the cantina," he thought, smiling at David.

"I think we ought to pay another visit to that small town of Clearwater soon," David said, making the end of his cigarette glow more brightly. He figured that the town was ripe and ready for him to take whatever it had to offer. Even though it had not offered anything to him, he was still planning on taking it.

"But I'm going to need more help than just Ramon here," he thought, as he took another drag off his cigarette.

He saw Ramon look his way and hearing no objection continued. He went on to tell Ramon of his grandiose plans to rob the town once again. He also mentioned the possibility of getting others to join his gang.

"Those pig farmers will not be expecting another robbery so soon after the other one," David said, throwing more sticks on the fire.

"Si, Señor Hawk," Ramon spoke slowly, while looking off into the night air. "But I cannot help . . ."

"Help what?" David asked, sitting up straighter and looking at Ramon with deadly eyes. Eyes, that seem to bore into your very soul. These eyes made Ramon think of the ones his mother was all the time talking about.

"Nothing, Señor," Ramon said somewhat timidly. "Unholy eyes, or the eyes of the Devil!" Silently Ramon crossed himself. "I'm going to learn to keep my thoughts to myself," he reflected, as he bent over to fill his cup again. He breathed a sigh of relief as he noticed David lean back more fully on his bedroll.

Ramon finished his coffee and then turned over to lie on his side as he let sleep overtake him. David folded his hands behind his head and looked at the stars shining brightly in the heavens. In a moment, he also went to sleep.

TWENTY-ONE

Chris was busy hammering on a red-hot horseshoe that he had removed from the forge. The sparks were flying from the anvil each time he struck the shoe with his iron hammer. He was careful to make sure that no sparks reached any of the straw in the stables.

After he had pounded the shoe into the proper shape, he took it over and plunged it into the water. The sound of hissing and the vapors coming up from the vat caused him to smile. This sudden bath made the shoe temper itself.

He had only three shoes left to complete the set he had promised to the Thomas woman. It would take him more than an hour to do the job right.

"Enough time to finish and go home to the waiting arms of my new bride," he thought.

The prospect of that happening made him want to hurry more. But he knew, you didn't rush making the shoes. If you tried to cut corners, you would be sorry if you did, for you would get shoddy merchandise. Besides, word would get around and he did not need any adverse advertising. Even though he had the only livery for miles around that still did not make him want to give bad service.

"Say, mister," a small voice broke through his reverie. "Don't you ever get tired?"

Chris turned in the direction of the voice and saw a youngster that was new hereabouts. A small boy around nine years old stood in the doorway of the stable; black hair, enormous brown eyes and a mouth that when he smiled, showed his missing two front teeth. He had on knickers, a straw hat and shiny new black boots.

"And who might you be?" Chris asked, knowing full well who it was, but wanting to hear something outside of his own voice for a spell.

Lately, he had stopped his muttering, but still felt the need for any kind of diversion. Chris's new bride had helped fill the void he had previously been feeling. But, as almost all men yearned for, he had no son.

"Sure, Kim and I have figured on starting a family, but there always seem to be something in the way. Someday, was all he ever heard, not only from Kim, but he himself had voiced the concern," he recalled. Chris promised Kim that when their finances were ship shape, they would consider a family. She knew that Chris had a special fondness for children, especially the new arrivals.

"Ryan Davis, sir," the boy said.

He stood straight as an arrow and removed his hat. He looked at the big blacksmith unflinchingly. The youngster was not afraid of the man, but he did not believe in taking chances either. Therefore, his feet were ready at a moment's notice to take flight. He did not know where, just anywhere but here.

"Hmm," Chris said, putting the shoe aside for the moment. "You must be Bob Davis's son."

"Yes sir," Ryan said, pride in his voice.

He was elated that everyone seemed to know his father. His family had been here in Clearwater only a short time, but already the youth felt at home. It was to him, a lot better than where they had lived previously. Too much loneliness for him. Here there were lots of boys to play with and have fun.

Chris admired this young man. He inwardly smiled at the boy and thought, "least he has been taught manners." Chris had taken an instant liking to Bob Davis and that fondness extended to the family as a whole. Bob's wife, Susie, often stopped by and chatted with Kim. The two had become fast friends, as had Bob and him.

The Davis children, Ryan and Melissa, or Missy everyone called her, took great delight hiding in the haystacks and were forever playing tag out back in the corral. Horses and mules seemed to pay them no mind as the two darted among the creatures. The animals continued munching hay.

"C'mere son," Chris motioned to the lad, laying his hammer down and sitting on a hay bale.

"I wouldn't want my Father to think I was keeping you from your work, sir," Ryan spoke, hoping against hope that the big blacksmith wouldn't care. He did not get to talk to adults much and this big smithy was kind.

"No, son, you aren't," Chris laughed, patting the spot beside him on the bale of hay. "I think I may be getting tired after all. Anyway, I need a breather."

The two started to talk of the boy's evident aptitude at the art of throwing horseshoes. Chris was amazed at the boy's unerring aim at the horseshoe stake. It seemed, the boy could make a ringer every other time. Chris couldn't achieve this feat and knew of no other who could. After three games with this young athlete, in which Chris lost, he could only sit back on his haunches and scratch his head in bewilderment.

"Ho, Chris," Gary said, walking into the livery, "could you get my horse for me?"

"Sure thing, Gary," Chris replied, as he arose from the hay bale beside the youngster. "Excuse me, son, but duty calls."

Ryan liked this large liveryman who, no matter what happens, always seemed happy. Ryan especially liked it when this towering oak, stopped long enough to talk to him as an adult, not like his father, who could be very short with him. And like a child, the magic of the moment seemed to elude him, as Ryan quickly darted out of the stable in search of his sister for another game of tag.

"That boy's sure a handful," Gary stated.

"That he is," Chris chuckled, returning with Gary's horse. "He surely is, but I myself wouldn't have it any other way. I'd much rather have one full of life as that one. It beats hang dogging around all the time."

"You've got that right," Gary chuckled, as he mounted his horse, flicked the reins and wheeled about the livery's opening.

Gary did not say where he was headed and Chris did not feel as if it was any of his business. So he returned to the anvil. Gary clicked his tongue, rode out of the livery and headed south toward the Red River.

Chris went back to finishing the shoes for the Thomas woman's horse. He spent time pounding the hot metal, then give it another bath and hammer some more until the shoe was finally the shape wanted. The jolly man was busy hammering another shoe, then taking it to the forge, where he stuck it into the glowing coals. Chris had just reached for the bellows, when Bob Davis walked into the stable to ask about his son.

"He's here just a moment or so ago," Chris replied, while pumping the bellows to make the coals glow cherry red. When the forge was ready, he shoved an unfinished horseshoe into the fiery coals. He let the heat soften the metal, before taking it out and placing it on the anvil. Swinging his heavy hammer, Chris pounded the metal causing bright red sparks to fly from the anvil.

"Say, Chris," Bob asked, dragging a hay bale closer to the forge. "As one of the founding fathers, what's your solution to the town's salvation?"

Chris stopped his task, reached into a back pocket and removed a bandana. He wiped the sweat from his brow, replaced the handkerchief and sat beside Bob. He had also been thinking of the town's predicament. The circumstance around the plight of Clearwater was foremost in his mind.

Chris could sit back and let Tom, the mayor handle it alone, but Tom was his friend and friendship didn't work that way. Besides, he was on the town council along with Abner Hershey, Levi Yates, Haskell Aldridge and Ralph Rawlings.

"Don't rightly know, Bob," Chris stated, picking up a piece of straw and placing it between his lips. "But as they always say, it'll work itself out."

"Maybe so," Bob breathed with a sigh, taking a piece of straw himself and following Chris, placed it between his teeth. "But patience hasn't been my long suit. My wife says not to worry, but I can't seem to help it."

"Tell you what," Chris said, looking up at his finished work, rising and removing his leather apron. "Let me hang this up, then we will go and see if our wives have any fresh lemonade handy. Maybe even get in a quick game of chess."

"Sounds good to me," Bob said, as Chris hung his apron on a peg by his office door. They started from the livery, then stopped, as Bob turned and spoke to Chris "Our little game of chess will have to wait as well as my visit. I just remembered, I've promised the sheriff to meet a person on the stage this afternoon."

TWENTY-TWO

The Wells, Fargo stage lurched through the early morning hours as if it was some sailor on a storm-tossed sea. Inside the coach, the harried passengers were trying to hold onto the sides for dear life. Two men, a woman and a small child seemed trapped in the public conveyance. They were packed tightly as sardines in a can.

"A little rocky," a man said, who was sitting across from the woman and child, as he was busy trying to secure a better handhold.

The woman could only roll her eyes heavenward, as she wrapped her arms around the shoulders of the young girl. One of the men reached into his valise and removed a small flask. Uncapping it, he motioned to the speaker and getting a nod of a no, placed the flask to his lips. The pungent smell of the whiskey permeated the small enclosure. The woman gave the drinker a look of disapproval, as the dainty child stared at the men with large brown eyes.

"Pardon me, Madame," the man said, as he doffed his derby. "I haven't introduced myself. I'm James J. Jeffries."

"Mrs. John Kessler and my daughter, Amanda," the woman shyly answered, while trying to secure a firmer handhold on the child and her seat.

Jeffries noticed she did not have a wedding ring, which caused all sorts of images leap to the front of his mind, all of them honorable.

"Maybe she forgot to put it on last night," he thought, "or maybe she wants everyone to think of her as unmarried or maybe the child's governess. Either way, she's an attractive woman. Not a beautiful one, but attractive enough to make a man stop in his tracks and look again," he thought to himself smiling.

"My Daddy's gone to Heaven," Amanda stated as a matter of fact, with her young innocence evident in her voice.

"Hush, Dear," her mother said, then looking at Jeffries. "I'm sure the nice gentleman doesn't want to hear about our misfortunes."

"On the *contra*, Madam," Jeffries smoothly said, tipping his hat again. "Just don't want to intrude where I'm not wanted."

Mrs. Kessler looked as if she wanted someone to talk to and giving Jeffries a small apologetic look started to say something, then she gathered her wits about herself and stared downward. Whatever she was going to say was best left unsaid

Sighing, Jeffries sat back in the seat and smiled at the two. He was a member of a Boston conglomerate which was being sent west to a small town in the Indian Territories. Clearwater was the name his superiors had mentioned to him as needing their type of help. Jeffries was to provide the means of salvation to the beleaguered town, even if it was found at the outside of civilization.

He hoped that there would be no trouble with wild Indians, outlaws, or scallywags. But in his vest pocket he carried a small derringer for an added sense of precautions. In the boot of the stage, a sizable sum of gold was to be made available to the town. No one knew of it except Jeffries and his company.

"The fewer people that know about it," Jeffries had told his associates, "the safer it'll be. I personally will make sure of the safety of it!" Jeffries was placed in charge of the money and he took his charge very seriously. "There'll be no danger to the gold," he thought, "as long as I am able and willing to protect it."

"My name's Hogarth H. Hottle," the man with the flask said, as he tipped his derby also, mimicking Jeffries.

At a nod from Jeffries and a smile from Mrs. Kessler, Hottle sat back and resumed his drinking. Jeffries notice the apparent displeasure emitting from Mrs. Kessler and to make time go by quicker, he pointed out a flock of Canadian geese winging there way north.

As Mrs. Kessler and Amanda were busy looking out the window at the geese, Jeffries thought back to the time he was a child and first caught sight of a flock of Canadian geese. He smiled in recollection. But was quickly jolted back to the present when he heard the stage driver call out their destination.

"Clearwater ahead!" the jehu shouted, as he was busy tugging on the reins of the horses.

Jeffries looked outside the window and saw Clearwater for the first time. A typical western town, according to what he knew from reading dime novels of the West. There were a few dwellings in back of a thriving business district. There were also the customary saloon, bank and hotel. A man with a badge on his vest and a dapper looking gentleman were standing in front of the stage depot.

After helping Mrs. Kessler alight from the stage and swinging Amanda down to the ground, he reached into the stage for his satchel. Jeffries turned to meet the welcoming committee.

"Mr. Jeffries?" the sheriff asked, with his hand extended for a handshake.

"Why yes, sheriff," Jeffries replied, taking the proffered hand and shaking it.

"I am Sheriff Lee Wildman. Welcome to Clearwater, Indian Territory. This gentleman is Bob Davis, a Pinkerton man."

"Retired, I must add," Bob said, removing his hat and sticking his hand out for a handshake also.

After shaking hands, Jeffries turned to find to his dismay that Mrs. Kessler and her child had already entered the hotel. Shrugging his shoulders, Jeffries turned back to the sheriff, thinking he would make sure he was afforded the opportunity of meeting Mrs. Kessler again.

"As a man of action," he thought, smiling, "I'm sure to find or possibly make an opportunity of renewing the acquaintance of Mrs. John Kessler or die trying!"

"Sheriff," Jeffries asked. "Do you think we can unload the property and discuss this more in your office?"

"The property?" Lee asked, then smacking himself in the head. "Oh, the *property*, by all means."

The trio raised the canvass covering on the boot of the stage. Lee and Bob carried the strongbox into the sheriff's office and then moved the box into a waiting cell. After lugging the town's salvation to a corner, Lee let the men out and turned to lock the cell. He motioned the others toward his office.

Once in the office, each took a seat. The sheriff sat behind his desk, as Davis and Jeffries sat in the chairs to the front of it. Davis placed his hat on the edge of the desk, Lee tossed his hat to land accurately on the top of the coat rack, while Jeffries kept his on, but reached up to loosen his cravat.

"Sheriff," Jeffries said, then stopped after being told to call him Lee and the other man Bob.

"Lee," Jeffries began again. "My group of investors, have decided to help Clearwater out in any way we can. I'm authorized to now place $50,000 in gold in your town treasury. Another $50,000 letter of credit to any of our banks back East. On top of that, I must admit, it surprises me, my employers have consented to, of course, upon the signature of the mayor and city council and you Sheriff, the almost unlimited use of their expertise in handling monetary measures of troubled financial institutions. To get the ball rolling, we only need the sheriff and the mayor to sign for the initial delivery I brought in on the stage."

"Jim," Bob said, moving his chair around to face Jeffries better. "I know that's a goodly sum, but what is the catch?"

"Ah," Jeffries replied, warming up to this debonair man. "As you so quaintly put it, *the catch*. Of course we are not in the market to be philanthropic, we naturally would want some return on our investments."

"Naturally," Lee said, as he leaned back in his chair and was seemingly lost in thought. This means of saving the town was all Greek to him. He was a lawman, not some financial whiz kid.

"Again, Jim," Bob asked, also sitting back in his chair. "What's the return we're talking about?"

"Like that in a man," Jim said, turning in his chair and giving Bob his full attention. "You know, bluntness. Get right to the heart of the matter I always say. Well, here goes. I'm sure you gentlemen have kept abreast of the latest developments of the proposed expansion of the West. My people want to be in on the groundbreaking of this venture. In other words, we like to be out in the forefront or have the option of buying prime real estate in this town. Of course, the surrounding area is included also."

"Then," Lee began, thinking of all the possibilities open to the town. "If I'm sure of what you are saying, now please correct me if I'm wrong. We take your money and in return we let you have first dibs on the property in Clearwater and as you put it, the surrounding area."

"Yes, sir, in a matter of speaking," Jim said, looking at the sheriff. "That statement boils it all down to a pill."

"A pill that might be hard to swallow," Lee said, seemingly lost in thought. Then he straightened in his chair. "But what about the little feller or the hardscrabble farmers? They don't have the money to match you big guys."

"True, Lee," Bob stated, moving his chair to the side by the sheriff. "But then again, the big boys don't have the federal government to back them either."

Bob saw the look of surprise on Jeffries face, as well as the look of hope on Lee's. Bob felt good at being able to help his adopted town. Now is the time to call on the training he had received as both a land speculator and land developer after the war.

"You see, Jim," Bob spoke softly. "We're no country bumpkins or have just fallen off the turnip wagon this morning."

Lee was elated with the way Bob had deftly seen the problem and had adroitly met it head-on. But, he could see a possible confrontation between the two men and in an effort to defuse the situation got to his feet.

"Jim," Lee said, smiling. "Why don't you go on to the hotel and freshen up a bit? I'm sure you are tired after your long journey. Anyway, I'll have to approach the town council with your proposal. Not that I'll need their signatures at first, but I don't cotton to surprises either. All the men on the council will have to be brought up to snuff on this crucial matter."

"Of course, sheriff," Jeffries said. "These aren't dummies," he thought, "either the sheriff or that other man." Then he looked at the men with more respect. "I'll retire to the hotel, refresh myself and possibly catch a quick bite. By the way, can either of you gentlemen recommend a good restaurant?"

Before the sheriff could reply, Bob offered Jeffries the hospitality of his home. Jeffries politely declined, saying that he would prefer to eat alone tonight and read some papers that he had brought with him. Actually, he was hoping to be able to achieve another meeting with Mrs. Kessler.

Lee walked Jeffries to the door and after the businessman man headed toward the hotel, shut the door and turned to Bob. He smiled and moved to his desk.

"What do you think?" Lee asked Bob as he was sitting.

"I think, Mr. Jeffries has a rude awakening coming to him."

"So do I. So do I."

TWENTY-THREE

David and Ramon halted their horses on a small hillock overlooking the peaceful town of Clearwater. Each had warily crawled to the hill's summit at dusk, after making sure their mounts were securely tied to a clump of sagebrush. At the crest of the hill, David dropped to lie on his belly. Ramon hunkered down beside him.

"What do you make of it, Señor Hawk?" Ramon questioned, squirming to get closer to David.

"Don't rightly know, Ramon," David said, readjusting his position so he could see better? "But I do know, there's a lot of activity going on at that one building with a bell tower on the roof."

"That, Señor," Ramon said, with pride in his voice at knowing something David did not. "It's the Church of Christ. I know, because my *mamacita* used to take me to one just like it in Texas."

"Anyway," David said, chagrined at being one upped by a Mexican. "You stay here and I'll go down and scope out the situation."

David scurried down the hill and went up an arroyo that led behind the Church of Christ. From there, he was able to crawl to a spot underneath an opened window. He could hear the murmur of voices. It took him awhile to maneuver so he could hear the voices clearer.

"Calm down, Friends!" Lee shouted, then getting nowhere, he sat. Frustration was on his features, his brows drew farther down as his face became more stern. Then he remembered their mission and realizing why they were gathered here tonight. Lee started to smile and became calmer.

The group assembled in the Church of Christ consisted of mostly men. A few women were also present, along with a scattering of babies. The people seated in the pews were talking excitedly. Some were talking like they have not seen each other in a long time.

"Come to think of it," Lee thought, then smiled, "they haven't seen each other for a long time. Some were ranchers and farmers, while others were townspeople. Time and distance being what it was, maybe this is the only time they were able to see each other."

Now the people seemed to be making up for the lost time and the great distance. The building seemed to buzz like an angry bee hive. But like the bees have honey in common, these people seemed to be concerned primarily with money, not others, but their own.

Lee would give them time to settle down. He thought back to yesterday when he had talked with Tom. He remembered asking if there was anything Tom could do in calling a town meeting for tonight.

Tom immediately gathered Chris and Bob in his office. He asked the two if they would spread the word of a town meeting the following night in the Church of Christ. The men had happily agreed to send out the news, even going so far as to send out riders to the neighboring ranches and farms in anticipation of a good attendance.

On the stage were Lee, Tom and David Curtis, the preacher. There was also seated between Lee and Tom, Jim Jeffries. Jeffries, who by this time had renewed the acquaintance of Mrs. Kessler. He had met her again at the hotel and after an enjoyable afternoon, they had agreed to see each other more often, therefore, her attendance tonight. Amanda was already taken with the handsome gentleman from back East. And to be known, the gentleman was taken with the darling little girl.

Lee posed a commanding presence; his flinty eyed stare broke no compromise. Tom, on the other hand, seemed to find the throng exhilarating, especially since he had been seeing a lot of Laurie Thomas. He was wondering just what her feelings toward him. The young lady in question was seated on the front row, staring at Tom with love in her eyes. Tom's eyes seemed to sparkle, as he knew full well, the effects of this newfound wealth. The preacher looked down on his flock with love in his eyes too.

"I know the Lord works in mysterious ways," the preacher thought. "Who's to say, this was not one of them? Ahem," the preacher intoned solemnly, standing behind the pulpit. "Can you people quieted down some? Thank you."

After the pandemonium subsided, the preacher turned to Tom and nodded. Tom was somewhat embarrassed, but approached the podium determinedly. He stood behind the wooden structure and grasped both sides with his trembling hands. Clearing his throat and taking a drink of water, he began.

"I want to thank you people for coming here tonight you on such short notice," Tom said, then his voice took on a vibrant voice. "Especially you folks from afar. I'm the mayor of this town and am not beholden to you, but I hope to be your friend. I want to extend our whole town's welcome to you for your trip here. But after you hear of our latest news, you'll be delighted that you made the effort."

Tom then continued to inform the crowd of the arrival of Jeffries with the town's solution. He went on to tell of the town's prosperity waiting for them around the next bend. Tom also cautioned them about being optimistic. He looked to the group of farmers and cattlemen and explained the town' fortune rode with them also.

"If we, the town, prosper, so do you. And on the downside, if we fail, then it won't be much longer before each of you fail. We all mean that we all need each other.

Or as it says in the Good Book, 'no man's an island'. Sure, we can remember our pasts, plan for the future but we've got to live in the present. A sort of help me and I'll help you." Tom said, as he hastily took another drink of water, then he launched into more detail.

While Tom was in the process of extolling the success of the town in finding such a generous benefactor, David was seeing dollar signs dance before his eyes. He had already figured on *borrowing* the money. With this new found loot as an added treat, he could retire to South America. Once there, he would form another gang and continue with his life of crime. Having tasted of the thrill of taking risks, one does not want to return to the mundane aspect of a more sedate life.

Then Tom paused, took another sip of water, turned toward Jeffries and motioned for him to stand. He stood to one side, while Jeffries strode forward and took a place beside the podium and bowed to the assembly. He was now in his element. Jeffries loved to address people. That was what he was doing for his employers back East.

"A superb businessman," some would say, while others would say, "a good head on his shoulders."

"Here's Mr. Jeffries," Tom announced, waving his hand, said in a grateful tone. "He'll explain more fully."

Tom sat again while Jeffries approached the podium. He winked at Laurie and she returned the wink. Then she smiled at her good fortune in finding Tom. The young lady was happy as she could possibly be. She often thought of herself as, Mrs. Tom Schellenburg.

"Of course," she thought, "he hasn't asked me yet, but it's only a matter of time." Happy in her summation of the impending proposal, Laurie Thomas smiled.

"My good people," Jeffries said, in a well-modulated voice. "I want to begin by telling you that . . ."

David did not hear the rest of the story as he was busily running up the hill to Ramon. He quickly scooted down on the ground beside Ramon. After his heart had calmed down from the excitement and exertion, he looked at Ramon with devilment in his eyes. It took him a moment to catch his breath. Finally, he looked at Ramon and said with much enthusiasm.

"Ramon, my Friend," David breathlessly said. "I do believe we've come upon another goldmine. Yes Siree, I think we've waited long enough for our ship to dock. In fact, I thought we waited so long, our ship's been shanghaied or maybe sunk."

The two outlaws ran to their horses and mounted them. They put the spurs to the horses' flanks and galloped away into the night. Their shadows were swiftly swallowed up in the darkness. Only the sound of their hoof beats gave evidence of them spying on the people of Clearwater.

When the meeting was over, everyone broke up and went their separate ways. Chris asked his wife if it would be all right with her to have Davis's over to the house for coffee and cake. He knew she had finished a cake this afternoon and he wanted to show off her cooking skills to Bob and Susie, as well as get revenge for losing the last chess game.

"Sure thing, Chris," Kim replied lovingly, placing her arm inside of his. "I'm glad that we met that family. You love to play chess with Bob and I enjoy the company of Susie. Those children of theirs are as dear to our hearts as our own will be some day. That'll give me the opportunity of making plans with Susie for the upcoming picnic next weekend."

The picnic was actually a friendly get-together for the townspeople, ranchers, farmers and anyone else who thought to show up. It was to be held on the banks of the Red River. They would still be close enough to town in case of an emergency. The gentle slope of the hills would afford everyone ample room to spread out and would give the children the space needed to run and play.

Chris looked with fondness on his wife. Then, not paying any attention to who could be watching them, threw his big arms around her, picked her up and kissed her in front of God and everybody.

"Why Chris, I was beginning to think that you didn't want to show public display of your emotions," Kim said, blushing deeply and almost out of breath. She loved this tower of strength so very much.

"I don't really care what everyone thinks," Chris breathed softly into her hair. "Want you and everyone else to know how very much I love you."

"As if anyone could doubt," Kim laughed, squeezing this gargantuan husband of hers. She was proud of him and wanted to show everyone else, so she reached up and brought his head down to hers and kissed him for a long time.

Then the two lovers started walking arm in arm. Bob and Susie looked back and smiled. They interlocked their arms and walked hand in hand down the street. People would see the two couples and smile to each other. Before long, Tom and Laurie joined the hand holding couples as they too started to stroll down the street of Clearwater. Soon, it seemed as if the street was flooded with couples walking, holding hands and laughing. A festive mood soon enveloped the town.

"Kim," Chris said, while disengaging his arm. "Why don't you and Susie go on to the house and start some lemonade? Bob and I'll be along directly. I've a few questions to ask Bob and tonight when the news is still fresh on our minds I want his opinion."

Kim and Susie with the children walked ahead to the house. Chris and Bob walked slowly along the street. Each seemed lost in their own thoughts. They walked along the dusty silent street.

Chris was thinking of the good news, but something still bothered him. He meant to ask Bob about the situation. Chris had grown to not only like the dude from back East, but also to respect his judgment.

Bob had warmed up to this mild mannered mammoth. He also obtains a certain sense of comfort of knowing Chris. Chris was the big brother Bob always wanted but he never had. Together, they reminded one of the tall and short of the matter.

"That's some speech," Bob said, stopping to bend and pick up a small stone, which he threw off the boardwalk.

"Sure was," Chris replied. "But then again, do you think Mr. Jeffries answered the condition of the poor. You know, the farmers and sharecroppers, let alone us small businessmen?"

They had reached Chris's house and Bob quickly sought out his favorite rocker. He sat in the rocker while Chris was in the porch swing. Neither said anything, just sit and rock or glide back and forth. Finally, Bob looked at his friend and cleared his throat.

"To answer your question of Jeffries comments tonight, I believe he did, Chris," Bob answered, proud that Chris valued his opinion. He in return often sought out the friendship that Chris so feely gave. Then he went on to explain to Chris that the federal government had laws against land grabbing and monopolies. Bob farther talked to Chris patiently, the plight of the poor was the least on his mind now.

"Oh?"

"Yes," Bob said, while sitting in his choice of a rocking chair on Chris's front porch. "Me being a former security specialist, I can't help but think about the safety of our money. We haven't rebuilt the bank to suit me."

"But the jail is strong enough," Chris said, sitting also in a rocker. "Besides there are enough men to provide protection."

"Maybe so, but what if there isn't? What if," Bob said, as he rocked softly on the porch. He was all the time thinking about what, where and how many.

"Sometimes," Susie had once said, in a joking manner. "You, Bob Davis, will likely be the death of me. Honey, you worry too much. I mean, it might rain tomorrow, or snow, or any calamity you can think of happening."

"In that case," Chris grinned and remembering what Kenny always said. "Dog-rabbit."

Chuckling, the two men went into the house to see about the women. Chris could almost smack his lips at the thought of Kim's baked apple pie. Bob was thanking his lucky stars that he and Susie had met such nice people as the Barkers.

TWENTY-FOUR

Jim Jeffries walked Mrs. Kessler to the hotel. He was pleased with the warm reception he had received tonight at the meeting. When he first heard of the meeting, he asked if it was advisable.

"Advisable?" Lee asked, sitting more straight in his chair and looking at Bob and Jeffries closely.

"Yes, maybe a wrong choice of word," Jeffries answered. "More like caution. I mean letting everyone have first hand knowledge of the gold."

"Jim," Bob said. At a nod from Lee, he continued, "I've been here only a short time and I've learned to trust these people. Not to sound pompous or presumptuous, but in my capacity as an ex-Pinkerton operative, my very life depend on judging people. Therefore, in my professional opinion these people are solid."

"I must agree, Jim," Lee said, sitting back in his chair. "Plus, these people are the very ones who were robbed. It's their money in the bank. Besides all of that, they know the consequences of talking to the wrong person or persons."

Jeffries, after receiving the assurances of both the sheriff and a professional security man, felt better. Tonight, he had seen the faces of the people and felt more secure in the knowledge of the advisability of the conglomerate's investments. He would lose no sleep tonight in worry over the fate of his, no, the town's money.

Jeffries was remembering this earlier discussion with Lee and Bob as he walked up the steps of the hotel. He was at first hesitant at the large crowd at the meeting tonight, but he was rewarded with a smile from Mrs. Kessler. The other men noticed her sitting in front also.

They began to poke and nod at each other, all the time smiling at Jeffries.

Jeffries smiled as he recalled meeting her again at the hotel restaurant. He had invited and she had accepted to dine with him tonight at the hotel. They went to a restaurant and were seated by an older gentleman. After they were seated, Jeffries commented on the man's age. Mrs. Kessler laughed softly. They had a delightful meal and afterwards, he escorted her to the front of the hotel.

"Mrs. Kessler," Jeffries started to say, only to be stopped by her hand on his arm.

"Pam," she said. "Pam Kessler, but I would prefer for you to call me Pam instead of Mrs. Kessler."

"Pam," Jim said. "I'd also consider it an honor for you to call me Jim."

Jim saw her acquiesced and his grin got broader. He took her by the arm and steered her to the hotel porch swing. Ever being the gentleman, he took out a handkerchief and dusted the supposed dust from the seat.

Together, they sat and peacefully moved the swing back and forth. Jim got so bold as to place his arm around the back of the swing. It rested there for as moment, then he slid his arm down to encompass her shoulder.

The two talked for a while of their dreams and plans. Hers - to find true happiness again, maybe even open a dress shop and a good father for Amanda. His - to be healthy, wealthy and wise. So far, he was healthy and wise, but wealth seemed to elude him for the time being.

"But all of that is going to change soon, I hope," Jim said, with earnestness in his voice.

"Oh?"

"Yes, my dear," Jim replied. "As soon as I conclude my business here and return to Boston."

"You mean you're going back so soon?" Pam said, sitting up in the swing and looking alarmed.

Jim, seeing the look on her face, hurriedly added that he was going to return here to Clearwater. Especially since he had found her.

"A bit rough around the edges," he thought, "but I'm sure I can hone them down just fine."

"Let's not think about the morrow," Jim said, smoothly. "Let's just think about tonight and the good fortune of finding each other."

He knew that tomorrow, after the sheriff and mayor signed for the gold, the burden would be off his shoulders finally. His stomach had been as tight as an over wound spring in a pocket watch since he first took possession of the gold. Now, it seemed to settle down somewhat. He murmured a sigh of relief of that happening.

Lee and Tom had arrived at the jail early in the morning to relieve the guard who had been keeping an eye on the gold. Also, in preparation of signing the release accounted for them arriving early for Jeffries. Already the sun was beginning to peek over the rims of the eastern hills. The sunlight hitting the shadows made them run swiftly away. A rooster crowed to proclaim the day from its lofty perch on the roof of the livery.

People were starting to move on the street. Shopkeepers were opening their place of business. A few were placing barrels of merchandise outside of their stores, while others were sweeping off the boardwalk in front of theirs. Abner Hershey was placing a barrel of farm tools by the side of his front door.

Lee provided relief for the guard, who walked away quickly in the hope of being among the first at the breakfast at the hotel. Now that he knew the sheriff was going to be picking up the tab, he walked faster.

"By the way, Lee," Tom asked, going to the pot-bellied stove for coffee. "Where's Gary these days? Haven't seen him or Kenny for over a week."

"I think Kenny and him went on a hunting trip. At least I heard him mumble to himself of going on a hunting trip. Something or the other."

"I wonder what in the world's keeping Jeffries," Tom asked. "He's so adamant about making sure we were here this morning. Bright and early were his last comments."

"I think it's not what, but who," Lee replied. "Mrs. Kessler's doing the honors this morning. I saw them at breakfast this morning over at the hotel on my way to the office. It seems, Mr. Jeffries has found a person worthy of his attention."

There was a knock at the door, Tom arose to let in a flushed face Jim Jeffries. His derby was at a rakish angle on his head and he had a smile plastered all over his face. He seemed to be in a jovial frame of mind.

"Top of the morning to you fine gentlemen," Jeffries said, as he reached into his jacket pocket and removed two sheaves of paper. "It's a glorious morning, the sun is bright and the men sitting on the front porch of the hotel all seem to be in good sprits. It's a wonderful day, don't you think."

This last statement was spoken, as a statement not a question. It needed no more emphasis. Jeffries was in an exuberant mood this morning. He was bristling with excitement and in a hurry to conclude his mission. He reminded one of an expectant mother. Sad, but happy. Sad at her condition, but happy to be able to bring a new life into the world.

"Good morning to you too, Jim," Tom spoke. "And what seems to be the rush?"

"Yes, Jim, what's your hurry?" Lee asked, knowing full well what the rush was for and what had given a lift to Jim's steps this morning.

"Well, let me tell you two first," Jim said, drawing himself up higher. "It may be a little premature, but I am seriously thinking about a move out here. Maybe not right in town, but close enough to keep my finger on the pulse of the town."

"It wouldn't be on the account of Mrs. Kessler, would it?" Lee asked, tongue in cheek.

Jeffries began to blush and looked about shamefacedly. Tom grinned with Lee and quickly arose to join Lee in shaking Jeffries hand. Tom even slapped Jeffries on the back.

"You ole son of a gun," Tom said, with humor in his voice. "You've been here only a couple of days and already you seem to have found a sweetie."

"I can't blame you a bit, Jim," Lee said, sitting. "That Mrs. Kessler's a looker. Pardon me . . . no offense given."

"No," Jim laughed, letting out a sigh he had been holding. "None taken. She is quite attractive, if I say so myself."

"What I meant to say if I was a tad younger and more available . . . well," Lee said haltingly.

"I think if our poor sheriff says anymore, he'll swallow his foot," Tom laughed as well as Jim. Finally the sheriff joined in the merriment.

"Enough levity, Gentlemen," Jim said in a more somber tone of voice. "Need these papers signed so I can be on my way. Your public conveyance leaves your fair community soon."

"Our what?" Lee asked.

"He means the stage," Tom laughed, then he pulled out his turnip pocket watch and flipped open the face cover to glance at the time. "In fact you have about an hour to make it."

"Oh dear!" Jim exclaimed, rushing to the desk and placing the papers down. "Please sign this for me now, I've to finish packing, pay my bill and a whole host of other things that require my immediate attention."

"Not to mention saying good bye to Mrs. Kessler," Tom laughed, as he finished signing the papers.

Jeffries hurriedly gathered the papers, placed them in his vest pocket, shook hands with the sheriff and rushed out the door. Tom and Lee watched his back as he rushed to the hotel. He dodged two little boys, skirted around a shopkeeper and tipped his hat to a lady before he entered the hotel.

"That man's going to have a heart attack if he doesn't slow a mite," Tom said, smiling.

"That he is," Lee chuckled as he walked back to his desk. Sighing now that the hard part seemed to be over.

"Well, I for one," Tom breathed heavily, sitting in a chair, "am certainly happy that hurdle is behind us?" The town now had a savior and a shiny one at that.

Lee and Tom spent the morning discussing the various ways of moving the money to the bank. They were not aware Chris and Bob was discussing the same thing. In fact, everyone was concerned about the gold.

"I think," Chris said, as he was busy moving a water barrel closer to the forge. "The gold's going to be safer in the bank than the jail."

"Maybe so," Bob replied, moving to sit on a hay bale so he could watch the mighty smithy at work. "But it still bothers me. Also, the bank's not finished yet."

"Of course, but let me ask you a question?" Chris asked, filling his water tank.

"Sure fire away."

"You say the bank's not completed and I agree with you. Let me finish. The structure is all repaired and the vault is secure, so it still needs some woodworking to be done on the inside. Your idea of additional bars on the windows was a good one. Outside of that, what more can be done to make our gold any safer?"

"Now hat you put it that way, nothing I guess," Bob said, while he was whittling a piece of wood. He was making a toy for his young son and possibly one for his daughter too.

"Then it's settled," Chris spoke. "Right? Okay, now please help me load those plows on the buckboard. Once I get them delivered to Mr. Hadley, swing by the Emporium so I can pick up Kim's grocery list and get back here it will almost be dinnertime. Say, why don't you and your family join us for dinner? Afterwards, we can get in a game of chess. I still owe you one for checkmating me so easily the other night."

"I can't speak for Susie, but it's all right with me," Bob answered, rising from the hay bale. "Let me check with her. In the meantime, think I'll saunter down by the jail and see if the sheriff is in his office. I've some concern on the bank's safety to discuss at great length with him."

After Chris drove off in his buggy, Bob headed toward the sheriff's office. He walked in the street and came abreast of the burned leather shop. He stopped, then looked at the structure more closely, advancing to the edge of the boardwalk, where he peered up.

Since the robbery and fire, the bank was being refurbished and the Emporium also, but the leather shop was still in shambles. Bob had heard that Daimon Dickerson, the owner, had moved back East to be with his daughter. Since then the leather shop had been vacant. Now it stood out for being the only building on Main Street that was not being repaired after the fire; a slight mar on the beauty of the town businesses.

Bob knew their finances and they were situated fine. Nothing to shout about, but adequate. He had made money in his latest land dealings and with the generous retirement settlement from Pinkerton's, he was doing all right. He had told Susie of his plans to buy a business here in Clearwater and she was elated with the news.

Bob stepped up to the boardwalk and moved toward the boarded opening of the shop. As he was peering in the broken windows, he caught sight out of the corner of his eyes the shape of Abner Hershey. Abner was watching Bob from the doorway of the Emporium next to the leather shop.

"Hello, Abner," Bob said, tipping his derby to the portly man. "Happen to know who owns this property?"

Abner was watching Bob warily, but let his avaricious nature overcome his trepidation, he quickly removed his apron and donned a smart looking waistcoat, forgetting to take off his green grocer shade. He stepped out of his doorway and approached Bob. Abner took care to stay up on the boardwalk. He had read somewhere, that being higher than a prospective customer was an advantage.

"Well?" Bob asked, remembering trying to get information out of Abner was near nigh to impossible. He also recalled, that Chris once telling him of Abner's of apparent slowness.

"That man could have both feet on fire," Chris said, laughingly, over a game of chess. "And it'd take at least a day for the smell to reach his nose, let alone the pain to his brain!"

"Whatcha want to know for?" Abner asked, wiping his vest of an imaginary piece of lint and assuming an air of importance. He walked closer to the edge of the boardwalk and peered down at Bob.

"Well, friend," Bob thought smiling, "two can play at this game." He looked shrewdly at Abner and did not utter a word. Bob glanced up and down the street as if he had all the time in the world. He ran his hand over his chin thoughtfully, he appeared to be lost in deep thought.

Finally, Abner cleared his throat and pulled at his collar. He began to shuffle his feet, started rocking back and forth on each leg. He also looked up and down the street before taking a deep breath. The grocer placed his hands in his vest pocket, seemed to strut and cleared his throat.   Looking at Bob with an attitude of privy knowledge, he spoke.

"It so happens, I do," Abner replied smugly. "Why?"

Bob could have taken the answer either way.   Abner did own the shop or Abner knew who owned the shop. He also remembered also Chris telling him that Abner did own the premise, but after the fire, was left holding the bag.   Abner had tried in vain to unload the shop on some unsuspecting   outsider,   but   so   far   he   had   been unsuccessful.   Anyway Bob went into his horse-trading form.

"I happen to know of a, well not rich, but he's at least well off, a person who is interested in this place.   That is for a reasonable price."

"You do?   Who?" Abner said, his voice raising in hope.   "At last I have a bite," he thought smugly to himself.   He was rubbing his hands behind his back as he inwardly gloated at the prospect of finding a buyer.   "At long last," he thought, "I'll be able to unload this white elephant."

"Here, let's not be so hasty," Bob said, hoping to place Abner off guard.   "I mean this person wants a main street piece of property and especially one next to the bank.   Of course, it will have to be remodeled."

"I can see that being done," Abner said, greed taking hold of him again.   "In fact, I can almost assure you of it being done."

He was already figuring on making a fine profit from the before burned store.   "So far, I've not had even a nibble.   Now it seems as if this young man's ready to bite and take the bait.   I'll let him bite and swallow the bait and like the good fisherman I am, I'll play out enough line to let him run with it.   Then wham, I'll flick my wrist, plant the hook deep in the mouth and slowly reel him into my waiting net,"   Abner let his mind wander as he was busy wringing his hands in anticipation of making a sure sell.

"Know just what you mean, my young sir," Abner said, drawing himself up higher on the boardwalk. "This's prime real estate. Why I was just telling my good friend, Chris Barker, you know the town blacksmith. Anyway, I was just telling him the other day about this store. I was going to expand my business, but now I can't. You know, a bad back and all."

"Do tell," Bob said, starting to turn. "Well, as I said –"

Abner was too busy envisioning his newfound wealth to take notice of Bob walking away. When it finally dawned on him that his quarry had been spooked, it was too late. The last Abner saw of his intended victim was Bob's back as he entered the sheriff's office.

"Hrump!" Abner said, then went wearily back to his labors of sweeping the porch, pausing long enough to place a well-aimed kick at the local stray mongrel, which deftly avoided the intended blow. The dog slunk off to its hiding place underneath the Emporium's front porch.

TWENTY-FIVE

David traveled south with Ramon by his side. They ride their horses below the summit of the hills so as not to be outlined against the horizon. David did not believe in taking any undue chances either. Like Hawk, he was making sure he wouldn't be detected; his feeling of importance having gone to his head.

"Ho, Señor," Ramon said, reining in his horse. "Look."

He glanced in the direction Ramon was pointing and saw a small puff of smoke rising from beyond the next hill to their left. He was glad, as he was hungry and thirsty. Jeremy was still sore from his arduous climbing back at Clearwater. That exercise and him being thankful for a rest, made him rethink the way that he had been treating Ramon so badly. But, that was all it was, rethinking, it was not in his nature to be sorry for any human. So he reverted to his former ways of looking out for no one but himself.

David had cursed Ramon for being so forgetful. Ramon had forgotten the foodstuffs and extra water. A handful of dried corn and a piece of moldy black bread were their fare now.

"At least, over there will be refried beans and possibly some tequila," David thought, as he spurred his horse forward. "Maybe, a sweet señorita or two, who knows?"

They rode up to a crest of the hill overlooking the tiny village. David and Ramon looked down at the small village. There were at least eight huts, a stable and a combination general store and cañtina. Smoke was coming from the roof of this cañtina. The outlaw looked carefully around and saw nothing to be alarmed about.

David started down the hill with Ramon right on his heels. The two horsemen pulled their steeds to halt at an adobe cantina. David motioned for Ramon to hold the reins of his horse as he strode to the front door. Quickly, he pulled aside the blanket used for a front door and entered the cantina.

True to habit, he immediately stepped to the side of the doorway. After his eyes became adjusted to the dimly lit enclosure, he glanced around. The inside of the cantina was the same as a thousand others in the southwest. Two tables and stools and a piece of an old railroad tie that spanned the top of two cracked wooden barrels was the only furniture in the place. To David's left was an iron cauldron hanging over a fire. It was partially full of beans bubbling as they were boiled. The smell was slowly permeating the small cantina. It was making his mouth water.

A droopy-eyed bartender wiped the bar slowly with a piece of burlap and acted as if in a daze. From the nodding of his head, he seemed almost asleep. Every now and then, his head would slowly drop to his chest and with a start he quickly brought it up. Then he began his ritual of wiping the bar again.

"Lost in his own little world," David thought. "Well, to each their own I guess. I could rob this place easily, but by the look of things, I wouldn't get anything, except maybe an upset stomach from the beans."

The dirt floor was uneven due to the recent rains that had washed channels throughout the bar. David could see the fat bartender was alone in the cantina. He hitched his gun belt up higher on his bony frame and walked to the bar. He took care to navigate the ruts.

"Leastways," he thought, "there's no chickens. Must be really poor, for them not to even make an appearance?"

"Tequila," David grunted to the bartender, who stared at him with one eye closed and the other was barely open.

The sweaty Mexican reached under the counter and placed a filthy bottle in front of David.

David uncorked the bottle and turned it up to his lips. He did not see a lime or salt as he wiped his mouth with the back of his hand. He glanced about and saw there were two empty tables, one window and an open hearth for the beans.

Ramon chose that time to come through the slot of a door. He had a flopping chicken hawk in his hands. Not bothering saying anything, he ambled to the bar. He then placed the bird upon the bar where it squawked, flapped its wings and flew to the back of the cañtina where there was an open window. Fluttering, the bird flew through the opening in the wall and off to the azure sky, screeching all the time.

"All right, Amigo," David asked in a soft voice, as he cast a baleful eye upon his friend. "What's your idea of that?"

"I think two hawks are better than one. Si, Señor Hawk," Ramon answered grinning. Then he raised the bottle to his fat lips and took a large swig of the fiery tequila. Ramon wiped his mouth with the back of his dirty sleeve and belched loudly in the face of the bartender. The Mexican thought it best not to mess with these strangers, so he continued making circles with his rag on the bar.

David considered it best to let Ramon have his fun while he could still enjoy it. After one more job, he figured on cutting loose of Ramon, perhaps to even kill him and keep all of the gold to himself.

"Maybe, I'll spend my treasure at some place somewhere else in the good old U S of A. Speaking of gold," he thought, "I wonder just how I can lay my hands on those yellow bars in that little backwater town after all."

It was while David was pondering the theft, some strangers walked into the small cañtina. There were four of the banditos and the smell emitting from the outlaws raised a stink to the high hills. They sat by the door and nodded to the fat barkeep, who quickly supplied them with a dirty bottle of tequila.

David warily glanced to where one of the banditos was sitting. He noticed that Ramon had moseyed off to one side of the bar.

"A good boy," he thought, "that way in case of a ruckus, we'll have them in a crossfire. I may have to change my mind about Ramon after all," he thought, adjusting his shooting side away from the bar.

One of the banditos looked toward David and Ramon, turned back to his companions and whispered something. The biggest of the bunch lumbered to his feet and advanced toward David, who by this time had planted his boots firmly on the ground.

The Mexican that approached him had two bandoleers criss-crossing his immense chest, .45 pistol stuck in a wide piece of moth-eaten leather belt at the waist of his stained large trousers. A sombrero was pushed back on his head revealing greasy black hair. The Mexican's salt and pepper moustache drooped over his crooked mouth.

"Ah, Señor," he said, grinning to reveal yellow teeth. He was also watching David's hand hovering over his gun. "My compádres are wondering what's you doing so far south of the river."

David knew he was in a tight corner. This small cañtina harbored no safe refuge in case of a gunfight. There was too much of a chance someone would get lucky and hit him. He had already figured on the safe place for him to be and that was behind one of the barrels.

When David did not answer right away, the speaker looked back over his shoulder at his friends. As he was looking, David noticed his hand slowly move toward the gun in his belt. Thinking fast, David drew his gun and shoved the barrel of it into the protruding belly of the Mexican.

"We can do this two ways, friend," David softly said, shifting his weight to shield his body with the hapless outlaw. "We can either shoot it out, which means you get the honor of being the first killed; or we can sit at the table and discuss some things. Very rewarding things, if you catch my drift? It's all up to you, Amigo. The cards are on your table. Stand pat, raise, call, or maybe fold. It doesn't mean a thing to me, but you can feel my response in your side right now."

While David was getting the drop on the outlaw, Ramon had quickly drawn his gun and was covering the trio at the other table. He had moved around the bar to get the protection of the barrels.

"Si, Señor. I fold. Manuel will sit and talk," the outlaw said, raising his hand's chest high and grinning.

"Over there then," David said, replacing his weapon in his holster. "Ramon, try to keep them boys occupied while I chew the fat some with Mr. Manuel."

Ramon nodded and placed his gun on the bar still pointing at the three. He glared at the others not to make a move. He motioned for them to sit still and place their hands on the table. The trio quickly complied and placed their hands on the dirty table top, smiling all smiles at Ramon and David. Then one pulled the cork from his tequila and passed it to the one on his right. After all had finished their drink, they motioned for Ramon to join them.

As David and Manuel walked to the table, the bartender reached under the counter, then hurried over to the table. He appeared with a fresh bottle of tequila, fresh limes and a saltshaker to boot. He then returned to the bar and picked up his dirty rag and began to polish the counter vigorously again.

While David and Manuel got to know each other better, the town of Clearwater was preparing for their picnic.

TWENTY-SIX

Susie Davis and Kim Barker were busy making preparations for the upcoming picnic. Susie was frying chickens that she had received from the neighbors. She asked Kim's help in plucking the chickens, as Ryan and Missy were nowhere to be found.

"Probably out playing somewhere," she thought as she was moving around in Kim's kitchen.

Kim had also prepared a bowl of potato salad. Together, they had plucked the hens, fried the fowls and made fruit pies. Chris had provided the dried apples that he had brought up earlier from the root cellar.

"I'm sure glad Chris dug that cellar," Kim said, wiping her brow with her apron and moving to the large wooden table. She placed a bowl of potatoes to be peeled on the table.

"Me too," Susie stated, moving to the table also. "You never know when it will come in handy."

Susie was used to a storm cellar from where she came in the Midwest. There was all the time the imminent threat of a tornado or some sort of bad weather descending on them. "It pays to be prepared," she concluded.

Kim was clueless as to the weather, her being raised in California; earthquakes yes, twisters, no way Jose. It was just enough to trust Chris's judgment in these matters.

"So far he's been right in everything," she thought smiling at her recollection of her husband.

"Wonder what the men are up to?" Susie asked, sitting and starting to peel the potatoes. She moved her chair to the side to give Kim room to sit also.

"Got me," Kim answered, sitting herself to help Susie with the chore of peeling. The two peeled the potatoes, washed them and placed them in the cast iron skillet to fry to a nice golden brown.

Chris and Bob were talking to Lee and Tom about the latest move of the gold. It was to be moved from the jail to the bank. This morning, a group of men transported the gold from its resting place under the watchful eye of Lee. Bob helped in setting up the simple security system at the bank.

"Is it safe?" Tom asked, moving to sit beside Chris.

"Safe as a new born babe in his mother's arms," Bob replied, stepping aside to show off his handiwork.

Bob had rigged between the teller cages, a wire that ran from a trip lever on the floor up to a hole in the ceiling. From there, the wire went across the bank's attic to another wire connecting it to a small bell cord that hanged down in the sheriff's office. Whenever it was engaged, the bell in the sheriff's office would jangle. It was so simple that the others castigated themselves for not thinking of it themselves.

"Seeing as I'm just next door," Lee said, looking askance at Bob. "Why not holler?"

"Simple," Bob said. "This way the perpetrators will not be aware of the alarm and could be caught red-handed. Also, it does not hurt anything to be attentive of any situation."

"Maybe so," Lee replied, still not sure of the new-fangled contraption. He was from the old school where just being able to out draw a man, or beat him to the punch would make all the difference in the world. Especially here in the West.

"Now," Chris said, with pride in his voice, standing and motioning for Tom to stand aside also. "We're going to show you our job."

The gold had been moved from the jail next door to its final resting place at the back of the vault in the just finished bank. It had been removed and stacked in neat rows on the shelves in the bank's vault.

"I'd feel better if I didn't have this uneasy feeling something bad is going to happen," Lee said, as he walked to examine the vault's new steel doors.

"I know the feeling," Bob said. He looked at Chris, then went to the vault doors as well. "These doors are made of heavy gauge steel, like the kind they use at big banks back East. They weigh at least a ton a piece. They also have a new invention, a three-day time lock. Besides all of that, it has newly double wall fire-resistant walls."

"Pshaw," Chris stated, looking directly at Bob, "Bob's a worry wart. He and I have been going over the what ifs until I am about ready to smack him in the side of his head to get him to shut up about it."

This last was said teasingly by Chris, as Bob and he had developed a grudging respect for each other. Chris knew that Bob would lay down his life for him and vice-versa. The whole town knew it and grinned when the two walked on the street together.

"Tweedledee and Tweedledum," one would say in good-natured fun. And like the twins in the Lewis Carroll story of 'Alice Adventures in Wonderland', the two would mimic each other. The men often thought of the same thing at the same time. One would think that they were married, because of their uncanny ability to think what the other's thoughts were before they we even uttered.

"Like twin foals," another would comment.

Bob and Chris were the talk of the town. They were two firm pillars in the community. There was even talk of creating a new post in the city council. It was to be called the Director of Utilities, reportable only to the mayor. Bob had been approached by Tom and the city council about assuming that job. Bob had shown his willingness to help out in any way he could be of assistance.

The former private detective was thrilled at the prospect of a new job, but informed Tom, he would have to talk to Susie about it. He also wanted to ask Chris's advice on the new opportunity and subsequent headaches that went with such an opportunity.

The two men were almost inseparable. Bob had ended up buying the leather shop from Abner. He had remodeled the insides now with Abner's money and was in the process of making fine-tooled leather saddles. He supplied Chris with leather harnesses, reins and any other leather goods Chris or the town and the surrounding area needed.

The town was going to need someone, now there was talk of getting gas piped to the businesses and repairing the streets, to do the directing. Bob Davis had been approached by Tom about it. Bob had told Tom that he would think it over and let him know soon of his decision.

Clearwater was fast becoming a small city. The town had formed an all-volunteer fire brigade. It was in celebration of the reorganized fire department that Clearwater was going to have a community picnic the following Saturday.

TWENTY-SEVEN

David and Manuel were in a deep discussion as Ramon had joined the other outlaws at their table. The banditos had seen their leader grin and sit with David. They had relaxed and invited Ramon to join them. Ramon was having a good time passing the bottle around to his newfound friends.

"You say you've just come through Clearwater?" David asked, while pouring Manuel another glassful of the tequila. He glanced to where Ramon and the others were sitting. They were passing the bottle, laughing and talking. The quartet seemed oblivious to Manuel and him. "Good," he thought.

"Si, Señor," Manuel said, then reached for the glass, picked it up and tossed back the burning liquid.

"Well?" David asked.

"My compádres and I stopped off at a saloon up there," Manuel responded. Then looking craftily at David asked why he wanted to know?

"I was just wondering," David said nonchalantly.

"A person don't just wonder. He wants some information. No?"

David did not want to reveal his hand too quickly, but at the same time, he needed help in the worse way. Ramon was fine, but having more was better. Taking a gamble, he told Manuel of his plans to rob the town again. Also, he told of overhearing of gold being in the town.

"This gold," Manuel asked, pulling his stool closer to David. "She's in the bank now?"

"I hope to shout it is," David replied, then he moved his stool closer to Manuel. They were almost touching foreheads now. "It's stored in a cracker box of a bank. A vault that's paper thin. In fact, I imagine I could waltz in there and blow gently on the walls and they would come tumbling down. The gold is lying there, just begging to be picked up. I figure five or six men could handle the job just fine and dandy. Now, there are five of you and two of us. That makes seven good men. What do you think, Amigo?"

The Mexican sat back and then reached up to stroke his mustache. He looked over to his companions and barked out an order. Then he resumed drinking with David. Immediately, one of the outlaws came to the table and after a whispered conversation, went outside. In a moment, he came back in and nodded to his leader. Then he rejoined his companions.

The Mexican grinned widely at David and pulled the bottle to his side of the table. He uncorked the almost clear liquid and poured David a glass. He took his glass and raised it in a salute.

"Here's to a good venture," Manuel said, looking at David.

"So you're in?" David asked, grinning now as he raised his glass in acknowledgment.

"Si, we are in," Manuel replied, taking a hefty swig of the burning liquor, wiping his mouth with a dirty sleeve and leaning back in his chair.

"Good," David echoed. "Now, of course I'll be the leader."

"Oh?" Manuel asked, turning to fix his gaze more fully on David. "And why's that? We are five," he looked about and smiled at his compádres. "And you are only two."

"Simple, Amigo," David said in a menacing voice, giving Manuel an evil stare. "It's my plan and besides, you are going to let me or I will blow a hole in you big enough to ride your horse through sideways. You see, your life doesn't mean diddle squat to me. I'd as soon kill you as look at you, my friend."

The last was said as David stared hard at Manuel. He knew he needed additional firepower, but at the same time, he had learned long ago that there was no such thing as a free lunch. David was also prepared to start shooting as much as he was ready to fall in with the Mexicans. He did not believe in tomorrow, only today.

Manuel glanced toward his companions, looked back at David and was all smiles as he filled both glasses. He took his drink, raised it to his lips, threw back his head and the throat searing liquid traveled down his throat. He was already thinking of killing this Gringo and his friend, stashing their bodies and riding off into the sunset with his amigos.

"Done," Manuel said, dragging his filthy, swarthy hand across his fat lips as he placed the empty glass on the table.

David smiled and finished his drink. Then he leaned forward as Manuel motioned for him. Manuel informed David of the up coming picnic of the town. He had heard the bartender speaking of the event to another patron of the bar.

David nodded to Manuel and filed this little bit of information to the back of his mind. "A celebration would provide an ideal time to hit the bank. Everyone would be at the picnic and no one to speak of would be in town guarding the bank. What, with his band of desperados, the town of Clearwater would once again know how the Romans felt, as Attila the Hun descended on them. Only this time it would be The Hawk that would be plummeting to plunder!"

TWENTY-EIGHT

The day of the picnic, Bob Davis approached Lee Wildman and asked of the safety of the gold. Lee told him that there would be two guards inside the bank and another guard outside standing on the front porch of the bank. That, along with him and a few of the townspeople being within shouting distance to hear any alarm would provide more than enough protection for the gold.

"I hope you don't think of me being unduly alarmed, Lee," Bob said, as he was walking beside the sheriff to the saloon.

"No, I'm not," Lee responded with concern in his voice. "I'm just glad someone besides me is worried about the gold."

They both knew that their feelings were well known about town. Chris had told Lee that he could call on the burly blacksmith anytime, to help in any way needed. Tom had said the same thing. Even Abner Hershey had voiced concern and had offered his help too.

The men walked into the Green Parrot and at once stopped. On the walls were banners, crepe paper and replicas of flags. The once proud wooden Indian now stood stoically with tinsel draped on his stiff shoulders. His wooden eyes seemingly to stare off into space. The piano of all things, had flowers arranged on top. There was bunting draped over the windows and streams of brightly colored material snaked its way up the banister, weaving in and out of the columns.

"Looks like Big Tim's going all out in this celebration," Lee said, looking around the establishment in awe.

"Sure does," Bob said, as he started to weave in and out of the sea of tables. The chairs had been arrayed against the wall, leaving a large vacant area in front of the bar. "Space to dance I guess?" Lee wondered.

The biggest surprise to the men was yet to come. Big Tim rose from behind the bar with a shiny red fireman's hat on his head. He was dressed in large rubber coated trousers that were being held up by red canvass suspenders. He placed a yellow funnel looking device on the bar and turned to grin at them.

"What'll it be, Gents?" Tom asked, taking a damp rag and beginning to wipe the bar. It seemed that he never forgot this time-honored tradition. Or maybe, it was a sort of comfort to him. Either way, he rubbed the bar vigorously.

Bob and Lee stood amazed and looked at Big Tim with wonder in their eyes. Both men had sparkles of merriment in their eyes. Bob seemed to be tickled and Lee started to laugh out loud.

"Where's the fire?" Lee laughingly asked.

"No fire," Big Tim laughed also. "I'm supposed to give a demonstration of our new fire fighting equipment this afternoon at the picnic."

"Er ... what is that?" Lee asked, pointing to the glimmering yellow funnel on the bar.

"That, my friends," Big Tim said as he was picking the funnel from the bar and placing it to his lips. "Is my new speaker!"

Big Tim, seeing the baffled looks on the men's faces, explained the reason for the contraption. He told them of the need to be able to shout orders and directions to the men fighting a fire. With this new speaker he would be able to clearly and precisely give instructions to the volunteers.

"How's it going to look, if my men can't hear my orders?" Big Tim said with emphasis. "I can hear it all now. Madam, why did your house burn down so quickly? Weren't the firemen there to help? Ah, yes they were, but they could not hear the fire chief shout orders. Now, all of my worldly goods have gone up in smoke! O woe is me!"

The men chuckled. They could just envision the poor woman and her burning house; firemen scurrying around, falling over themselves and the constant chatter from the crowd as they stood and watched the antics of the firemen.

"Alas, my dear," Big Tim said, going into a mock stage posture, with his hand held up to his forehead.

"My word, Madam," Bob said, getting into the act. "What of your children? Of course, they were all rescued."

"All, but one," Lee said, getting into the act too "But he's the worst of the lot. He won't be missed. Besides, he was the very one who set the fire in the first place!"

The trio started to laugh as Big Tim drew a schooner of beer for Bob and Lee. He filled the tall glasses with the foaming liquid. Then he took a large wooden ladle and scraped suds off the top into a sink behind the bar.

In a more serious tone of voice, Big Tim asked of the picnic and who would make it. Lee told him that the word had gone out to the surrounding area. The ranchers and farmers would be sure to attend. He counted on people from miles around the town coming to enjoy the festivities.

"Everyone and their dog will be there, I hope," Lee said, taking a sip of beer and wiping his mouth with the sleeve of his shirt.

"I also heard through the grapevine," Lee said, looking sideways at Bob. "Chris's not only going to bring his horse shoes for your son to regale people with, but that he also said something about revenge on you for besting him the other day at the King's game of chess."

"I certainly hope so," Bob replied, pride in his voice. "I'm quite proud of my son and I think Chris deserves a chance at winning a game of chess, even if I know that beyond a shadow of a doubt, he's going to lose again. Only this time I aim to beat him royally."

"Well, everyone drink up," Big Tim spoke, placing his fireman's coat over his lanky frame. "We've a picnic to attend."

David and his gang crossed the Red River during the early morning hours. Meadow larks were flying peacefully in the clear blue sky as nearby ducks were quaking at being disturbed so early. To David's left, a roadrunner was catching up to a snake as the reptile squirmed across the road. Both bird and the deadly snake disappeared in the tall foliage at the side of the road. He could see the bushes shake as the victor had made another conquest, or maybe at the outside, the snake had reached its hole quick enough.

"No matter," David thought, as he could see in his mind's eye, the riches that would soon be his. "And mine alone," he thought, already his devious mind had conjured up double-crossing the Mexicans. "But only after they have helped me," he smiled.

The small band of desperados stayed close to the wooded hills east of Clearwater. David remembered teaming up with the Mexicans. At first, he thought there might be a problem with him assuming leadership, but after seeing Manuel handle his men, David felt better.

"Manuel," David said, as they were riding down a slope to the edge of the woods. "We'll stop there by the bottom of that hill."

"Si, Señor," Manuel said, directing his men to the hillside. The four plus Ramon rode quickly to the hillside. They dismounted, tethered their mounts and squatted in a circle. David noticed that Ramon was not included in their little circle. He stood by the horses instead, patiently watching David and Manuel as they ascended the hill.

Once near the top, David dropped on his belly. He then hurriedly placed a dirty telescope to his right eye. Manuel had followed David up the hill and followed suit by dropping down beside David.

"What's you see, Señor?" Manuel asked.

"Here, take a look yourself, Amigo," David said, handing the telescope to Manuel. He then took out his canteen and drank lightly from it, the tepid water soothing to his parched throat. "I got to quit smoking them cigarettes someday," he thought, as a spasm of coughing made him spit the phlegm onto a nearby bush.

Manuel brought the telescope up to his eye and squinted to make out the blurred shapes in the distance. David sighed and reached over, pulled the telescope out more fully and adjusted the lens so the images would come into sharper view. He knew that the Mexican would not have had an opportunity of spying on others as he was now afforded.

"Si, Señor," Manuel said, shifting his body to lean more on his elbows. He quickly adjusted his body and brought the telescope up to his eye.

Manuel watched as a group of people strolled across the grassy knoll. He saw more of the community gathered around a large bonfire. An immense iron pot was hanging on a tripod over the coals of a smaller campfire. He saw where someone had brought a beef to roast over the embers of the large fire. Right now, there were small children scampering at the fringes of the campsite. Manuel could see women; some having spread out tablecloths, while others seemed to stroll around the edge of the camp twirling their parasols.

"They're unaware that we are going to be visiting them soon," Manuel asked. "We go to town now?"

"No, not yet," David said, taking the telescope from Manuel's outstretched hand and placing it to his eye.

"Want to be sure I see the badge of the sheriff before we make a solitary move."

David looked down at the group, then swung around to see the outline of the town. He could barely make out the shapes of buildings. He adjusted the lens again and was able to see the object of his desires more closely. The bank was sitting there in the shadows like some fat hen on a nest. And like a hen protecting her eggs, the bank was sitting there protecting her gold.

"My gold," he thought, smiling at his good fortune. David was going to be like a farmer's wife collecting eggs, only he was going to be retrieving the gold.

David and Manuel stayed on the hillock for almost an hour, alternating turns at spying on the town and the picnic. It was while Manuel was looking, he stiffened. Shuffling a little, he spoke.

"Señor?" Manuel said softly, handing the binoculars to David. "Lookee over there."

David quickly took the telescope and cast his gaze in the direction Manuel was pointing. He saw a small contingent of men coming from town in a wagon with one man mounted on a horse riding at the side. The carriage held three men. David got excited! The one mounted had a gleaming badge pinned above the left pocket of his vest!

"That's the one I have been waiting to show," he thought. Then he nudged Manuel in the side and together they scooted back down the hill.

When the outlaws arrived at the bottom, the others were sitting on the ground playing cards with Ramon. David motioned to Ramon to get mounted as Manuel waved to his group.

"I'm glad to be going, Señor," Ramon whispered to David, as he swung into the saddle. "I think them Mexicans were cheating me."

David smiled, thinking, Ramon seemed to forget that he was a Mexican too. He taking offense at the others made David's smile get broader.

"Maybe there's hope for poor Ramon after all," David thought, as he nudged his horse into a canter toward the town.

The seven men rode a circuitous route to the outskirts of town. They dismounted at the back of the livery and carefully sneaked around to the alley separating the saloon from the bank. David motioned for the others to wait with the horses as he crept down the side of the bank.

He reached the bank corner and paused. Taking off his hat, he looked around the corner. He saw his first disappointment. The windows had bars on them! He looked farther and saw his second heartbreak. All the windows of the bank had bars on them! The final disappointment was sitting in the shade on the front porch in a chair. A deputy with a shotgun!

David cursed the shadows for not permitting him to see these obstacles. He would have to report to his gang of his discoveries. It was possible that new plans would have to be formulated. He had already thought them out and smiled as he brought them to his mind.

TWENTY-NINE

Lee was riding to the picnic area on a horseback. Chris, Tom and Bob were riding in a bouncing wagon. Lee had left instructions back with his newly deputized man at the bank that if anything, no matter how small, happens out of the ordinary, he was to fire his shotgun into the air and Lee and the others would come a running.

The wagon held enough firepower to start a small revolution. There were shotguns, guns and rifles resting on one side while the other held ammunition. Tom was sitting behind Chris and Bob. He held onto the seat tightly, his black hair streaming in the wind as Chris drove the buckboard a tad briskly.

"Slow down some, Chris," Tom shouted, taking a firmer grip on the back of the seat. He had already braced his lanky legs against the floor of the carriage. He smiled when he saw Bob brace his legs against the floorboard also.

"Oops! Sorry about that Tom," Chris said, pulling back a little on the reins. He was in a hurry to beat a lot of people, as he wanted to get first dibs on a good place to set up his horseshoe game and secure more room for the ladies to set up their fare. His wife had admonished him to be sure to find a place in the shade. Chris had visited the place yesterday and had easily picked out the best spot.

Bob was glad that Tom had hollered, for he was getting worried about the wagon tipping over by Chris's fast driving. He liked Chris a great deal, but at the same time, he did not trust Chris's driving all that much anyway.

Lee also was worried about Chris's fast pace. "That's all I need now," he thought, "for the buggy to tip over and someone to break his fool neck. Talk about raining on a parade, that would be sure put a damper on things."

Chris pulled the wagon to a stop on the banks of the Red River. Tom and Bob hopped down and each took an armload of blankets to spot underneath a spreading maple tree. A stand of cottonwoods was to their left and back up the slope aways.

"Now," Chris said, while scanning the area. "This's more like it."

He tied the reins to a small sapling and pulled back on the brake to make the wagon more secure. Then he turned and looked to where Lee was sitting astride his horse gazing back toward the town. He inwardly chuckled at the sheriff.

"Can't stop worrying for a minute, sheriff," Chris laughed, pushing the crown of his hat up on his forehead?

"Nope," Lee said, trying to see if he could catch a glimpse of town from his perch in the saddle. He was disappointed in that he could not make out the bank more clearly. But, he had faith in the men he had posted at the bank.

Bob had been staring across the river and was happy to see the water was flowing nicely. Almost as if it had stopped, only he could see the current was moving fast out in the middle of the great expanse of water. He turned as he overheard Chris and Lee.

"I'm feeling somewhat uneasy also," he said, tugging at his shirt collar. "Of course, to hear Chris and my wife talk, I am a worry wart. All I can say in my defense, my worrying has kept me safe more times than I can remember."

Tom walked to the group of men. He had caught the tail end of Bob's conversation and was promptly alarmed. His whole hope was riding on the gold. It was the town's salvation, his future, and his upcoming announcement of his engagement to Miss Laurie Thomas.

"Expecting trouble?" Tom asked, concerned evident in his face.

"Always expect trouble," Lee said, turning in his saddle and looking down at Tom. "That way, if it happens, I won't be surprised."

"Look, if I'd wanted to hear all this Jonah talk," Chris said, as he was busy carrying the horseshoe game over to a small clearing. "I'd have stayed home. Kim can talk about the end of the world all day long. Sometimes, she even scares me with her talk of disasters, plagues and the misfortune of other people."

The men laughed and the mood was broken. Tension seemed to fade from their faces. They began to pitch in and help Chris. Lee dismounted, tied his horse to the back of the wagon and went on to help Chris lay out the stakes for the horseshoe game. He dutifully paced off the proper steps with Chris directing him. Then he took out a stake and started to drive it into the ground.

Chris and Lee finished laying out the stakes. Chris wiped his brow, walked to the trunk of the maple and sat with his back to it. Bob followed suit by leaning against the other side. Tom stretched his lanky form out in the grass and announced to everyone that he was going to catch forty winks. Lee squatted next to Chris, reached out and pulled a blade of Johnson grass. He stuck the green shoot between his teeth.

THIRTY

David hurried back to his gang and informed them of the bank's added defenses. The Mexicans started to murmur and cast suspicious eyes toward David and Ramon. Manuel made a motion to David and the two walked away from the group.

As they were walking and talking in hushed tones, David was thinking how to cut his losses and Manuel was wondering if now was the time to take charge. He also, was planning on a double cross.

"Señor," Manuel said, in an oily sounding voice, as he moved up closer to the leader of the gang. "Think that I've something to help you out."

"Oh?" David said, trying to be prepared for anything, his hand constantly hovering over his gun. He still did not trust this Mexican or his colleagues; or for that matter, Ramon. After all, they were all Mexicans.

"Si, do you remember when we first met at the cantina and I did not offer me or my men until one had gone outside to check something for me?" Manuel said, whispering slyly to David.

"Continue," David said, remembering the episode.

Manuel told David that he and his compádres had just robbed an army post and they came away with no money, but they did have a small amount of dynamite. Manuel had sent the man out to check on the volatile sticks, to make sure they were well lashed to the backs of the pack animals. The man had returned and with a nod, assured Manuel everything was fine.

"You mean you got dynamite?" David asked, overjoyed beyond belief. "This's what I need now more than anything," he thought, running the possibilities through his mind.

"Si, Señor, but we may have a little problem," Manuel spoke in a low voice. "My men do not think they are going to get a fair share of the bank's money. You understand what I am saying?"

David understood only too well. "After the robbery, Manuel and his friends would likely kill him and Ramon. Why would they need us anyway? We've already told them about the gold. Once we steal it, there will be no farther use for us. I'm only mad at myself for not thinking of this plan earlier."

Then, as always, he grinned and slapping Manuel on the back confided in him that when they were done they would split the gold fifty-fifty. David knew from the talks he had with Manuel that Manuel felt no love lost between him and his compádres. Manuel was like David in that respect. Let the others take chances and when the time was right, just walk in and shoot every mother of them. Each man walked back to the gang thinking of the death of the other. David smiled evilly, while Manuel's grin made his mustache quiver.

David motioned to Ramon to help him unload the packhorse, while Manuel gave similar orders to his men. As Ramon was tugging on the ropes lashed to the animal's back, he was muttering to himself.

"What's your problem, Amigo," David asked, taking a piece of rope from the horse's saddle?

"Them Greasers are making me feel uneasy, Señor," Ramon said, walking around to face David.

"They're not making me feel any better, Ramon," David answered over his shoulder as he walked toward the pack animal Ramon had brought.

Manuel was unloading the sticks from his horse. They were wrapped in an oilskin pouch. He handled the package gingerly as he turned to David and smiled. He did not know much about dynamite.

"Let the others handle it for me," he thought.

"Do you know how this's to work, Señor?" Manuel asked as he gingerly placed the deadly cargo on the ground.

"Sure," David replied with more confidence than he felt. "We'd a con man back in stir that was an expert with this stuff."

He failed to mention the two derelicts J.O. and Clovis. "They'd handled the nitroglycerin while he hid safe and secure, but they were dead and he wasn't. Besides, they'd already finished their work for him." He smiled inwardly at the recall of such precious memories.

David gently picked the bundle up and motioned for the others to follow him. The killer walked slowly down the side of the bank building. He stopped and peered around the corner. Seeing the seated guard, he turned back to his companions.

Taking the bundle apart, he unwrapped the sticks, cut off a length of a fuse and placed a primer in the end of one stick. As an added caution, he wrapped the extra length of the fuse around the tightly packed bundle.

"Now listen closely," David said in a whisper. "Here's the plan. As we discussed on the trail, Ramon and I'll go into the bank, blow the safe and get the gold. Then . . ."

"That's fine, Señor," Manuel said. "But there's still a deputy sitting out front. He's not going to fall over dead, no matter how much we wish it to be."

"True, Amigo," David said. "That's where you and your compádres come into the picture. I want one of you to start out of this alley and stagger toward him. Then when he stands to talk, try to get him to turn his back to us. That done, one of you'll sneak up behind the man and knock him out. We'll go into the bank and make a withdrawal. Waltz right out the front door, jump on our horses and be on our way to the border and safety. Safe and rich that is!"

The Mexicans looked doubtful, but Manuel was able to coerce them into the plan. One of the Mexicans shrugged his shoulders, took a deep breath and staggered out the alley. As he was staggering toward the guard, the guard stood. The deputy was pointing a scattergun at him and demanded to know where he thought he was going. When the guard turned away from the alley, another Mexican crept up behind him and with a long bladed knife went on to give the lawman another mouth below his chin.

The man started to say something but nothing came out his mouth but a gurgle as he chocked to death on his own blood. The two Mexicans let the guard fall to the ground and turned toward the alley grinning widely.

David was angry at the Mexicans for not obeying his orders to knock the guard out. He wasn't upset over the death of the guard. David was simply mad for the Mexicans at not following orders.

"If they won't follow his orders now, what of the future?" He made a vow to himself, not to trust the Mexicans again.

David and Ramon ran across the front porch and entered the bank. They started across the lobby toward the vault. Suddenly another deputy stood up and pointed a greener at them. This guard grinned, thinking of the accolades heaped upon him at the capture of the bank robbers.

"Hold it right there," he said, aiming the scattergun at them.

Instead of holding his hands up, David quickly grabbed Ramon and shoved him toward the guard. The deputy cut loose with a load of double ought buckshot. The blast took off the biggest part of Ramon's head. David had shoved Ramon hard and the big man's momentum carried him into the deputy. In the meantime, David dropped to the floor and quickly plugged the guard in the stomach.

The shot man dropped his weapon and clutched at his belly. Bright red blood came seeping between his fingers as he pivoted on the floor and fell, upsetting a wooden chair placed by a desk.

Stepping over Ramon and pulling the dead guard from the front of the vault, David knelt and placed the sticks of dynamite on the vault handles. He lit the fuse and scurried to his right to hide behind a desk farthest from the vault.

The resulting explosion blew out all of the bank's windows showering David and the street with tiny shards of glass. Only David having a thick duster prevented him from being cut to pieces. As it was, he did receive a few superficial cuts on his neck and across the backs of his hands where he had placed them to cover his head.

THIRTY-ONE

"Hear that?" Lee shouted, as he was running to his horse. He swung up in the saddle and put the spurs to the horse's sides. The creature quickly bolted almost tossing Lee out of the saddle. He leaned forward to cut down on the wind resistance, as he slapped both sides of his mount with the reins.

"Sounds like an explosion," Tom said. Then looking dumfounded at Bob and Chris, "*The bank!*"

Lee had already started for town as Bob and Tom quickly harnessed Chris's wagon. Then they jumped into it and were barely seated when Chris flicked the reins and shouted to the horses. Off to town they headed, Chris applied the buggy whip to make the horses move faster. The four arrived in the town square at around the same time.

The center of Clearwater looked as if a giant iron fist had smashed into it. The gazebo was knocked off its foundation and lay on its side. A stone statue of a horseman was now headless. Smoke was beginning to come from the inside of the bank and the adjoining buildings.

The bank had a hole punched into the middle of it. Its large doors were lying askew in the street. Smoke was starting to billow in the clear sky. Townspeople were running for cover and shouting for the water wagon. The town was up in arms, as they began to lay down a hefty return fire.

As the men rode into the square, they were attacked by the Mexicans. Tom was the first injured. A bullet gouged out a part of his upper arm. Tom winced as the blood began to flow freely. Bob quickly tore the sleeve of Tom's shirt and made a tourniquet for the bleeding arm.

He told Tom to keep the bandage on tightly, as he dodged bullets flying about his head. Bob grabbed the tiny derringer from its resting place in his vest.

"Even then," he thought, "I've got to get awfully close for this weapon to be useful, but be ready's my motto." He thought again quickly and retrieved a spare gun from the buggy. Then he sought out the nearest cover available to him.

Lee meanwhile had run across the street firing at the Mexicans. One of the Mexicans, stood from his hiding place, behind a water trough and took a bullet in the belly. He pirouetted, clutched his stomach and fell into the horse trough sending water spraying over the sides. His feet were sticking obscenely out of the end of the trough.

Another of the robbers tried to scamper down the alle, to the waiting horses. Abner Hershey, standing by his opened back door, raised and fired his shotgun. The pellets from the shotgun hit the would-be-escapee in the arm and upper torso. The shot bandit leaned against the bank wall and feebly got off a shot toward Abner. He missed and Abner quickly ducked back into the safety of his store, slamming the door behind him. Then the fatally wounded outlaw slowly slid down the wall leaving a red streak behind him.

Tom hurriedly ran to his newspaper office and going into the building quickly pulled out the top drawer of his desk. On top of old papers rested a Smith & Wesson Frontier model .44-40 caliber revolver. Everyone claimed this weapon, to be next to useless in looks and feel, but i was still deadly.

"It may be clumsy, hard to handle and feel heavy, but I like it," Tom spoke to his critics. "It was my Father's and he gave it to me as a gift upon me becoming mayor."

Tom grabbed the gun and ran out the back door. He was planning on coming at the culprits from the back, hopefully catch them in a crossfire. Sort of a surprise, he reasoned, as he rushed from the office. At least, he hoped it would be a rude awakening to them.

Lee had reached the corner of a building next to the Emporium. He rested his back against the wall and hurriedly reloaded his gun. Then he peered around the edge of the building and saw two Mexicans on the porch of the Emporium. They were hiding behind barrels of farm equipment. He took a chance and ran to the horse trough, in front of Bob's leather shop.

Rising from his position, Lee began to fan the hammer of his gun peppering the two outlaws. One caught a round in his forehead, as the other was gut shot. Both fell to the boardwalk, as dead as last winter's cold. And like the trees felt the cold of the winter, the dead outlaws felt the cold and clammy hands of death upon their bodies.

"I wonder where their leader's gotten off to?" Lee muttered, as he advanced warily toward the dead men. He knew the outlaws did not have enough time to rob the bank, as his group was on the scene quickly after the explosion.

Answering gunfire from the bank told the sheriff of the leader's position. Lee paused to reload again. After this chore was done, he knelt to examine the dead men. He reached down and removed a few cartridges off the dead man's bandoleer'. Lee started toward the bank. The sheriff had just come abreast of the damaged doors, when he suddenly came face to face with David.

Lee automatically pulled the trigger of his gun. The hammer came down and nothing! David seeing a reprieve thought fast and tried to fire his weapon. The gun misfired. Thinking quickly, he swung his gun and struck Lee aside the head. This blow dazed the sheriff, bringing him to his knees. Lee saw stars for a moment. He shook his head to clear it and saw the back of the bank robber disappear.

David whirled on his feet and started inside. He ran through the door and headed toward the back. When he finally got outside, he was chagrined to see Manuel. He was mounted on David's horse and whipping the reins on the horse's shoulder. He was spurring the animal out of town. Manuel was making a good escape from the town of Clearwater.

David did not waste anytime to curse the fleeing bandit, as he hurried to the livery. "I can get a mount there," he thought. He reached the livery and was surprised to find it empty! All of the livestock had been used for the picnic. Even the mules were gone. A lone sheep bleated at him. He turned and went back to the opening of the livery.

David started to run from the livery when he saw Lee approaching. "Should've made sure that sheriff was dead," he mused. He ran to the ladder leading up to the loft and scurried up it. When he reached the top, he quickly rolled to his right and crouched behind some hay bales that were stacked by the opening of the hayloft. David stopped as he saw the sheriff had reached the livery. Quickly he hid behind the bales of hay. He quietly pulled back the hammer on his gun.

Lee entered the dimly lit barn and stopped. He let his eyes become adjusted to the dimness as he scanned the inside of the structure. Lee was trying to make out the form of the outlaw. Lee stepped forward, then stopped again. Falling hay and dust particles told Lee that someone was up in the loft. He rolled sideways and got into a stall underneath the bandit.

"Better give it up!" Lee shouted upwards, as he crabbed sideways to a better place of safety. He pulled his gun from its holster and quietly pulled the hammer back. He surveyed the area once more.

"Now," Lee thought, looking upwards to the floor of the hayloft. He thought that he saw specks of dust and pieces of straw falling from the ceiling. "Where's my quarry?"

David did not say anything. He was quiet as a sepulcher. He was not going to give himself away. Crouching, he suddenly started to reminisce about the days spent at the correctional place. It was dark and damp like this hayloft. Smiling when he remembered what few times he had enjoyed and wincing as he thought of the nightmares. Now he was caught in a nightmare of sorts. A Mexican who ran away with his money and a sheriff that wants him to hang. But he also knew that like overcoming the former nightmares, this one will work out all right too.

"Sort of between a rock and a hard place," he thought. "But a man of my intelligence will not let little things hold me back. If that sheriff will move into the sunlight," he thought, "he's good as dead. I can't miss from this range, it'll be like shooting fish in a barrel." Gleefully, he aimed his gun to where he thought the sheriff would appear. Then he thought again, "there's no money in killing him." He replaced his gun in its holster. "If I can just escape," he thought, "I'll kill that dumb Mexican, recover my loot and then come back here for another attempt at this jerkwater town."

The outlaw glanced about him and in the dim light spied the opening of the hayloft. He saw his chance and pondered on the gamble.

"If I can jump from here, I'll still have an out," he thought, as he began to tense his leg muscles. "I've jumped from taller places and still lived to tell about it. Got to create a diversion first," he considered. "That lawman's bound to see me when I make my move."

David remembered the heavy gold chain wrapped around his neck. It was given to him by a pretty señorita two days ago. His eyes lit up in anticipation of making the right move.

"Now it's going to come in handy," he thought. David reached to his neck and removed the chain. "I'll throw the chain against the far wall of the stall where the sheriff is, and when he turns at the sudden noise, I'll make my break!"

Lee had moved to a vantage point where he could barely make out the shadow of the bandit. He took aim at the silhouette and started to squeeze the trigger, but stopped. Lee then started to say something, but halted.

"This guy has no mercy, so why should I. Because I'm the *sheriff*," he remembered. "This outlaw will shoot me if I move into the clearing."

Thinking this way, Lee holstered his gun and silently moved to another stall. At a quick glance he could see that this stall was empty except for a hogshead in the corner.

"I can use that for cover," he thought, as he quickly ran to hide behind it.

David hurriedly made his decision, he then threw the chain as hard as possible toward the stall. When he heard the clatter of the metal hitting the stall, he made his move.

David stood and started to run for the opening. In his haste, he did not see the rope used to swing the hay bales out of the loft, hanging from the rafters until it was too late. He tried to quickly halt, but his boots skidded on the damp hay and his momentum carried him too fast toward the opening. The rope settled gently, almost as a caress, around his scrawny neck. As he reached up to remove the rope, the floor boards that Tom was going to get around to repair one day, started to crumble abruptly and gave way. He pitched forward toward the opening.

Suddenly, he was falling out of the hayloft. Only this time, he did not escape. There was to be no getaway for him now. David felt the rope tightening and then heard the brittle sound of his neck bones breaking. A cracking noise, a sharp pain and then darkness settled its dark cloak over his eyes.

Lee rushed from the stall to the doorway and looked up to where David was hanging. The lithe body was gently swaying in the morning breeze. A quick quiver, a shudder and the corpse became still. David Shannon White had cheated the hangman once, but he finally kept his long delayed appointment. He was hung in...

THE END

SynergEbooks

Taking Books to New Heights!